MURDER FOR LUNCH
A Reuben Frost Mystery

"Crisp, suave, and wry ... Murphy's sketches of Wall Street law-life are shrewd, deglamorizing, drily amusing .... wise, droll Reuben could become a welcome series presence."

The Kirkus Reviews

"Reuben Frost is an original and appealing invention."

The New York Times

"A first mystery worth a prolonged stay in an armchair."

The Washington Post

MURDER
FOR
LUNCH

Haughton Murphy

FAWCETT CREST • NEW YORK

A Fawcett Crest Book
Published by Ballantine Books

Library of Congress Catalog Card Number: 85-22134

ISBN 0-449-21276-9

This edition published by arrangement with Simon and Schuster, Inc.

Manufactured in the United States of America

First Ballantine Books Edition: April 1987

For Martha,
with much love

GRAHAM DONOVAN

1

STEVE WATSON STOOD OUTSIDE THE DOUBLE FRONT DOORS OF 928 Park Avenue, Manhattan, and discreetly stretched in the warm September sun. He knew that stretching, or scratching, or any similar catlike movements, would not be considered acceptable staff behavior by the stuffier residents of the fancy cooperative building. But he felt relatively safe since all the early morning traffic—the joggers and the striving Wall Street brokers—had already passed through the lobby.

Despite a large and fearsome mustache, Steve looked no older than his twenty-two years. A three-year veteran at 928 Park—the job was his way of putting himself through college—he knew the tenants well and their extremely regular habits even better. Right now, at 8:45 A.M. on a pleasant Tuesday morning in September, he was reasonably sure, when the elevator bell rang, that Graham Donovan was calling it. He was equally sure that a half hour later Anne Singer, an increasingly frequent visitor to Donovan's apartment, would emerge. (Tony, the nightman, had alerted him that "Mrs. S" was in residence.)

Steve was indifferent to Mrs. Singer's visits. He was very fond of Mr. Donovan—a terrifying presence if angered, but normally both a genial and an amusing man. Not at all overbearing, as so many of the tenants were and as a successful Wall Street lawyer might be ex-

1

pected to be. And he had remained cheerful even after the death of his wife two years earlier. So if Mrs. Singer soothed the old boy, it was fine with him.

The elevator door opened and Steve's first prediction proved right. Out strode Graham Donovan, still three years short of sixty, gray-haired in a most distinguished way and almost but not quite overweight. Donovan, who had had a mild heart attack five years earlier, had been sufficiently frightened by that experience to make an effort to control his weight. Just under six feet tall, he managed to conceal his bulk, except for a formidable middle with which neither his efforts to diet and exercise nor Dunhill's custom tailoring could adequately cope.

Donovan was carrying a letter-sized leather envelope under one arm. Steve, generally a shrewd observer of the social scene about him, did not understand the subtle symbolism of the tiny envelope. It said: This man does not need to establish himself by carrying home pounds of work in a giant attaché case. He *is* established and all he has to do at home is to review the carefully distilled work product of others. All of which, in Donovan's case, was on the mark. In thirty-odd years of practising law with Chase & Ward, one of New York's leading law firms, he had graduated from the large attaché case toted by ambitious young associates to the thinner, sleeker model favored by young partners and, finally, to the skinny envelope that denoted senior status.

"Good morning, Mr. Donovan," Steve called out, half saluting him as he did so.

"Good morning, Steve," Donovan responded.

He smiled at Steve with what he fancied was a perfectly straightforward and friendly smile, quite unaware that those years of shrinking briefcases had engraved a toughness and determination in his face and eyes that his smile did not entirely offset.

From past experience Steve knew that Donovan would not want him to flag a taxi; he would do that himself.

"Most of the taxi drivers in New York are maniacs or idiots or both," he had once told Steve. "The only possible chance you have for safety and comfort is to look them over in advance as best you can. Never flag a cab with an advertising sign on the top. That cab belongs to a fleet owner more interested in buying a new Jasper Johns than new shock absorbers. And the driver will probably have been in this country about six weeks. Go with a cab with a 'radio call' light; chances are the driver has a family and a mortgage and a decent respect for human life.''

Donovan moved past Steve and out the door to Park Avenue. He made an impressive figure at the curb, with his protruding middle pointing into the street. Seeing that the nearest approaching cab met his standards, he waved his leather envelope and the cab pulled over smartly.

"Good morning, driver. Down the Drive to One Metropolitan Plaza, please," Donovan commanded, after arranging his bulk in the back seat. "Get off at Broad Street."

"Yes, sir," the driver responded over the cacophony created by a music program on his regular radio and a dispatcher's calls on his two-way radio.

"And one more thing, driver. Either turn off the music or your dispatcher. One or the other is fine, but not both."

The taxi driver was about to argue but thought better of it. Donovan was not smiling, and the toughness and determination that Steve had noticed signaled a man who was not to be trifled with. The music was turned off and the cab's radio messages continued.

Donovan sat back in the taxi, *The Wall Street Journal* in front of him. After a quick glance at the front page he put the paper down and closed his eyes. A headline about a Securities and Exchange Commission crackdown on "insider" stock trading reminded him of an unsolved mystery—and potential scandal—at the office. Once again he considered, as he had done so often in recent weeks, who could have exposed the firm to potential embarrassment, and possibly to legal liability.

Many American fortunes had been based on the skillful use of "inside" information; many a robber baron had not been a fabled captain of industry at all, but an inside dopester adept at using facts not generally known to the public in selling or buying stocks to and from the unsuspecting. But both ethical standards and the law of the land had changed so as to make the use of "inside" information unseemly and, in at least the most flagrant cases, illegal.

Chase & Ward, like its sister firms at the top of the Wall Street hierarchy, was extremely sensitive to the "insider" problem. Not, God knows, because ethical standards were low within its confines, but rather because of the high volume of potentially volatile information the firm collectively possessed. Of the Fortune 500 corporations, a fair share were Chase & Ward clients; an even larger number were, at any given time, engaged in transactions with its clients—borrowing money from them, selling securities through them, even (though it was rare) acquiring them. Chase & Ward had what its partners called "associations" with—and what envious competitors called tentacles into—virtually every major industry in the United States. The result was a collective pool of valuable information that, in the hands of those willing to violate their professional confidences, could readily be used for self-enrichment.

All of these considerations went through Donovan's mind as he once again reviewed the facts of what he had come to think of as the "Stephens matter." Early in August his old friend and client, Joe Mather, President of Stephens Industries, had sent him in strictest confidence a draft press release. It announced sharply lower projected earnings for Stephens during the current year due to production problems with its computer peripheral equipment. Subject to Donovan's approval of the text, the release was to go out over the Dow Jones wire immediately after the summer meeting of Stephens' board of directors.

The news was expected to create turmoil in the market for Stephens stock. A public company for less than three years, its stock price had risen spectacularly as it announced one innovative product after another, all designed to perform various computer functions better and faster than comparable equipment produced by others in the industry. The fact that "bugs" had developed with its new low-cost, high-speed modem—a product with great potential sales among home computer hobbyists eager to "talk" to each other through their machines—was the first adverse development since Stephens' public launching. Its stock was then selling at a multiple of earnings astronomical even by computer industry standards; bad news could be expected to have a devastating effect on its price.

Donovan had read the draft press release sent to him by Mather and had suggested some judicious cutting of several euphemistic phrases designed to obfuscate the true import of the news being announced. As usual, the public relations department had substituted fluff for the precision that made lawyers comfortable. He then sent the draft, with his handwritten marks on it, to the Chase & Ward files and thought no more about it until two days later when he received a call from a broker at Bennett Holbrook & Co. asking if it was true that Stephens Industries was about to show a drop in earnings. With some anger, he had told the broker in no uncertain terms that any such matter was none of his business. He had been forced to curb his indignation, however, when the broker told him that he possessed a copy of Mather's letter addressed to Donovan at Chase & Ward, and the accompanying draft of the press release.

Subsequent investigation showed that the broker indeed had a Xerox copy of the draft release, with Donovan's penciled notes on it. So someone at the firm had sent the copy anonymously to the Bennett Holbrook employee.

Even though Donovan made clear to the stockbroker that any use by him of the information about Stephens would be grounds for potential action by the SEC for improper use of "inside" information, the price of Stephens stock dropped sharply, forcing the company to announce its unfavorable news even before its board had met.

Someone was trying to force down the price of Stephens stock—presumably someone who had sold the stock short and now wanted, in order to make a profit, to cover his position with stock purchased at a lower price. But who? A messenger who had taken the Stephens material from Donovan's office to the file room? A file clerk? Donovan had no idea. But he suspected, sadly, that it was probably some two-bit operator playing around with a few hundred dollars. Someone making a minuscule profit, but in the process causing a not so minuscule problem for Chase & Ward. Or was it someone trying to embarrass him? He couldn't believe that that was the reason, but then, he couldn't rule it out, either.

Could it be Arthur Tyson? He tried to dismiss the thought; it was petty—or worse, paranoid—to think such a thing of his contemporary and partner. He had known Tyson as long as he had been at Chase & Ward. Both were the same age, the same class at law school (Donovan at Columbia, Tyson at Harvard). Both had become partners of Chase & Ward the same year. But despite all this, they had never really been friends; their personalities were just too different. Donovan was a man of some elegance and much grace. Tyson, by contrast, had been an all-American lineman at the University of Michigan and treated most personal encounters in his life, whether at home or at the office, like scrimmages at the goal line. He was an arbitrary tyrant, short-tempered, impatient and sarcastic with everyone but his clients and (except on rare occasions) his partners. But to be married to him, or to work for him, or to be his son, was trying indeed.

"Arthur loves to kiss up and kick down," Donovan had once observed to a colleague. "Someday, though, he's going to get confused and make the wrong gesture at the wrong time."

Tyson's kissing up occurred most often as the senior partner in Chase & Ward's trusts and estates department. He was the epitome of charm with his demanding, wealthy clients. Rich widows and titans of industry alike found him responsive and irresistible when discussing their personal affairs; many refused to deal with anyone else at the firm when matters involving their personal fortunes were at stake.

Except for the occasional outburst when things were not going his way, Tyson was reasonably polite to his partners—not because he respected them or their intelligence, but because he had decided that he wanted to cap his career as the Executive Partner of Chase & Ward. There were many within the firm—including Donovan—who regarded the job of Executive Partner as more of a burden than an honor. But at an early time Tyson had learned that it was better to be the captain rather than merely a player, so he wanted to be not only a respected senior partner but *the* Executive Partner.

With his impressive roster of well-to-do clients—and the prospect for the firm of several hefty commissions from their estates when they died—Tyson had a fair claim to the title he wanted. Only two things stood in the way—a long-standing tradition at Chase & Ward that the Executive Partner come from the ranks of the firm's corporate department and the presumed consensus among the partners that Graham Donovan should succeed to the job when George Bannard, the present holder of the title, retired in two years.

Donovan of course knew of Tyson's barely concealed ambition. But now he shook his head, as if to drive out the thought that Tyson might be seeking to embarrass him. It really was unworthy, he told himself; Tyson was extremely aggressive, but Donovan could not imagine him being underhanded enough to set up the Stephens caper. No, it was unthinkable, Donovan concluded.

But who was it? Ross Doyle, the private detective Chase & Ward had retained on occasion over the years for "sensitive" matters, had been called in, but so far had produced nothing other than bad feelings on the part of Grace Appleby, Donovan's secretary, and the messengers and file clerks Doyle had interviewed. Donovan resented the whole business. Partners of his senior eminence were not supposed to be troubled by such irksome matters.

Donovan's musings were interrupted as the taxi's radio came on again full blast. They had reached One Metropolitan Plaza. Donovan paid the driver and headed for the marble facade of One Metro. Each morning he marveled anew at how the Chairman of the Board (and largest stockholder) of Metro Bank, owner and principal tenant of the building, had acquired his reputation as a sensitive connoisseur of art and architecture. To Donovan, the heavy pink marble suggested Mussolini rather than Medici.

As Donovan reached the revolving doors to the building, he met his partner, Roger Singer. Roger Singer, cuckolded husband of Anne Singer. Encountering him had become immensely painful to Donovan since the beginning of his affair with Anne. Although they were both corporate lawyers at the firm and practically contemporaries, they had never worked together closely. Singer's practice was more international in scope than Donovan's and they had not shared the same clients. And beyond that, Donovan found off-putting Singer's taciturn reticence, which seemed to have gotten worse in recent months.

This reticence was not something only Donovan had noticed. It had been a subject of considerable comment within the firm. Week after week Singer sat through the Thursday luncheon meetings of the partners without saying a word or even making small talk with those sitting around him.

It was an open secret at Chase & Ward that Singer had been recruited for Central Intelligence Agency work back in the 1960s. By a series of coincidences, Singer had ended up spending virtually all his time in those years on Latin American business. Such business had never been particularly important at Chase & Ward, but one deal seemed to lead to another in those optimistic days of the Alliance for Progress, and Singer had become known as an "expert" in the legal intricacies of doing business in Latin America, both within and without the firm.

Donovan did not know precisely when Singer had been recruited by the Agency. But in the 1960s Singer had started leaving on extended trips, his absences explained in the flimsiest of ways. From all Donovan could gather, it was a commonly held assumption among his partners that this clandestine activity had severely depressed Singer and resulted in his silent behavior. As far as Donovan knew another likely cause, Donovan's affair with Anne, was not generally known—and if Anne was correct, not known to Singer. But Donovan of course could not be entirely sure of what Singer knew, and this made him uneasy whenever they met.

"Good morning, Graham, how are you?" Singer said, as Donovan gestured him through the revolving doors.

"Fine, Roger," Donovan responded heartily—perhaps too heartily. "Coming in from the country?" he asked, pointing to Singer's overnight bag.

"Yes. Decided to stretch out the weekend. Nice weather."

No mention of Anne, who had come back to the city from Sagaponack late Sunday and had been at Donovan's for two nights.

The two men fell silent as they went up in the elevator to the fifty-first floor. Donovan felt very much the hypocrite but knew that neither he nor Anne had the courage to confront Roger with the fact that they wanted desperately to get married. Anne feared that Roger would completely fall apart if he knew the truth. Donovan would gladly have let him know the truth but he, too, had a fear—of his partners. One's personal life was none of Chase & Ward's business, but scandal so close to home might be.

Donovan did his best to conceal the emotions provoked by these delicate thoughts, but was relieved when the elevator stopped. After a series of "good mornings" —the receptionist, a stenographer, an associate, none of whom he knew by name—he reached his corner office with its commanding view of the harbor.

The last "good morning" was to Miss Appleby, an austere and formidable—some would say disagreeable—presence, but a woman who had served Donovan discreetly and well as secretary for the past twenty-five years. He knew she was regarded as a witch by his colleagues, but he didn't care as long as she continued to coddle and protect him. And besides, he was sure that those who complained about her did not know of her almost daily volunteer work at St. Blaise's Hospital, an acute care institution where it could not be terribly pleasant to work, as a volunteer or otherwise.

No, Miss Appleby was just fine with Graham Donovan, and he said good morning to her with gusto. It was the last time he would do so. Less than four hours later, he would be dead.

GEORGE BANNARD

GRAHAM DONOVAN HAD ONCE BEEN ASKED BY AN ATTRACTIVE but persistent dinner partner to describe how Chase & Ward was run. Donovan explained that the partners of the firm basically operated as a democracy, with "one man, one vote" the governing rule. His dinner partner did not believe him; a very successful cosmetics industry executive herself, she expressed disbelief that Donovan's ideal could really be the governing principle for thirty-seven articulate—and egotistical—lawyers. Pressed by his companion, he finally admitted that the firm was in actuality "a one-man band, as long as the band doesn't play too loud."

For six years, George Pierce Bannard had been the one-man band, the Executive Partner of Chase & Ward. Bannard looked the part—jet black hair despite his sixty-six years (there was some, but not much, intraoffice cattiness about the genuineness of the color), topping a six-foot, two-inch frame that had once been sleek and athletic but now reflected its owner's abandoning of strenuous exercise. His ruddy complexion echoed his sturdy New England farm ancestors, but there was nothing rustic about him. Bumptious and sometimes ill-mannered, perhaps, but not rustic.

If someone had asked George Bannard how he had come to be the first among equals—the one-man band—at one of the country's preeminent law firms, he undoubt-

edly would have said "merit," echoing Jefferson and
Horatio Alger in the bargain. In a way he would have
been right; his linear progression from Yale under-
graduate to successful law student at Penn to diligent
Chase & Ward associate to eager young, then older,
partner certainly plotted an upward graph that indicated
success.

But there were those at Chase & Ward who might
have substituted "luck" for "merit" as the essential
propellant to Bannard's rise. He was, after all, the son
and the grandson of successful Wall Street lawyers.
That alone had given him a certain acquired-at-the-dinner-
table ease with the jargon and outward mannerisms of
the successful practitioner—plus the financial backing to
cushion life's early shocks, whether in the form of inedi-
ble college meals, a railroad flat in Greenwich Village or
a meagre apprentice's salary at Chase & Ward.

Bannard had been lucky, too, in being born in 1918,
and born with poor eyesight at that. As a result, he had
finished college in 1941 and begun law school at a time
when his contemporaries were being drafted (law school
at Penn; Bannard's preoccupation with Scroll and Key's
antics and similar amusements at Yale had foreclosed
admission to a more prestigious law school). Deferred
from selective service because of his eyesight, Bannard
finished law school in 1944 and went to work at Chase &
Ward immediately. (Luck had helped here. Bannard had
done well enough at Penn Law School, but it was not
then a prime recruiting ground for firms of the caliber of
Chase & Ward. Timely intervention by his father with
Phineas Ward took care of all that, however; merit, in
those days, was a malleable concept where the son of a
good friend was concerned.) So Bannard arrived at Chase
& Ward with plenty of time to ingratiate himself with his
seniors before the arrival of a flood of GI-bill law school
graduates who had served in the war.

More good luck followed. As a successful young man-
about-town he met and soon married Eleanor Coward,
an attractive Smith graduate three years his junior. Thoroughly conventional—to the point of boredom in the

view of some—she was exactly the kind of wife who appealed to Phineas Ward and the other aging WASPs who then ran the firm.

Bannard's selection as a partner in 1954, after what was then a normal, underpaid ten-year apprenticeship, was thoroughly predictable. No one said Bannard was brilliant or even very imaginative. But he had acquired a reputation for dispensing sound, straight and practical legal advice, qualities that had in recent years made him one of the most sought-after business lawyers in New York. His ability to cut through complex problems, to clarify issues and to suggest workable solutions was well known. At the same time, he was an indifferent legal draftsman and impatient with the minute details required to bring transactions to fruition; as far as he was concerned, these matters could be left to subordinates who were more accomplished technicians. It was enough that he was there to enshroud often nervous and unsure clients with the bright beam of the self-confidence he always projected, at least in public.

A college friendship at college with Alan Young, one of the first and leading conglomerateurs, sealed Bannard's claim, if any sealing was necessary, to the Executive Partner position. Starting out with a small family business in Massachusetts, Young created a multibillion dollar company through an aggressive and continuing acquisition program. He had sought out Bannard early, and Bannard had been his personal lawyer as the company grew to be one of Chase & Ward's largest, most active and most lucrative clients.

As Chase & Ward's Executive Partner, Bannard was expected to "show the flag" on the firm's behalf, which he did as the director of several corporations and as a Trustee of the Museum of Modern Art. The Museum trusteeship he had in effect inherited from his father, a thoughtful, cultivated man and an art collector in a modest way, who had served with distinction for many years on the Modern's board, almost from the time of the Museum's founding. George Bannard did not share his father's enthusiasm for modern art; indeed, given his

poor eyesight, there was some question about just what
he saw when looking at a Picasso or a Braque, let alone
an Agnes Martin. In private, he had been heard to en-
dorse the any-child-can-do-this theory of modern art, but
he was nonetheless an enthusiastic, if not terribly well
informed, supporter of the Museum and, with his wide
business contacts, a diligent and successful fund-raiser
for the institution.

On this particular Tuesday morning, George Bannard
was standing at the corner of Park and Seventy-ninth,
waiting for the Wall Street express bus. As a senior
partner of Chase & Ward, Bannard could well have
afforded a more elegant means of commuting to his
downtown office. A private limousine would have been
affordable, and a taxi certainly would have been. But
with his inheritance of New England frugality, he regarded limousines as ostentatious and taxis as simply
not worth the money. The premium-fare Wall Street
express bus was just fine, saving him as it did from the
vagaries of the subway system which, when Bannard
had stopped using it the year before, had seemed to be
deteriorating on a daily basis.

This morning he was carrying both an attaché case (he
was oblivious to the small envelope theory) and a small
overnight bag, since he was leaving later in the day on a
business trip to Chicago. When the bus arrived, Bannard
pushed toward the door, using both the attaché case and
the overnight bag as offensive weapons, in a manner
best described as aggressive. Given his size, he was
something of a menace in crowds and queues, particularly when armed, as he was this morning.

Seventy-ninth Street was one of the first stops for the
bus, so Bannard had no trouble getting a seat. He un-
folded *The Wall Street Journal* and, like Graham Donovan, was attracted to the front-page story on "insider"
trading. He, too, was mentally confronted once again
with the Stephens press release mess, but his attitude
was different from Donovan's. Bannard's thoughts were
ones of anger, directed at Donovan's carelessness in

sending the sensitive release to the Chase & Ward files through the normal distribution system. That system was usually reliable, and not as a rule subject to leaks, but the Stephens release was sensitive enough, Bannard thought, to have been kept locked up in Donovan's own desk until after the Stephens public announcement had been made.

Donovan was probably too busy thinking about Anne Singer, Bannard concluded, damning his partner's foolishness. He was sure Donovan thought no one knew about his little dalliance, but secrets like that simply could not be kept in the small town that is New York. What had happened in Donovan's case was fairly typical: their partner, Fred Coxe, while dining with his artist son in SoHo, had seen Graham and Anne together in a remote and rather offbeat restaurant. The office busybody, Coxe had immediately sought to gain Bannard's favor by reporting what he had seen. Bannard thought nothing more about the matter until several weeks later when he heard a similar report from another partner. Then a picture of Graham and Anne appeared in *W*, the high-society gossip sheet—noticed by Eleanor—and there remained little doubt in Bannard's mind what was going on.

Bannard hoped against hope that the steam of the Singer/Donovan affair would evaporate of its own accord. As Chase & Ward's Executive Partner for six years, he had managed to survive in that thicket of egos without a major blowup, and he had hopes that the remaining two years of his tenure, before he was required to step down at age sixty-eight, would be placid as well. He was less concerned about Roger Singer's reactions—Roger was so burnt out and beaten down that Bannard didn't believe Anne's behavior would upset him—than about those of his partners. There was Marvin Isaacs, who could bring an almost terrifying Old Testament righteousness to questions he viewed as moral issues. Or Peter Denny, Knight of Malta and straight arrow (Donovan's being a lapsed Catholic not helping in this department, either). Or Nigel Stewart, pursed-lipped Calvinist. Yes, there was an ecumenical coalition that would readily conduct Donovan's auto-da-fé if the chance arose.

Not that Chase & Ward was precisely a Sunday school. Many of the partners, if not a majority, had been divorced, some more than once. (Even the young ones, Bannard reflected. Marrying early and shedding a wife during or right after law school seemed common. Bannard had noted, for whatever it was worth, that this was particularly true of Stanford and Berkeley graduates.) But old or young, a partner simply did not take up with another partner's wife.

At the Second Avenue stop, Bannard saw Tom Agnew, a partner in Harvey, Handelsman & Linde (a respectable downtown law firm but, in Bannard's view, no Chase & Ward), approaching down the aisle. Roughly the same age, Bannard and Agnew had been classmates at Penn, where they had had a class or two together, but had not been friends. Rutgers (Agnew's alma mater) and Yale simply did not mix, at least not in the 1940s when they had been at Penn. Bannard and Agnew had begun work at their firms the same year and had become partners within months of each other.

For reasons that Bannard could never understand, Agnew had become increasingly friendly over the years. Since he found Agnew a total bore, this disturbed Bannard. Did it mean he was a bore, too, with likes attracting? When they had started out in New York, the two were barely nodding acquaintances. "Hello, George . . . Nice to see you, Tom" was about the extent of it. Then Tom became increasingly active in Pennsylvania Law School fund-raising activities and solicited Bannard with some frequency for money—the law school annual giving fund, a memorial scholarship for a classmate killed in Korea, dues for the alumni association, reunion gifts, and so on and so on. Each solicitation and each encounter brought their friendship, at least in Agnew's mind, to a new level of intimacy.

Bannard quickly opened his *Journal* and buried himself in it, but it did no good.

"Mind if I sit down, George?" Agnew asked, doing so before Bannard could reply.

Bannard had never figured out whether Agnew was smart or stupid; if pressed, he would have said that he was dim. If pressed further, he would have admitted that this was based as much on Agnew's physical appearance as anything else—his large, round head and slack face, all offset with a grin that could without much exaggeration be described as moronic.

Agnew's clothes heightened the unfortunate effect. This particular morning he was wearing a badly fitting and hardly pressed brown suit, scuffed brown shoes and a shiny rep tie that decidedly was not silk. A bit of Agnew's composition shirt peeked out from under his vest, which did not quite meet the pants, and a bit of flesh showed above his anklet hose when he crossed his legs and settled into his seat.

Bannard was no fashion plate; his clothes were tailor-made and expensive but unimaginative, and most outsiders would have been shocked to know how few suits the highly successful Executive Partner actually possessed. Yet he knew slovenliness when he saw it. He was repelled by Agnew's hayseed appearance. How could a Wall Street lawyer, and presumably a prosperous one, dress this way?

Bannard tried to conceal his distaste, grunting a barely audible good morning to him.

"What's new, George?" Agnew asked, in his flat, South Jersey accent. "Busy these days?"

"Yes, thanks, I am. And you?"

"I've never been so busy in my life."

Bannard ignored the fact that Agnew unfailingly said this, leading Bannard to think that business at Harvey, Handelsman & Linde might not be as brisk as Agnew would lead one to believe. Besides, even if Agnew were busy, his work was, at least in Bannard's opinion, exceptionally tedious. Bannard enjoyed the trust and confidence of the top officers of his clients, advising them on interesting and often delicate matters of policy. Agnew, by contrast, was a scrivener, turning out thoroughly routine loan agreements for insurance companies and other institutional purchasers of corporate debt. Perhaps there was an excitement there, but it had always eluded Bannard. As far as he could see, the principal traits of Agnew's practice were to be obsequious to often self-important house lawyers at the insurance companies and to be able to articulate the word *no* in a variety of ways to the hapless borrowers from those companies.

"Still doing private placements, Tom?" Bannard asked.

"Oh, sure. Can't get away from it. Everybody's got money to lend and they don't seem to have any trouble pushing it out there."

"Well, I'm glad to hear you're busy. If you weren't you might get into mischief."

"Oh, George, always the joker," Agnew guffawed. "Just the way you were in law school."

Agnew's statement was absurd, Bannard fumed to himself. He was not then, nor was he now, by any stretch of the imagination a "joker." And besides, Agnew had not the faintest idea of what he had been like at law school.

"By the way, George, are you going to the reunion?"

"Law school, you mean?"

"Yes, it's our fortieth, you know."

"I guess I did get something in the mail about it. But no, I'm not. I can't think of anything more painful. All the class losers will be there, hoping to drum up some referral business from their successful classmates. And all the successful ones—or the ones that think they are successes—will be standing around preening and waiting for the losers to flatter them."

"Oh, George, it isn't like that at all. Have you ever been to a class reunion?"

"No. But I just know what they are like. I just know—oh, aren't you our class president or something?"

"Reunion chairman, George," a subdued Agnew replied. "Well, here we are. Sorry you won't go to the reunion. But I'll give you a full report on all the losers." Again the guffaw and the simpleton grin. "It was good to see you, old fellow."

"Good-bye, Tom. And, all kidding aside, I hope all our classmates who go down to Philadelphia have a splendid time." It seemed the least Bannard could say to the hurt reunion chairman of his class, even if he disliked him.

As he got off the bus at the Battery, he thought of his colleagues in midtown firms and for a moment envied them. They could walk to work and have elegant and leisurely lunches at the Four Seasons or Le Cygne. But he checked his hedonistic thoughts. Downtown was the place to be. Uneventful, but that was good; it let you concentrate on your work without distraction. And the simple, no-nonsense fare at the Hexagon Club was better for you than the tempting excesses available in midtown. Having convinced himself anew, he strode purposefully toward One Metropolitan Plaza.

Bannard's analysis of life downtown was to prove wrong that Tuesday. For, at Chase & Ward, there was to be a very large distraction in the dramatic death of Graham Donovan. And in the Hexagon Club at that.

REUBEN FROST LOOKED UP FROM THE MORNING *TIMES* AS his wife, Cynthia, handed him a large glass of freshly squeezed orange juice. He took the cool glass eagerly and downed its contents with what, had he been in public, would have seemed ill-mannered haste. At seventy-four, he was much too old to have experienced the "rushes" modern young people said they experienced when taking drugs. The lift from rapidly drinking a glass of orange juice first thing in the morning (and the satisfied burp that usually followed) were quite enough for him and the effect, he was sure, was not unlike that of sniffing cocaine.

The combination of the *Times,* delivered each morning to the door of his East Seventieth Street townhouse, and his glass of orange juice, prepared unfailingly by his wife, formed a ritual that had been followed since his wedding thirty-nine years earlier. The *Times* did not always fill him with contentment, but the orange juice did, both physically and psychologically.

The day they had returned from their honeymoon, Cynthia Frost had bought a juice squeezer and, on almost every day when they had both been at home since, had prepared a glass of orange juice for her husband. He regarded it, rightfully, as a loving domestic gesture from a wife who had many other things to do to fill up her day.

Frost's marriage to Cynthia Hansen had created much incredulous surprise among both his friends and hers. He had first met her when she was a promising star of the newly founded Ballet Theatre. Her vivacious, lighter-than-air technique, employed most notably in the title role of Anton Dolin's new production of *Giselle,* had caused much favorable comment in the dance world (a smaller world then than now, but nonetheless the world that mattered above all else to young Miss Hansen from Kansas City, Missouri). She had made a distinctive mark at age twenty-three, and the city's balletomanes adored her. Equally vivacious offstage, she seemed an unlikely bride for a fledgling Wall Street lawyer.

Frost first met his bride-to-be in 1940, at the very start of her career in New York. A college roommate of Frost's at Princeton, working as an investment banker in New York, had known her growing up in Kansas City and had introduced Reuben to her on a double date. Frost, who knew nothing whatever of the ballet (dancing lessons were perhaps familiar in Kansas City, but not in the Adirondack mountains in Upstate New York, where he had grown up), was intrigued by his new acquaintance. Soon he found himself attending performances at the City Center and shyly asking the ballet's star for late suppers afterward. Or, on more than one occasion, dashing to the City Center stage door after a late evening of work at Chase & Ward.

Reuben Frost was a serious young lawyer at Chase & Ward. Orphaned while still in his teens, he had worked his way through Princeton and Harvard Law School with a combination of scholarships and odd jobs. Determined not to return to Upstate New York, he had been jubilant when Phineas Ward, himself a Harvard graduate, had offered him a job at Chase & Ward at the magnificent salary of $2,000 a year. In the Depression year of 1935, getting *any* legal job was considered something of a triumph, but a chance to work at Chase & Ward was good fortune indeed.

Frost had worked diligently and attracted favorable comment from those he worked for. But his apprenticeship was a long way from being over—though his salary had risen to $7,500—when he met Cynthia Hansen. The diligence he showed at the office, and which inevitably colored his manner outside it, concealed a romantic streak that had never before had a chance to display itself.

Soon the couple were seeing each other daily, or as near to daily as was possible with their conflicting careers, Cynthia's touring and Reuben's business trips out of town. Frost became a confirmed balletomane, and a knowledgeable one as well. Cynthia came to admire his taste; he did not, like so many dance addicts, like everything, and she not only respected, but came to value, his critiques. And they both had the drive not to return to their roots, to be successes in the world beyond Missouri and Upstate New York, and to enjoy the fascinations and pleasures of New York City as if they were eager immigrants from lands more distant.

Only Pearl Harbor kept them from getting married. Within months of the beginning of the war, Frost was commissioned as a lieutenant in the Navy and was sent off to the Pacific. From then until war's end his courtship of Cynthia Hansen was frantic—endless V-mail letters, the occasional badly connected telephone call and, somehow, a dozen roses at the stage door whenever she was performing a new role.

Cynthia, despite infinite opportunities to do otherwise, remained loyal to her romantic sailor/lawyer, and they were married just before Christmas 1945 in the Little Church Around the Corner in New York. Their thirty-nine-year marriage was one of the durable wonders of the circles in which they traveled in the city, not always the healthiest environment in which to cultivate marital bliss. Totally independent in their own careers, each was nonetheless supportive of the other in valuable ways. Cynthia sympathized with Reuben when the volume of work he was doing, particularly in his younger days, occasionally seemed overwhelming, especially when done for unappreciative clients. Reuben not only encouraged his wife as she went from one artistic triumph to another, but often pointed out flaws that members of her company might either overlook or (perhaps deliberately) ignore—sloppy corps work, for example, or the visual blindness of a particular costume designer.

Cynthia Frost continued dancing into her thirties, retiring in triumph in the mid-1950s. She remained very much a part of the ballet world, however, working as an energetic ballet mistress for Ballet Theatre and then for a new company, the National Ballet, until a whole new, if not unrelated, career opened up when she became the head of performing arts activities for the Brigham Foundation. Martin Brigham, an extraordinarily successful inventor whose laser-beam techniques had revolutionized the manufacturing process in a score of industries, had been a client of Reuben's and, through his urging, had established a private foundation, active primarily in making grants to performing arts organizations. In addition to being a client, he was a good friend of both Frosts. It had been his idea to recruit Cynthia to administer the grants program.

She had accepted the job with many misgivings—she had never been an administrator at Ballet Theatre or the National Ballet. But she had taste, and strong ideas based on a lifetime of experience and observation as to how the arts should be supported. The dancers-are-dumb cliché most decidedly did not apply to her, despite her lack of any formal higher education.

The result was the development, in concert with Martin Brigham and the advice (when solicited) of her husband, of a program in support of the arts generally conceded to be one of the most effective—and, given the magnitude of Brigham's generosity, the largest—in the country. Cynthia Hansen Frost became an articulate spokesman for the arts—testifying before Congressional committees, speaking at universities, pleading the cause for artistic support on television talk shows. Now in her late sixties, she had a reputation that continued to grow and a schedule that remained full to overflowing.

Reuben Frost's career developed at a comfortable pace too, though in a less public way than his wife's. His reputation as a fine legal craftsman, as contrasted with his partner George Bannard's gifts as a shrewd handholder, was well known. Within the legal profession, or at least that portion of it that dealt with corporate and financial matters, he was reputed to be the best legal draftsman around, capable of writing clear, concise legal prose that could be read and understood by lawyers and laymen alike. At sixty he had become Chase & Ward's Executive Partner, presiding with distinction over his firm's transition from a relatively small, homogeneous organization to one twice its size at the time he took over, a move to spacious new quarters at One Metropolitan Plaza, and an early, innovative beginning at automating many of its operations.

All this was accomplished smoothly, without the bickering among partners, the decline in quality of work, or the loss of the "family" feeling that had characterized the older Chase & Ward firm. The agrarian shrewdness that Frost had brought with him from the Adirondacks—he was not just a transplanted rube recently fallen off the hay wagon, as one of his partners once pointed out—fitted him well for the task. As did the sense, acquired from his wide acquaintance with life outside the law, that the firm must not be isolated but instead be a part of the world in which it existed—and prospered. He had insisted that the firm cast its net wider in seeking able young people, and its recruiters had sought out qualified minority and women lawyers at a quickened pace under his direction; also at his insistence and over some virulent but ultimately ineffective opposition, two women were admitted as partners. Frost had also encouraged his colleagues to take part in public service, whether through projects run within the office or by taking leaves of absence. The inconvenience of accommodating this activity, and its dollars and cents cost to the firm, were considerable, but Frost firmly maintained that the costs were worth it and his partners agreed, albeit some more reluctantly than others.

Through the dead hand of Charles Chase, the founder of the firm, Frost had had to retire as Executive Partner when he became sixty-eight and to give up his partnership altogether four years later, when he became seventy-two. By all accounts Chase had been a genius, and indeed he had visualized and created a firm with exceptional resilience and durability. But those closest to Chase had seen the other side as well—the completely autocratic decision making (Chase's loud, boisterous one-man band had continued until Chase was in his doddering eighties) and the old man's insistence upon a massive, paternal share of the profits. After his death, his surviving partners hastily agreed, and so rewrote the firm's partnership agreement, that no partner could remain as Executive Partner after age sixty-eight, and that, absent dire circumstances, all partners of the same seniority would receive equal shares of the firm's profits in lockstep, with that share declining after age sixty-five to zero at age seventy-two, when retirement was mandatory.

As happened almost every morning—only an early morning meeting of consuming urgency prevented it—Frost thought about his status at Chase & Ward as he sat at the breakfast table. As a young partner at the firm, he had been the direct beneficiary of the post-Chase reforms that had led to a more democratic sharing of the firm's profits. And, while he was too young to have been subjected to Charles Chase's autocratic ways, he had supported the mandatory retirement policies his seniors had decreed for the partnership.

Again this morning, as he looked up from the *Times* and gazed out over Seventieth Street, he reflected that the firm's policies were inherently right. Sixty-eight was plenty old enough for the compulsory retirement of the leader of a growing and active law firm. And seventy-two was an appropriate age for ceasing to be an active partner and a participant in the firm's income—especially when generous salary arrangements were made for those, like Frost, who remained partially active in the firm's business as "of counsel" to Chase & Ward.

Frost realized that the honorific "of counsel" covered a variety of situations. It could be a title bestowed, in

Chase & Ward as well as other firms, on those who were senile and gaga, a title that said to the outside world, "He's a dear old fellow and we all love him, but he may have lost his marbles and we are no longer responsible for his legal advice." Or it could simply signal, as it did in his own case, the mere fact that he was no longer sharing in the firm's profits as a partner.

In good health, although his hearing had started to fade, Frost was confident that those with whom he continued to deal would not consign him to the paperslipper, gaga category. But there still were the annoying intangibles, aggravated by George Bannard's "reforms." True, he had given up his magnificently large corner office, befitting the Executive Partner, when Bannard had succeeded him. But his more modest quarters were more than adequate and still looked out on the beauties of New York harbor; not for him were the indignities inflicted by another firm he knew well, where three retired partners of his own vintage jointly shared a windowless office unworthy of a fledgling associate. And true, his secretary was not one of the old-school, efficient and literate nursemaids that a senior partner might command; the little, semiliterate girl from Hoboken who was his secretary did not meet those standards, but she was at least cheerful and, on the second or third try, could get approximately right the letters and documents he now produced in his reduced circumstances.

No, surrendering the surface attributes of power didn't really bother him. The hurt was more subtle. Bannard's decision to bar retired partners from the firm's weekly lunches, for example. He understood the reasoning—the old retired crocks tended to reminisce at too great a length, when the purpose of the weekly lunch was not fraternity but the discussion of current firm business in a crisp, expeditious manner.

Then there was the condescension. George Bannard, to one degree or another, condescended to everyone, always managing to pitch the level of his discourse just below the level of comprehension and sophistication of the person to whom he was speaking. Frost, for example, had done research at Harvard in the early 1930s that had assisted Felix Frankfurter and William O. Douglas in drafting the Securities Act of 1933, the basic Federal law that had served to redefine the public behavior of the country's corporate citizens and their officers and directors. As a member in later years of the City and American Bar Association committees dealing with securities law matters—he hated bar association activities in general, but these were committees of worth and substance—he had kept reasonably up-to-date on developments in this basic area of business law. So he did not need the explanation of the Securities and Exchange Commission rules on corporate tender offers that Bannard had gratuitously given him at lunch at the Hexagon Club the previous week.

Then there was the matter of being excluded from events occurring at the firm. He had been mortally embarrassed only days before when his old friend Joe Mather, over drinks at the Gotham Club, had obliquely alluded to a problem concerning a controversial press release apparently stolen from Graham Donovan's office. He had been truly puzzled by Mather's conversation and had had to draw the story out of Mather without letting on that he did not know of the incident. Why had he not been told? Granted, he no longer shared in the firm's profits, but shouldn't he have been told on general principles—and wasn't it just possible that he could have brought an elder statesman's wisdom to the problem? He had not confronted Bannard with his knowledge of the incident; if Bannard had not wanted to consult him, there was no point in seeking an embarrassing confrontation.

Frost roughly closed the *Times*, putting an end to his sour meditation. Cynthia, dressed for the day in a designer silk dress that did justice to her remarkably preserved dancer's figure, came in from the bedroom as he did so.

"Off to the office, I suppose?" she asked.

"Of course. Where else can an old man go in the morning? The movies don't open until noon."

"Oh, Reuben. Are you really happy traipsing down to that marble palace every day?"

"Of course not. But I'm still too young, dammit, to spend my lunches at the old farts' table at the club or napping in an easy chair afterwards. And I do, believe it or not, occasionally perform useful work at the office."

Cynthia refrained from saying "Like what?" and her husband continued: "You know, I've got a fairly interesting project right at the moment. Do you remember Perry Griffith?"

"Should I?"

"I know you've met him. He's an associate, been around for several years. Tall, blond, quite good-looking. Very sure of himself too."

"It sounds like you don't like him all that much."

"Well, you're right. A little too aggressive and ambitious for me. But he's had an interesting technical problem of drafting—converting an old-fashioned utility mortgage that's been around since Charles Chase's time into a document under which Frontier Utilities can issue mortgage bonds to the public."

"If you say so, dear."

"I know it sounds about as exciting as your old friend Myna dancing Juliet, but I'm trying to teach Mr. Griffith some drafting streamlining that may keep him from writing like George Will."

"Fine, Reuben. I'm delighted that some of those bright young Hessians still have the sense to draw on your skills. But you do seem to do a lot of staring out the window at breakfast and I was just wondering . . ."

"Look. That old fool in the White House running the country is almost precisely my age. So there's room for us old parties yet. Besides, it's good clean work, keeps me off the streets and—most important my dear—keeps me busy and out of a nursing home."

"Reuben, it's been clear to me for some time that I will be in a nursing home long before you. God knows I'm not trying to discourage you from going to the office, but I can't help thinking it's not quite the happy place it used to be."

Cynthia Frost was, as usual, close to the mark. But there was no point in sharing his complaints—they were probably silly and paranoid anyway—despite his confident knowledge that he could, and should, do so if his psychological scratches should become infected.

"Well, I am going to the office. I'll try not to drool on Griffith's mortgage and everything will be all right."

"Of course it will," Cynthia said, squeezing her husband's shoulder with affection.

"And what are you up to today?"

"Oh lord, a dreary ceremony at Gracie Mansion. The Mayor's appointed a commission to study bringing culture into the schools, and the members are being presented at a press conference. Mostly rip-off artists with axes to grind for their own 'public service' outfits."

"Sounds great."

"Well, the idea's good anyway and I want to show him—and his committee—that there are some of us watching what's being done."

"Good luck."

"Did you know, by the way, that there's a typographical error in those silly scrolls he gives to everyone he appoints?"

"No, what?"

"This will appeal to you as a lawyer. As I recall— Jean Meyer at the Mayor's Office pointed it out to me—the text ends with 'to have and to hold the said office with all the rights and emoluments thereunto legally appertaining unto.' "

"That's certainly distinguished legal prose. But don't tell anyone or they'll engrave a new batch at vast public expense."

"You're right. Are you going downstairs?"

"Yes. Just a minute, I want to get the bills that came yesterday. I'll fill out my day, assuming I finish with Mr. Griffith, drooling over my checkbook."

"Very funny."

The two of them went down the stairs and out into the

street. The couple embraced and kissed like striving, career-oriented Yuppies and then parted, he toward the subway and she toward Park Avenue, where she hoped to find an empty taxi that would take her uptown to the Mayor's residence.

Thanks to Cynthia's tutelage, Reuben Frost cut a fine figure as he walked the two blocks to the subway in the September sunshine. A careless, disorganized dresser as a young bachelor, he had become almost narcissistic about his appearance under his wife's prodding. As a result, he was able to combine Italian high fashion with Brooks Brothers basic without looking like either a Hollywood agent or an apprentice loan officer in a bank.

Reuben Frost had gone by subway to his job interview at Chase & Ward almost a half century earlier; it had never occurred to him since to go to work by any other means. Granted the fare was no longer a dime, and some of the equipment used today had surely been around at the time of Reuben's first ride, but he still regarded it with fascination. And, for all the discomforts, it was a way of feeling oneself a part of the bloodstream of the city.

The morning rush hour was coming to an end when Frost boarded the Lexington Avenue local. The train was not crowded, so he took a seat and resumed his reading of the *Times*. At Forty-second Street he had to make his first strategic decision of the day—whether to cross the platform and take the express to the Bowling Green stop directly opposite his office, or to continue on the local and walk the last ten minutes to work from Brooklyn Bridge. He was sure of a seat on the local, but the express would be faster. There was no express in the station, so he would have to wait. What was the weather? A nice day; he would stay on the local and walk from the last stop. Not much of a decision, Frost had thought one morning, but a more exciting one than deciding whether to take the buggy or the Studebaker into town.

The local train began to fill up as it waited at the Grand Central stop. Without any bidding on his part,

Frost found himself almost physically a part of an entourage consisting of a young black woman and two tiny children, a girl in a stroller and a boy at her side. The woman, barely twenty Frost thought, deftly manipulated the stroller, the wiggly boy and a large carryall with diapers and a baby bottle. With some relief, she sat down next to Frost, but had to move over as the boy climbed between them.

Frost continued reading his newspaper but soon became aware of two small dark eyes staring up at him. He looked directly at the elfin starer, whose look continued unfazed.

"Hello," Frost said.

The boy opened his mouth but without speaking.

"What's your name?"

No response; Frost repeated the question, looking at the boy's mother as he did so. She smiled back politely, pleased at the attention her tiny son was attracting, yet at the same time vaguely wary lest the seemingly nice man should turn out to be some form of monster or bigot.

"Eddie."

"Your name is Eddie?"

"Yes." Then, after a pause, "What's yours?"

Frost was slightly taken aback by his bold new friend, but replied nonetheless. "My name is Reuben."

"Reuben?"

"That's right."

"Where are you going?"

"I'm going to work."

"We're going to grandma's."

"To stay?"

"No, just to visit. Do you have a grandma?"

"Not any more. I used to."

"Used to. Used to." Eddie became more animated and jumped on the seat. "Used to! Used to!" His mother took hold of him and tried to calm him down.

"Come on, Eddie. We're getting off here."

"Used to! Used to!" the boy continued to chant.

"Sorry, mister. He's only three but he's uncontrollable already,'' the woman said to Frost as she gathered up her objects, animate and inanimate.

''Not at all. He's a very cute youngster,'' Frost replied. ''And so is the little girl,'' he added, gesturing to the tiny sleeping figure in the stroller.

''Thank you.'' She smiled and moved toward the door.

The children were indeed cute, the mother attractive. Where did they live? What did the father do? What would become of the children? Frost speculated on these questions for an instant before returning to the newspaper. He wished them well—mother, son, daughter, unseen father, and even grandma—and hoped that the perils of the city's underside would not claim any of them.

At Brooklyn Bridge Frost left the train, crossed beside City Hall and then walked down Broadway to One Metropolitan Plaza. As he did so, he thought enthusiastically about helping young Griffith with his drafting.

It was a beautiful day and Frost was determined to seize upon it and enjoy it, with the zest that only a septuagenarian can muster. It was too bad that enjoyment would not last through lunch.

DEATH AT THE CLUB

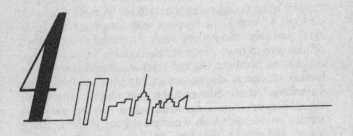

THE TRAINING TABLE. THAT WAS WHAT THE MORE IRREVERENT young associates at Chase & Ward called the round lunch table at the Hexagon Club reserved for partners of the firm. The theory was that partners not otherwise busy for lunch could come there for a fast meal, but one enjoyed in the relaxed surroundings of the club and in the company of their colleagues. And, it might be added, create a tax deduction to the firm for the cost of the lunches, at least in the view of Keith Merritt, the amiable southerner who was Chase & Ward's senior tax partner. After all, Merritt reasoned, the primary purpose of the luncheon gatherings was to provide a forum for the refined, collegial discussion of legal problems of mutual concern.

The practice did not quite live up to the theory. There were ten places at the table and thirty-seven Chase & Ward partners, not to mention Reuben Frost and four other retired partners. The end result was a pressing competition for seats on rainy days (the club was located on the top floor of the One Metro building where Chase & Ward had its offices) and on days when a large number of partners did not have lunch plans elsewhere.

Dorothea Cowden, the firm's receptionist, monitored the traffic to and from the Hexagon Club, assigning places at the table on a first-come, first-served basis. Her skills as a traffic director were considerable, but not equal to coping with those who did not register their comings and goings with her.

Ms. Cowden's biggest problems were the five retired partners (rather fancifully dubbed the Five Little Peppers by a flip young colleague, familiar with old-fashioned children's books). In keeping with long-standing tradition, partners who retired were permitted to keep their offices and to have lunch at the Training Table.

Another prerogative, the right to attend the weekly formal luncheon of the firm's partners, had been revoked by George Bannard the year before. There was no malice or ill will involved; some of the old boys simply talked too much. Unlike sessions at the Training Table, the weekly lunches, held in a private room at MacMillan's, a downtown restaurant, were devoted to firm business requiring relatively organized discussion. To keep the length of these sessions within reasonable bounds, most partners—and active retired partners like Frost—judiciously edited their own remarks. But at least three of the Peppers looked upon these lunches as a sort of picnic—a chance once again to talk and be listened to. Their irrelevant comment and reminiscing had started a mini-rebellion and forced George Bannard to disinvite them for the future; of course, to minimize the embarrassment, Bannard had banished all five of the retired partners, rather than just the three addled offenders. The result was to annoy Reuben Frost mightily and to make the Training Table lunches on other days a more valuable prize to all the retired partners and, it seemed, to increase the regularity of their attendance.

The Training Table was the scene of constant arrivals and departures during the lunch hour. Some preferred to eat early, others came to lunch on the late side. Chaos was the order of the day for the assigned waiter, who tried valiantly to take the orders of those just sitting down while almost simultaneously serving coffee and dessert to others. It was an impatient, demanding group; working the Chase & Ward table was considered a hardship post and one that no Hexagon Club waiter endured for long.

The quality of conversation varied widely with the

mix of participants. Often there was a lively discussion of a real legal issue (*pace* Internal Revenue Service); at other times talk revolved around whatever subjects the more dominant and outgoing partners selected. Often the partners' interchanges were highly civilized and intelligent, worthy of the best luncheon club; at other times they could become raucous and silly.

On Tuesday, September 12, at 12:30 P.M., events at the Training Table were fairly typical. Bannard, an habitué—he claimed it was his one means of staying in touch with the partners he was supposed to be leading—was sitting next to Arthur Tyson who, in his most brusque, playing field manner, was berating the table's waiter for bringing him trout when he had *distinctly* ordered sole. The waiter removed the offending trout—he was much too harried to argue that Tyson was wrong—and went off to the kitchen. Tyson nonetheless continued his tirade.

"I don't know where they get these waiters from. The last one we had couldn't speak English. Now we get one who speaks English but apparently can't hear. Or can't think. With the business we give this club, we ought to be able to get—"

"Oh, Arthur, come on. If the guy were any smarter he wouldn't be a waiter." The speaker was Marvin Isaacs, one of the firm's youngest partners, but one unafraid of tangling with his elders. His frequent settings-to-right were normally not resented because he was not in the least unpleasant in putting them forth. Indeed, his views were often welcomed because he had the sangfroid to express what others were too timid to say.

It was clear that Tyson would have continued the argument. But Graham Donovan, sitting across the table, deftly turned the conversation to a subject of great interest among the assembled partners—the stolen Stephens Industries press release.

"George, have you heard anything from Ross Doyle about Stephens?" Donovan asked Bannard. He lowered his voice when he did so, mindful that the partners' table for Rudenstine, Fried & D'Arms adjoined Chase & Ward's.

"No, nothing yet."

"I wish he'd get to the bottom of it soon. I just hope no part of the 'family' has betrayed us." Donovan avoided looking at Roger Singer, sitting next to him, as he spoke of betrayal. Roger, a cipher as usual, said nothing and reacted not at all.

"I do too, Graham. But we'll just have to wait and see," Bannard said.

"If there's a guilty party, I don't care who it is," Tyson chimed in. "If someone has been abusing his position as an employee, or lawyer, or whatever—maybe even as partner—there are only two possible things to do: get rid of him and call the district attorney."

"I hope it turns out as easy as you make it sound," Bannard responded.

"What are you boys talking about?" Reuben Frost asked.

"Nothing, Reuben. Just a problem we're having with one of the cleaning ladies. We think she may have taken some papers," Bannard explained.

"The cleaning lady took some papers? What papers?" Reuben pressed. From his conversation with Joe Mather, he knew precisely what his colleagues were talking about. But he decided to remain silent about what he knew.

"We don't know that, Reuben. Just a suspicion, and not important anyway. Nothing to get excited about."

"But Arthur was talking about calling the district attorney. Sounds pretty serious to me," Reuben said, still persisting with his feigned ignorance. "But that's all right, you don't have to tell me. If the thing's as serious as Arthur makes out, I can wait and read about it in the newspapers." He chuckled, and in a way not entirely free of malice.

"George, you mentioned cleaning ladies. I'm sure that's no longer what they're called," interrupted Keith Merritt in his mellow southern accent and habitually sardonic tone. "You'll get us up on a civil rights charge if you're not careful. Dis-crim-i-*na*-tion." He stretched out the syllables of "discrimination" and rolled his eyes.

As Merritt spoke, Bannard wondered to himself why

it was that so many southerners—including Merritt—sounded like histrionic actresses? Dis-crim-i-*na*-tion, indeed! Merritt, whom Bannard knew (or thought he knew) to be straight, nonetheless sounded at times like a refugee from a road company of *La Cage Aux Folles*.

"Yes, George, what do you call cleaning ladies these days?" Donovan, sitting between Roger Singer and Merritt, interjected. "Cleaning women? Cleaning persons?"

"Well, if you do it like those geniuses who run the City Bar Association, where they call their committee heads 'chairs,' they probably should be called 'cleanings,' " Fred Coxe chimed in.

"I would opt for 'environmental assistants,' " Donovan joked. "Very euphemistic, and trendy besides."

"Well, boys, you can have all the fun you want," Bannard said. "But I'm too damn old to start changing what I call people. Chairs—ridiculous! Cleaning persons—stupid! They were cleaning ladies when I came to work at Chase & Ward forty years ago, and as far as I'm concerned, they are cleaning ladies today."

"As opposed to plant ladies," Coxe added.

"Plant ladies? What the hell are you talking about?" Bannard shot back.

"Just what I said. Plant ladies. They come around once a week and water and trim the plants in your office."

"I don't believe it."

"That's probably because you don't have any plants to tend."

"As a matter of fact, I don't," Bannard said. "But where do they come from? Who pays them?"

"We do, George," Merritt said. "Two hundred dollars a week to Plant Gems, a nice little business specializing in watering plants for prosperous firms like ours."

Once again Merritt had shown his intimate knowledge of the minutest inner workings of the firm.

"Who hired these people, these plant ladies?" Bannard demanded.

"Kidde, of course," Merritt replied, naming the office manager.

"What in the name of God is wrong with having the secretaries water the plants?"

Oh, oh, George," Merritt said, reverting to his most histrionic manner. "Secretaries are *professionals,* not gardeners. They don't get you coffee in the morning, they don't do your errands, and they don't water your plants."

"Well, some do," Donovan said, rather proudly. "Miss Appleby gets me a Danish every morning. But you're right about the plant ladies. Why, two of them were in my office yesterday, trying to resuscitate some poor old thing that Marjorie gave me to put in my office before she died. Dwight Draper was visiting me at the time and said Marjorie's plant would need more than water to revive it."

"I am damned," Bannard said. "But chalk up one more thing done around here behind the Executive Partner's back."

"You probably don't know about the phone wipers either," Coxe said in his best tattletale voice.

"*Phone* wipers—"

"Yes, once every two weeks these women come around and wipe the germs off—"

"I don't want to hear it," Bannard shouted. "I simply don't want to hear it. Merritt, I suppose as usual you know all about this too?"

"I'm afraid I do, and I've been meaning to speak to you about it," Merritt said. "I found a payment to these people—Phone-genics I believe the outfit is called—in the accounts a couple of weeks ago. I asked Kidde about it and he said his friend, the office manager at Rudenstine, Fried & D'Arms, had hired them and he thought it was a good idea too."

"Well, I don't care what they do at Rudenstine, Fried & D'Arms and I don't care if every person there gets herpes from their phone receivers. It's the silliest damn waste of money I've ever heard of and I'll have Kidde stop it at once," Bannard said in a voice that caught the attention of the Rudenstine, Fried table.

"I agree with you, George, and told Kidde exactly the same thing. But . . ."

"But what, Keith?"

"But Kidde has signed Phone-genics to a two-year contract," Merritt answered.

"Damn, damn, damn. What will that idiot do next?"

Bannard's question went unanswered since, as he finished speaking, Graham Donovan began coughing violently, his chest heaving visibly. He became ashen and then his face muscles and arms started twitching. He clutched at his abdomen, rocked to one side and fell from his chair, first onto Roger Singer and then to the ground. Singer almost fell with him, but managed to clutch the table for balance. As Singer lurched against the table, he sent dishes and glasses to the floor, crashing around Donovan.

Donovan's colleagues were too stunned to react for an instant, but then they all began shouting and moving about at once.

"Get a doctor!" Bannard screamed out.

"Get an ambulance!" Coxe echoed.

Nine of the country's finest lawyers fell all over themselves in their efforts to assist their fallen colleague. Donovan was on his back, his arms and face still twitching.

Some order was brought to the scene by a take-charge woman lawyer from Rudenstine, Fried & D'Arms who ran over to Donovan, loosened his tie and began massaging his chest.

The Hexagon Club's headwaiter went through the dining room urgently seeking a doctor, but without success; no doctor was apparently seeing his lawyer or his broker that day.

Bannard kept asking if a doctor had been called. He was assured that one was on the way. The other lawyers from Chase & Ward stood around, somewhat ashamed at the cool competence of their Rudenstine, Fried colleague, who continued to press down on Donovan's chest in an effort to stabilize his breathing.

Many guests in the dining room left quietly; it seemed somehow indecent to continue eating while a man was dying in the same room.

A team of medics arrived with a stretcher, supervised by an overweight but most decisive woman.

"Okay, stand back," she called out as she and her two assistants approached Donovan. The Rudenstine, Fried lawyer continued her ministrations, even more frantically as Donovan's wails got weaker and his face changed color in a most eerie way from ashen gray to beet-red to gray-blue. The woman medic gently but firmly pushed the lawyer aside and quickly scanned Donovan's face, twitching arms and heaving chest. She pulled a stethoscope from her pocket and began listening to Donovan's heart beat, then pounded vigorously on his chest.

As she did so, Donovan became progressively quieter and then, with one massive, convulsive twitch, lay still.

The medic got up, surveyed the onlookers and instinctively turned to Bannard, the tallest man present.

"I'm afraid we're too late," she said quietly. One of the other medics covered the body with a blanket, while the second called the police on his walkie-talkie. "Did you know him?"

"Yes, we were law partners together. What was it, heart?" Bannard asked.

"I'm sure it was. Did he have a history of heart trouble?"

"Yes. He had a mild heart attack about, oh, five years ago. But as far as I know he had not had any trouble since. Did you, Keith?"

"No. He was always waging a battle of the waistline, but I thought he was basically in good shape," Merritt answered.

"Well, we'll have to wait for the police and a medical examiner anyway," the woman medic said.

"Police?" Bannard asked. "Is that necessary?"

"S.O.P., sir. Both police and a doc from the M.E.'s office whenever there's a sudden death like this."

"What happens then?" Bannard asked.

"They'll take the body to the morgue and do an autopsy. Then when the death certificate's signed, they'll release it. Will one of you gentlemen claim the body?" the woman asked, looking around the perplexed group.

"One of you really ought to stay here to answer questions about the deceased and then go to the M.E.'s office to claim the body."

Bannard now surveyed the group and called Arthur Tyson aside. Tough lineman Arthur Tyson, the ideal match for policemen and coroners.

"Arthur, can you stay around?" he asked.

"Sure. Let me call my secretary to postpone a meeting I had at three. But yes, I can do it. Leave it to me, George. I'll cut through the chickenshit in no time." No red tape was going to delay Arthur Tyson for long.

"I suppose the body should go to Frank Campbell's," Bannard said. "I'll try to reach Graham's son, but unless you hear otherwise that's what I'd do."

"Good. I'll call them while I'm waiting," Tyson said. "By the way, who was Graham's doctor, Stanley Hall?"

"I think so. In fact, I'm sure of it. Graham mentioned visiting him just a couple of weeks ago."

Leaving Tyson hostage, Bannard turned to the remaining partners and said he thought it was time to leave. Then he saw the Rudenstine, Fried lawyer who had worked over Donovan. She was still trying to collect herself as Bannard approached her.

"I'm sorry, we haven't met. I'm George Bannard."

"I'm Angelica Post."

"I can't thank you enough for what you tried to do."

"It was nothing. Really nothing, since it did no good."

"But you tried. That's what's important. And you knew more about what to do than any of us."

"Well, let's hope I won't have to do what I did again right away."

"I hope so, too. And Chase & Ward thanks Rudenstine, Fried."

Ms. Post smiled and turned away. Bannard turned toward the exit. His partners, like chastened—and slightly frightened—children, dutifully followed him out of the dining room.

ARRANGEMENTS

5

BANNARD REACHED HIS OFFICE, SHUT THE DOOR AND BEGAN organizing his thoughts. He must call Donovan's next of kin. Who was there? He thought a son—Bruce was it?—but was not entirely sure. He buzzed Mrs. Davis, his secretary, and asked her to find out if the boy's name was indeed Bruce and to try and locate him.

"If I'm not mistaken, he's a professor at New York University," Bannard told her. "Archaeology, I think."

Mrs. Davis was back on the line within minutes. The son's name was indeed Bruce, he did teach at NYU, and he was holding on the line.

Talking with Bruce Donovan was trying, to say the least.

"So the old man's dead is he? That's a surprise," he said to Bannard. Then, after a pause, he continued, "I can't really say I'm heartbroken, Mr. Bannard. We were not on very good terms. Not on very good terms at all, in fact . . . Funeral? Have any kind you want, Mr. Bannard. But I doubt that I will be there . . . Why do I feel this way? Because, to put it bluntly, he was unspeakable to my mother. Unspeakable to her at a time when I couldn't do anything about it. Made her suffer, made me humiliated. It would be the greatest hypocrisy in the world for me to go to his funeral. But thanks anyway for letting me know."

Bannard hung up on dutiful son Bruce with some

relief, although realizing that he would get no help from junior; the funeral arrangements, the obituary—everything—were squarely in his lap.

But how could he take care of all this and keep to his schedule? He was supposed to leave almost immediately for Chicago for an intensive meeting with his client, Bernard Sussman, and Sussman's financial people. Sussman's oil drilling company, Mid-Coast Enterprises, was in the process of considering the acquisition of a large and successful mail-order company. Not exactly a synergistic fit with oil drilling, but a chance to diversify and a chance to pick up a highly successful company that the smart young MBAs around the autocratic Sussman thought could be obtained at an attractive price. Sussman and his financial assistants and their investment banking advisers were scheduled to meet late in the afternoon in Chicago to review all the pros and cons of the proposed acquisition in preparation for a Mid-Coast Board of Directors meeting the next day. Bannard had to be there; it was a command performance. Sussman was excessively demanding but he paid his bills; Bannard could not beg off merely because one of his partners had died.

What to do? Bannard closed his eyes and rubbed his forehead, attempting to resolve his scheduling problem. Then he remembered that he had to open Donovan's desk as well. He had never been sure where the charming custom had come from, but at Chase & Ward, when a partner died, the Executive Partner was expected to supervise going through the papers in the dead lawyer's desk immediately. He had only had to do this once since becoming the Executive Partner, and while no surprises had been uncovered, he nonetheless found the prospect distasteful. Presumably there had been good reason for the tradition—some dark embarrassment deep in the past of the firm (which had been founded almost a century earlier) that could have been avoided had a prompt search of a deceased partner's papers been made—and so he would carry it on.

As he thought about his dilemma, it suddenly occurred to him that Reuben Frost might be able to help out. He knew that Frost thought he had been given short shrift when Bannard had taken over the firm and that Frost was still at best out of sorts. But he could still handle the details incident to Donovan's death and burial; indeed, he might even get some quiet satisfaction out of dealing with the funeral arrangements of a man so many years his junior. Besides, there were those within the firm who admired Frost's shrewd common sense and felt, he was sure, that Frost had been a better Executive Partner than he. So, dammit, let him do the necessary dirty work while he, Bannard, went off to do real legal work in Chicago. Bannard went down the hall to Frost's office.

"Reuben, can I come in?" Bannard asked, pushing Frost's door open.

"Of course, George. Sit down." Frost swiveled his desk chair around to face Bannard, who was slightly embarrassed at the amount of room his large frame took up in the tiny office. It was clear that being the incumbent Executive Partner was better than being a former Executive Partner, at least in terms of square feet.

"Helluva thing about Graham, wasn't it? But I guess there's nothing could be done. That girl from Rudenstine, Fried seemed to know what she was doing, and she couldn't save him," Frost noted. "Have you talked to his boy?"

"Yes."

"What about Anne?"

"Anne? Anne who?" Bannard's voice became higher as he tried to play dumb.

"Oh, come now, George. Anne Singer. Surely you knew she and Graham were fiddling around," Frost said.

I did, but how did you? Bannard felt like saying. But he let the matter pass. "No, I didn't. I figure Roger will tell her soon enough."

"Yes, I suppose you're right." Frost paused, then shook his head. "You know, I'm quite taken aback.

When my old friends die these days, there's no surprise there. Just what's expected. But I'm surprised about Graham. Except for his weight, he always seemed to take care of himself. Not like your ferret friend Coxe. He gets shakier every day, and I'm sure the shakes come in a bottle with 'gin' written on it.''

"Now, Reuben, Fred has always been a nervous type. I don't see any evidence that he's drinking too much.''

"You wouldn't. He's your little toady.'' Frost sighed. "But I guess you were just following my advice.''

"What do you mean, Reuben?''

"Remember, when you became Executive Partner, I told you to get two or three partners that you really trusted, that you really could rely on, and use them as a sort of executive committee? Well, you've done that, though I'm not sure the ones you picked are the ones I would have picked.''

"Maybe not, Reuben, but they're the ones I trust. Including Coxe.''

"Of course including Coxe. He's the biggest ass-kisser in kingdom come. Has he ever said no to you about anything?''

"No, I can't say that he has,'' Bannard said, a slight defensive edge to his voice. "But I value his advice and I want him there to help me.''

"Fair enough. But why have you come to see me?''

"Reuben, I'm in a helluva fix. I've got to leave for Chicago for an important meeting with Bernard Sussman later this afternoon. And there seem to be a thousand and one details about Graham that have to be looked after.''

"Such as?''

"Such as arranging his funeral. When I talked to his son, he informed me that he had no intention of attending his father's funeral, let alone arranging it. Seems he and Graham weren't on speaking terms.''

"Any reason?''

"The way Graham treated Marjorie before she died. Do you know anything about that?''

"Not a thing," Frost said.

"Then there's the matter of opening Graham's desk. And arranging the obituary. I know it's an imposition, but I want to leave all these things in your lap."

"Sure. Glad to," Frost answered. "Let's start with the funeral arrangements. Wasn't Graham a Catholic?"

"I think he was brought up as one. But you remember he was married twice. First time to a little Italian girl I scarcely remember; didn't last long. Then to Marjorie. I do remember he married her at City Hall, so it doesn't appear that he was much of a Catholic."

"I'm not so sure, George. I don't know much about it, but I gather the Church of Rome isn't quite as rigid as it used to be. But anyway, assuming you're right, what do we do?"

"We could have him cremated and have a memorial service later on, up at Columbia, or something like that," Bannard said.

"No, we should have a real funeral. There's my rector up at St. Justin's. I could ask him but he is so mellifluously unctuous that I would prefer not to. How about Dr. Clark up at Second Memorial? Very nondenominational, and he will bury anybody."

"You know him?"

"Sure. He used to be on the board of the Gotham Club with me. Want me to call him?"

"That would be splendid, Reuben. When should we have the funeral?"

"Well, there's no family to worry about, so I say the sooner the better," Frost said.

"Thursday morning? Is that too soon?"

"No, I don't think so. What time?"

"How about eleven?"

"Bad for the office, George. Means people have to come here first and then go uptown. Or worse, they don't come to work at all and go directly to the church. I'd vote for ten."

"Should we close the office?"

"What do you think?"

"I don't know," Bannard said. "I've never figured out when we do and when we don't."

"Oh come, come, George. Think about it. We closed the office when Holderness and McKeon died, but not when Larrimore did. What does that tell you?"

"Well, Holderness and McKeon both were very active right up to the time they died, while Larrimore didn't contribute all that much."

"Contribute. Contribute. You've got the idea. There are many intangible rewards to practising law as we do—it's good clean work and often exciting. But every so often dollars and cents make themselves felt, sometimes in subtle ways we don't even think about. Holderness brought business in and McKeon helped to hold what we had. Poor Larrimore did neither very effectively. So we didn't close the office for his funeral."

"I'm sure it's not that simple. Larrimore just wasn't very popular."

"But why?" Frost asked. "Because he was a drone and absolutely no good at bringing in business."

"Well, I would argue with you. But whatever the criteria, I guess we should close the office for Graham."

"All the more reason to have the service at ten."

"Should we march?" Bannard asked.

"Match? Match what?"

"No, Reuben, march. Should the partners all march in as a group?"

"What do you think?"

"I would say yes," Bannard said.

"I agree. Most often it's left up to the widow. But that doesn't apply here. Usually the widow has known her husband's partners over the years and wants that show of loyalty or solidarity or whatever you want to call it. But occasionally you get one who hates the firm, hates the demands it made on her husband, hates everything about it. Holderness's widow, for example. We were barely allowed to come to the funeral, let alone march in a body."

"Well, Graham was a stalwart of the firm and I believe loved it. We should march."

"What about the ushers?" Frost asked.

"Aren't they usually partners?"

"Yes. Usually contemporaries, except in this case you have the touchy matter of Roger Singer."

"Don't we have to ignore that? Wouldn't excluding Roger make things look worse?"

"You're probably right. And you'll also have to include Donovan's great friend, Arthur Tyson. He's a contemporary, though one could hardly call him Donovan's best friend. You should also be an usher, George, as you know the clients well."

"What about inviting people?"

"Absolutely. And someone should get started right away. How about your toady Fred? He'd be good at that."

"Reuben—"

"Never mind. Put him to work on it as soon as I clear the time with the minister. You should make sure all the people at Graham's major clients know about it. Joe Mather at Stephens Industries—"

"Harry Knight at First Fiduciary Bank—"

"And I suppose that fellow with the chemical company, what's his name?" Frost asked.

"Draper. Dwight Draper. Draper Chemicals. I've never liked the fellow myself. Every time I've ever met him he's always told me what a wonderful firm Chase & Ward is, how wonderful everybody here is, how wonderful I am, et cetera. And he says all those smarmy things in a manner about as sincere as Dick Nixon's."

"I know all that, George. Our lives all would be pleasanter if all our clients were people we would want to have as our best friends. But probably not at all as involving. Not all the interesting people in this town are to be found at the Racquet Club bar. Or even any of them, for that matter." Frost chuckled at his own joke. WASP though he was, the Racquet Club types were intensely boring to him.

"Reuben, you're probably right. But I draw the line at Draper. He tries so hard to ingratiate himself that he really makes you sick. I never could understand how Graham put up with him."

"My guess is that Graham put up with him because he was proud of having gotten him started. Draper was nothing, a chemical engineer from some tank-town university—in Pennsylvania, I think. No money, just a lot of hustle and apparently a damned good idea for making a line of industrial chemicals cheaper than the majors, like Du Pont or Dow. Somehow he made friends with Harry Knight, who loaned him enough to get started in the chemicals business. Harry told Dwight that he should get a good lawyer and recommended Graham. Graham took him on as a favor to Harry, but at the same time Draper was probably the first real client Graham had on his very own. In circumstances like that, it would have been very hard to get rid of him later, even assuming Graham wanted to. Draper got rich—at least in comparison to where he came from. And once he got rich he wanted to be buddies with the big boys—among whom he includes, rightly or wrongly, the likes of you and me. And besides, I've never heard that he was anything but honest."

"I suppose you're right. I still don't like him. But God knows he should be at Graham's funeral if anyone is."

Bannard got up and began pacing the room, as was his habit.

"Is that it?" Bannard said. "You'll call your minister friend, right? We'll try for 10 A.M. Thursday. I'll send around a notice asking the partners to march in a body and ask Roger and Arthur to be ushers with me. Why don't you and Fred try to draw up a list of those to ask? That would help me a lot."

"Of course, George," Reuben answered agreeably.

"Oh, and Reuben, what about the dinner dance on Saturday? Should that be canceled, do you think?"

"Good God, I forgot all about it. That's a tough one. You could postpone it, but it will be hard to get a decent place to have it at this late date. A lot of the younger lawyers would be disappointed too, I think, since they plan ahead for the thing. Besides, Graham always liked

a good party and would not have wanted to be the cause
of not going ahead.''

''I think you're right.''

''We used to have the dance around Thanksgiving,
you recall. I remember the year John Kennedy was shot
and we were supposed to have the dance a week later.
We went ahead with it, but it was a little embarrassing.''

''I had forgotten that. I say let's go ahead as planned.''

''Sounds like you've got everything under control,
George. But what about Graham's desk?''

''I know, I know. I was hoping you could take care of
that, too.''

Frost nodded.

''How the hell did that ghoulish custom start, anyway?'' Bannard asked.

''I don't know whether there was a specific reason or
not. I suppose one theory is you might find an unex-
pected suicide note, or burial instructions, or something
like that.''

''I suppose.''

''All I can say is, during the years when I was Executive Partner, I went through the ritual four—no, five—
times and the only thing I ever found of any interest at
all was a small pornography collection locked in Ray
McKeon's desk. I suspect performing the ritual this time
will be pretty uneventful.''

Bannard agreed with his predecessor and left, telling
Frost that he could be reached if necessary at Sussman's
office or the Chicago Ritz.

After Bannard's departure, Reuben Frost felt a curious sense of well-being. Was it simply because he had
been found useful once again? Or perhaps because George
Bannard was demonstrating that arranging a funeral was
beyond him? Whatever the reason, he must get organized. What to do first? He guessed he should talk to
Grace Appleby, Donovan's secretary. She deserved to
be told about her boss's death and could also tell him if
he had been a practicing Catholic.

(Besides, Frost was more than a little curious to see

Appleby. She had been around the firm for years and he had known her from the earliest days when she had been in the typing pool. But now he wanted to talk with her, knowing that she might be the culprit in the Stephens Industries matter. She could easily have diverted the controversial press release on its way to the office files and made a copy without anyone else knowing. There was no reason to think Miss Appleby was anything but an upstanding—if, from many accounts, a somewhat disagreeable—woman. But she still was a suspect.)

He called her on the phone and she said she would come to his office right away.

"Yes, Mr. Frost?" Miss Appleby said, as she opened his door. "What can I do for you?"

"Sit down, Miss Appleby. I'm afraid I have some bad news for you."

"What is it?" She seemed unperturbed.

"Graham Donovan is dead. He had a seizure of some sort at lunch and died immediately."

"Oh my. What a shocking thing. How did it happen?"

"He was sitting at the firm table at the Hexagon Club when all of a sudden he started coughing. He grabbed his stomach, fell on the floor and within minutes he was dead."

"How awful. Was it his heart?"

"I suppose so. Had he been ill lately, Miss Appleby?"

"No, to the contrary. He had really watched his health since that heart scare he had a few years ago. His only problem was his stomach—he had had at least two ulcers in recent years—but that was under control. He took Tagamet and that seemed to help."

"Tagamet?"

"Yes. That antiulcer drug that has become so common. It treats ulcers without surgery. And has been a big success for Smith Kline & French, the manufacturer."

"My goodness, how do you know all that, Miss Appleby?"

"Oh, just something I read somewhere, I suppose. But I heard about the wonders of Tagamet from Mr. Donovan very day. I brought him a Danish pastry every morning. That and some awful powdered iced tea and a Tagamet were his breakfast.''

"Iced tea?"

"Yes. He couldn't have coffee because of his stomach. So he drank iced tea instead. Made it himself with the powder he kept in his desk. I have never tasted it, but it must be awful.''

"Grace, I mean, Miss Appleby—"

"Oh, good heavens, Mr. Frost, after all these years you may certainly call me Grace—"

"Grace, I seem to be stuck with making the funeral arrangements. But before I do that, I need to know one thing. Was Graham a Catholic when he died?"

"He was a Catholic once, but I don't think he'd been to church in years, Mr. Frost. Not since his second marriage anyway.''

"What about this son of his, Bruce? He's the only next of kin, I gather?"

"That's right. Of course he and Mr. Donovan were not on very good terms, you know," Miss Appleby said.

Frost did not let on that he knew this. "What was the difficulty?" he asked.

"It all started when Mrs. Donovan had her stroke, about two years before she died. She was in terrible shape—could hardly speak at all, memory impaired, and very little use of her arms and legs. Mr. Donovan decided she had to be put in a nursing home, but Bruce objected violently. He was very close to his mother and he felt she should remain at home. It was easy for him to say, of course, because he didn't live there. But Mr. Donovan was adamant, and his wife was in a nursing home all the time until she died.''

"It sounds to me as if maybe the son was right. Certainly Graham could afford whatever it would have cost to keep his wife at home.''

"Oh, but Mr. Frost, you don't know how depressing it is for a healthy person to be around a stroke victim. I know, I had my father living with me for seven years after he had a stroke. And I see it all the time at St. Blaise's.''

"St. Blaise's?"

"Yes, the hospital. I do volunteer work there on the weekends, and I must say sometimes it is an effort to deal with patients who have become vegetables."

"I see."

"So I understand how Mr. Donovan felt. But Bruce never did. As far as I know, they have barely spoken since Mrs. Donovan's death."

"Most unfortunate."

"Yes, it was very sad."

"Well, thank you . . . Grace."

She got up from her chair and headed toward the door.

"Oh, and Grace, don't worry about your future here," Frost said. "I'm no longer in charge of things, as you know, but I'm sure something can be worked out for you. Mr. Kidde can talk to you about that when all this settles down."

"I'm not worried, Mr. Frost. But I'd just as soon wait until I get over the shock of Mr. Donovan's death, too. You don't just work for someone for twenty-five years and then start in for someone else, or doing something else." She paused, but there was no sign of tears or losing control. "I've never been married, Mr. Frost, but I can't help thinking that such close work for so long a time is a little bit like marriage."

"Perhaps so, Miss Appleby. In any event, I'm very sorry. Graham was a valuable member of this firm and we are going to miss him.

Miss Appleby left, leaving Frost to muse upon their encounter. What a cool customer Grace Appleby had become! No tears, and barely even a suggestion of sorrow at Graham's death, despite the remark about twenty-five years of "marriage." And a deliberate fastidiousness in conversation that seemed to him to conceal some sort of hostility or resentment. But was she responsible for the Stephens escapade? It did not seem in character.

Frost called his friend Dr. Clark and the funeral was arranged as planned for Thusday morning. Hanging up the phone he sighed, as a result of both Dr. Clark's cheerful-in-the-face-of-adversity manner and the dreary prospect of going through his late colleague's desk.

He sighed still again, thinking how boring the impending task would be. Reuben Frost, a man of great wisdom, was for once not quite correct.

A NASTY SPILL

6

Frost called Wayne Kidde, the office manager, and asked to meet him at Donovan's office. "George Bannard has asked me to go through Graham's desk, and I think now would be a good time," he said.

Kidde, a veteran of these gruesome rites, said he would be there at once.

Donovan, as a senior partner of Chase & Ward, had a large corner office on the north side of the building. Frost reflected, not without some amusement, on the rigid seniority system that prevailed in assigning offices at the firm, a system that had prevailed as well in the firm's earlier locations where he had also worked: first a shared double cubbyhole, sitting by the door; then a shared double cubbyhole, sitting by the window; then a single cubbyhole; then a partner's office two windows wide; then a partner's office three windows wide; then a corner office with so many windows that one could not, as Donovan had often said, find a shelf on which to put anything. (There was, of course, the next, and final move, to smaller quarters for those who became "of counsel," but Frost saw no reason to dwell on that.)

Frost strode purposefully down the corridor to avoid being interrupted by those wanting to discuss Graham's death, the news of which he was sure had passed along the office's amazing grapevine by now.

The Miss Appleby he encountered outside Donovan's

office was a changed woman. From cool detachment she had gone to deep, noisy and practically uncontrolled sobbing. Her face was ashen, her makeup a runny stream on her face. Had there been a genuine change of mood or had she simply decided that some theatrics were in order? Frost had no way of telling.

"Miss Appleby, Mr. Kidde and I are going to open Graham's desk. Is it locked?"

"Yes. He always locked it. But I have the key."

Nearly in tears, she rummaged in her own desk and pulled out a pair of keys on a silver ring. Kidde, who had joined Frost, led the way into Donovan's office. From appearances, it was hard to think that its occupant was dead. It was almost compulsively neat. Frost, himself favoring modern furniture, nonetheless had always recognized that the traditional furnishings in Donovan's office were of the first quality. He now recalled sadly their kidding on the subject, with Donovan flinging the adjective "Hollywood" at him and he tossing "fusty" back at the younger man.

The top of Donovan's desk gave the impression that its user had only stepped away for a moment. A thick document was open in the middle of the blotter, a pair of reading glasses folded on top of it and a pencil beside it. On examination, it turned out to be a contract to which Stephens Industries was a party, with notes in Donovan's small, careful handwriting in the margin.

There was little else of interest on top of the desk. A pen and pencil set inscribed with the details of a debenture financing dating back almost a decade. A *London Economist* desk calendar. The standard issue water carafe given to all the partners. ("One of the few perks of being a Chase & Ward partner," Donovan had once joked to Frost, failing to mention the take-home pay.) On the tray holding the carafe was a used glass with traces of sugar in the bottom, presumably left over from Donovan's morning Danish—iced tea—Tagamet ritual.

Frost opened the desk calendar. It was virtually blank for the week, except for a capital A entered on both Sunday and Monday evenings. A? Anne Singer, Frost assumed. He then tried the middle drawer and found it locked.

"Do you have the key, Miss Appleby?" he asked. She handed him the silver ring and she and Kidde watched as he opened the desk.

If any of the three witnesses had either prying or prurient urges concerning Donovan's personal effects, they were disappointed. Frost picked out of the middle drawer in succession a box of cough drops, a Mont Blanc pen, a Morgan Guaranty checkbook, a Chase & Ward office directory, a folder of traveler's checks. There was also a sheaf of bills, all addressed to Donovan, from expectable sources—American Express, his laundry, Saks Fifth Avenue—a telephone message form with a doodle and the words "Draper—negative pledge?" written in Donovan's handwriting at the bottom, a pair of theater tickets for the following evening.

Frost moved on to the top drawer on the side, which contained nothing but paper clips, rubber bands and sharpened number two pencils. In the drawer beneath were the paraphernalia for Donovan's iced tea fixes—a bottle of instant iced tea ("with fresh lemon added") and a box of individual sugar packets. Finally, in the large drawer at the bottom of the desk were a series of file envelopes of papers, which Frost removed one by one.

"This seems to be a copy of Graham's will," he noted, lifting a document with a blue back from the first folder. He leafed through it.

"Well, Miss Appleby, Graham appears to have left you twenty-five thousand dollars," Frost said, turning to the distraught secretary.

"Oh, Mr. Frost. I don't know what to say. I didn't expect a thing . . ." She burst into tears anew. Frost felt quite helpless. As lord of the manor (or at least acting lord of the manor), he didn't feel he could physically comfort her and was grateful when Kidde, being more or less of the same social station, put his arm around the sobbing woman and, to Frost's great relief, calmed her.

Frost resumed looking through the folders in Dono-

van's drawer—past income tax returns, his copy of the
Chase & Ward partnership agreement, the ownership
papers for his cooperative apartment. He scanned them
all rapidly as Miss Appleby and Kidde watched. Then,
becoming impatient with the whole process, he began
looking through the remaining folders even more quickly.
While doing so, he came across a red-covered folio he
recognized as being the most recent Chase & Ward
financial statements. He attempted to shove them back
into the folder that had contained them but in his haste
only managed to drop them on the floor. Kidde, ever the
obliging underling, quickly stooped to pick them up. But
Frost was not about to let him so much as touch the
financials, the most closely guarded secret of the partnership, and lunged to grab them before Kidde could do
so. In the process, Frost knocked over Donovan's water
carafe. The top of the carafe fell off, covering the desk
blotter, and Frost's pants, with water.

Frost cursed as he attempted to rescue both the red
folder and his trousers.

Kidde, having been rebuffed in his attempt to retrieve
the fallen document, straightened up and then shouted
"Good God! Look at that!"

Frost also straightened up and looked where Kidde
was pointing—at the blotter with the spot of spilled
water. The blotter was not simply discolored, but covered with a deep brownish stain. Frost quickly looked at
his pants. They too had become discolored in a way that
would not have been possible with pure water.

"What the hell do you suppose was in that water?"
Frost asked.

"I don't know, but it's very strange," said Kidde.

Miss Appleby, who had observed the whole sequence
of events, was silent.

"Do you know anything about this, Miss Appleby?"
Frost asked.

"No, sir. I can't explain it at all. Do you think . . .oh,
it is too terrible even to think about," she said, shaking
her head.

"Do you think what, Miss Appleby?" Frost snapped.

"Nothing, nothing. Except . . . except . . . Mr. Donovan drank from that water, or made his iced tea from that water, this morning."

"Are you sure of that?"

"I saw him."

Frost waited no longer. He took out his handkerchief and used it to pick up and replace the cover to the carafe. He then picked up the tray holding the carafe and a used glass, his handkerchief still covering his hand, and dashed for the door, calling over his shoulder, "Don't either of you say a word about this. I'll talk to you later."

He was so flustered that he forgot the secret financials, which sat in their folder on Donovan's desk for all the world to see. But the faithful Kidde picked the folder up, replaced it in the drawer, and locked the desk with the key that Frost had forgotten on the desk. Needless to say, he didn't look inside the folder, pretending that he was not aware of its significance. Besides, whatever Frost might think of the sacrosanct status of the firm's financial statements, their contents were not exactly a secret to one who had been Chase & Ward's office manager for more than ten years.

"Grace, I think you'd better keep this key," Kidde said to Miss Appleby.

"If you think so, Wayne," she replied.

"And maybe you'd better lock the office too," Kidde added.

"That's a good idea."

They went outside and Kidde left. Neither one spoke to the other about the possible meaning of what they had just seen.

Frost returned to his office, the offending—and very probably poisonous—objects on the tray in his hand. He marched by Miss O'Hara, his secretary, and went directly into his own office and closed the door. He buzzed Miss O'Hara on the intercom and told her that under no circumstances was he to be disturbed.

He slumped into his desk chair, trying by relaxing to

drive out the insistent, nasty forebodings from his head. In one instant the death, already a dramatic one, of Graham Donovan had perhaps become something else.

Frost fought against the suspicion—suspicion, hell, the conclusion—that Donovan's death had been murder. Murder by poisoning. Was it really possible that this had occurred in the offices of Chase & Ward? He looked at the carafe and the glass beside it with horror.

He picked up the telephone and tried to reach Bannard. But he was unreachable, en route to Chicago. He had to discuss his horrid findings with someone. His fellow retired partners? No, he thought impatiently, they would be useless. What about George Bannard's Executive Committee? Not exactly his favorites, but this was no time to stand on personal feelings. Pressing his intercom once again, he asked Miss O'Hara to ask Keith Merritt, Arthur Tyson and Fred Coxe to come to his office at once.

Before she had made the calls, he buzzed her again: "On second thought, Miss O'Hara, have them come to Bannard's office. There isn't room enough in here."

If they were going to discuss murder, they might as well be comfortable.

EMERGENCY SESSIONS

7

JUSTICE BRANDEIS ONCE OBSERVED THAT IN MOST CASES BE-
fore the Supreme Court the actual decision did not really
matter; the important thing was getting the controversy
in question settled. The same was true of most problems
at Chase & Ward. Someone—the Executive Partner—
had to resolve them, but no one really cared very much
about the result.

There were certain matters, however, that the Executive Partner most emphatically could not decide by himself. Most questions involving profit distributions, for
example. Or the delicate question of who—if anyone—
the firm should represent when two clients found themselves in conflict. These had to be decided by informal
consensus or, if sufficiently serious, by the firm as a
whole. Chase & Ward was after all a democracy, with
"one man, one vote" applicable to each of its partners.
That is what its partnership agreement, signed by each
member of the firm at the time of his admission, said.
But there were in fact few decisions that could not be
made by George Bannard acting alone or by Bannard
and his so-called Executive Committee.

Following Reuben Frost's advice, Bannard had set up
an informal "Executive Committee" consisting of Fred
Coxe, Keith Merritt, Arthur Tyson and Graham Donovan. It was a body with no recognized status at Chase &
Ward and was in no sense representative of anything—

including the firm's departments or the age or ethnic characteristics of the partners. (One could not even say that it was Bannard's cronies. He had once told his wife Eleanor that his "Executive Committee" was of great help to him, but he was just as happy he did not have to see its members other than at the occasional meetings for cocktails at the Hexagon Club.)

Each of the members contributed something different to Bannard's governance of the firm. Coxe, as Reuben Frost had rightly noted, was a busybody, a gossip and quite possibly a drunk. But he was able to bring to Bannard's attention bits of information and rumors that might not ordinarily reach the Executive Partner's ears.

Merritt had an odd cast of mind that somehow led him to take a genuine interest in the nuts and bolts of firm administration. The amount of a raise for a particular secretary, the purchase of a new Xerox machine, an analysis of this year's accounts receivable compared to last year's, all were matters that interested him. As a result, he knew more about the firm—and about its finances—than anyone else. He was thus indispensable to Bannard, who was perfectly happy to rely on Merritt's constant probing into the operations of the office.

Tyson was the wild card in Bannard's hand. His personal ambition usually tempered his behavior to his partners, though he seldom if ever displayed to them the deferential charm he seemed to reserve only for his trust and estates clients. He was also capable of temper outbursts that were unpleasant to see. As a result, he would not normally have been anyone's choice for a group designed to reach a consensus on the issues before it. But Bannard, with uncharacteristic shrewdness, had decided, as Lyndon Johnson had once said, that he would rather have Tyson inside the tent pissing out than outside pissing in.

Donovan had been a member of the committee as Bannard's heir apparent. His good humor was also invaluable—Bannard was not long on humor—in resolving whatever squabbles arose among the members.

Merritt and Coxe arrived in response to Frost's summons almost simultaneously; Tyson was absent, presumably still engaged in the distasteful business of claiming Donovan's body. The two partners found Frost sitting on the sofa in Bannard's office—he did not choose to sit behind Bannard's desk—drumming the edge of the coffee table in front of him as he gazed out the window.

"What on earth is this, Reuben? What's going on?" Coxe asked, as he sat down beside Frost on the sofa and Merritt sat in a chair opposite them.

Frost ignored the question. "Gentlemen, we have got trouble. We have got very bad trouble indeed."

The two men's eyes were upon him as he reviewed how Bannard had asked him to open Donovan's desk and as he described the water carafe incident. As he came to the end of the account, their attention refocused on the offending carafe and glass, which Frost had brought with him to Bannard's office, afraid to let them out of his sight.

"Reuben, are you telling us that someone poisoned Graham Donovan?" Coxe asked, in a tone that may or may not have implied that Frost was senile.

"Fred, I don't know any more than you do," Frost replied. "But it is certainly odd that Donovan takes a drink of iced tea made with contaminated—or poisoned—water and then dies two hours later."

Merritt had become visibly agitated as the conversation progressed. His right hand trembled slightly as he lit a cigarette. "Are we sure it's poison?" he asked.

"Keith, as I just said, I haven't any idea. But I think we have got to find out."

"I agree, Reuben," Coxe chimed in. "But how do we go about it?"

"Well, I assume they will do an autopsy on Graham and find out that he was poisoned. But independent of that, I had in mind calling in Ross Doyle and getting him to get a lab test performed on the carafe and the glass. Maybe by the time we know whether Graham's death was linked to the carafe we'll be able to think more clearly and decide our next move."

"Oh, that's a good idea, Reuben," Coxe burbled. "A

very good idea." Coxe was showing the fine, independent judgment Frost had long admired. But at least he was supportive, he thought.

"What do you think, Keith?"

Merritt remained silent, though puffing nervously on his cigarette. "Oh. I agree," he finally answered. "I agree all the way, Reuben."

"Well then, I'm going to call Doyle right away."

"I certainly hope he can help us. I certainly do," Merritt said, now excited and sounding more than a little like the late Truman Capote.

"What about Bannard?" Coxe asked. "Shouldn't we tell him about this?"

"I've tried once," Frost said. "But he's in transit at the moment. I'll call him later when we can track him down in Chicago."

Ross Doyle was in Frost's office within three quarters of an hour. A dapper little man with nondescript features appropriate to a private eye, he nonetheless seemed a trifle seedy. There was reason for this. For years Doyle had made a very comfortable living, specializing in gathering evidence for publications sued for libel. All the major newspapers and magazines had used his services at one time or another. If a newspaper said that Frankie Filmstar was lying in the gutter drunk on Thursday night and Frankie sued the newspaper for libel, Doyle was the man to call if it turned out Frankie was drinking tea with his aged mother on the Thursday night in question. Invariably, Doyle was able to prove that, whatever Frankie was doing on Thursday, he had indeed been drunk in the gutter on Monday, Tuesday, and Wednesday. And molesting underaged girls in between. Armed with Doyle's "research," as he called it, the offending newspaper could easily persuade Frankie to drop his case.

Doyle's tales of tracking the famous were legendary in the communications business. But the Supreme Court had made him technologically obsolete. In *New York Times v. Sullivan,* the Supreme Court decided in 1964 that a public figure could not succeed in a libel case unless he could prove that the offending publication had maliciously printed a falsehood about him. In the usual libel case, Frankie Filmstar no longer stood a chance of collecting and there was no more need for Doyle's persuasive "research."

The other mainstay of Doyle's business, divorce cases, had also disappeared. Not because divorce had vanished, heaven knows, but because the grounds for obtaining one had so drastically changed. Twenty years earlier, the only grounds for a divorce in New York had been adultery, which was normally proved by the testimony of a private detective who had caught the offending spouse in flagrante delicto with a "corespondent." Absent such testimony, the divorcing New Yorker had to go to Nevada or Mexico or some other equally remote and inhospitable jurisdiction to shed a spouse. Then all that changed when the state legislature adopted what was essentially a "nofault" divorce law, cutting Doyle's business in the process.

Despite these setbacks Doyle continued to squeeze out a living from his work, aided in part by the desire of companies subject to unfriendly takeovers to get the goods on their potential suitors. But Doyle was always grateful for a chance to help Chase & Ward with difficult problems.

"Reuben, what can I do for you?" Doyle asked. "I thought you'd retired and didn't have troubles anymore."

Frost ignored Doyle's attempted—and as far as he was concerned, unfunny—jest.

"Have you heard about Graham?" he asked.

"Graham?"

"Graham Donovan. He died suddenly this noon. Keeled over at the lunch table at the club upstairs."

"Reuben, I didn't know, and I'm sorry to hear it. He was a very nice man. Heart attack?"

"I'm awfully afraid not. But that's why you're here," Frost answered. For the second time in as many hours he recounted the carafe incident.

"So you want me to get these things analyzed, right?" Doyle said at the end of the story.

"Yes. And I assume you can do so discreetly," Frost said.

"No problem. I know a lab that will work at night. We should have an answer tomorrow."

"Terrific . . . I guess. I'm not sure I really want to know the result."

"I sympathize, Reuben."

Frost, on the basis of a remark half-overheard at lunch, then ventured into new territory.

"Chase & Ward seems to be a good source of business for you these days, Ross," Frost said.

"Mmn."

"Anything new on the other front?" Frost asked.

"Other front?"

"Stephens."

"Oh, you know about that?"

"Something."

"I was hoping to surprise George Bannard on that one, Reuben. The fact is I'm due over at Bennett Holbrook this afternoon. I'm going to talk to the broker that got the press release, and by the luckiest chance my sister-in-law works in the back office there. She's promised me a peek at their customer records and I'm going to take a look this afternoon. After dealing with your drinking utensils, of course."

With that, Doyle opened his briefcase and pulled out a cloth bag. He put the carafe, the glass and the tray that held them in the bag, covering his hand with a handkerchief as he did so, as Frost had done earlier.

"Do you always travel with a spare bag, Ross?"

"In my business, Reuben, you do. I'll talk to you tomorrow."

After Doyle had left, Frost considered trying to call Bannard again; he should be in Chicago by now. But why bother him? He was undoubtedly already closeted with Sussman and his team. Yes, Frost thought, he should wait until he had something more concrete to

report. Instead he left word for Arthur Tyson to call him
if he returned to the office or called in from outside. In
what seemed a matter of seconds, Tyson burst into
Frost's office.

"Christ, what a mess," Arthur Tyson said straight
off, without any preliminaries.

Frost leaned back in his desk chair as Tyson sat down
opposite him.

"Reuben, I've just seen bureaucracy at its best. You
can't even die in this town without a mountain of paper-
work," Tyson complained. He reviewed the frustrations
of the last few hours—waiting for a homicide detective
and a medical examiner at the Hexagon Club (not such
great fun, with the body of his partner lying uncomfortably near by); an argument with the medical examiner at
the morgue over whether an autopsy was necessary and
when it would be done; a frantic search for Stanley Hall,
Donovan's doctor, to acquaint the medical examiner
with Donovan's earlier heart attack; and, finally, release
of the body to Tyson's custody.

"You'd think Graham had died of leprosy the way
they acted," Tyson said. "Questions, questions, questions. And then no idea when the autopsy would be
done, until I made it clear I would be around at my
obnoxious best until the damn thing was over."

"They did an autopsy?" Frost asked.

"Yes, after a good, long wait. The thick-headed jerk
who did it seemed more interested in filling out papers
than getting it done. But I finally got hold of Hall, who
conviced the ghoul that Donovan had had a heart attack
in the past and that surely that is what he died of. The
whole thing was over very fast once Hall gave him the
business."

Frost smiled and then told Tyson that he really
shouldn't be smiling in the circumstances.

"What circumstances?" Tyson demanded.

"Arthur, were you really at your obnoxious best?"
Frost asked.

"You're damn right. Graham's body would still be up

there on a marble slab if I hadn't pushed things through. Stupid paper-shuffling bastards.''

"Arthur, you probably managed to turn yourself into a murder suspect," Frost said, trying again to submerge the smile that would not go away.

"Murder suspect! What the hell are you talking about?" Tyson rose as he shouted across the desk at Frost.

"Unfortunately, just what I said, Arthur. You and Hall and your ghoul friend were wrong. Graham Donovan did not die of a heart attack. He was poisoned. And I suspect your leading the medical examiner away from the cause of death will not be taken lightly.''

"Reuben, explain to me what you're talking about. And quick, too," Tyson barked, as if confronting a hostile witness.

Frost did, after which a uniquely subdued Arthur Tyson mutely left Reuben Frost's office.

REQUIESCAT IN PACE

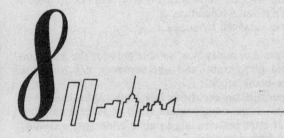

REUBEN FROST FOLLOWED HIS USUAL RITUAL WEDNESDAY morning, drinking his large glass of fresh orange juice with perhaps even more zest than usual. When he had finished, he turned to the obituary page of the *Times*. Like many his age, Frost in fact turned to the obituary page first every day, scanning not only the news stories, but the fine print of the paid death notices as well. He was always amazed at the number of acquaintances— not to say friends—who showed up there: long-forgotten chums from Navy days, law school classmates, even a Congressman from Upstate New York.

This particular morning Frost was eager to see how his dead colleague had been treated editorially. Bannard and Frost had agreed that Nigel Stewart, a Chase & Ward partner with some literary flair, should write the obituary. Despite Stewart's efforts, however, and the hand delivery of the text to an editor Frost knew well socially, the story on Donovan closely resembled what had become known as the all-purpose Wall Street lawyer's obituary:

_____, a member of the New York law firm of _____, died at his home yesterday. He was _____.

Born in _____, _____, 19___, he was graduated from _____ College in 19___, and _____ Law School in 19___. Immediately after law school he joined the firm of _____, where he became a Partner in 19____. He specialized in _____ law and had served as chairman of the _____ law committees of both the American and the City Bar Association.

He is survived by _____.

Donovan's obituary was notable only for the inclusion of an old photograph and one sentence not from the fill-in-the-blank model:

"A specialist in securities law matters, he had acted as counsel in the development stage of several corporations that later became large public concerns, including Stephens Industries, Inc."

Cynthia Frost came in as he finished reading.

"Well, poor Graham got the cookie-cutter treatment," Reuben said.

"I know. I was up before you and read it."

"It's a pity, you know. Graham was one of the most distinguished lawyers in New York, but his obituary makes him sound like the most mundane hack in the world."

"Well, Reuben, it may be just as well," his wife said.

"What do you mean?"

"Well, if your poison theory is true, the less interesting and prominent Graham Donovan was the better. Otherwise, my dear, you'll be on Eyewitness News—very fitting name in this case, since you were an eyewitness."

"To Graham's death, not his poisoning," Frost said curtly.

"By the way, have you called George Bannard yet?"

"Not this morning. I tried all last night, as you know, but couldn't reach him."

"You could have left a message to call anytime."

"Yes, I could have, and been awakened in the middle of the night so that I could tell him my inconclusive news."

"Inconclusive?"

"Well, the autopsy said Graham died of a heart attack. We won't know about the poison thing until our private eye Ross Doyle reports back.''

"Oh, Reuben. I see it all. You want to be in charge of this exciting mess, but you've got to tell George. You would have been furious if someone had not told you when you were the Executive Partner.''

"You're right, as usual. I'll try him again now." Frost got up and went into the library. He pulled a slip of paper from his pocket with the Ritz's number written on it, dialed, and was through to Bannard quickly.

"George, I'm sorry to disturb you so early in the morning, but I did want to reach you before you left the hotel.''

"As a matter of fact I was just going out the door; I'm running late. So what is it, something about Donovan's funeral?" Bannard's impatience was easily transmitted across the wires.

"It's about Donovan all right, but not about his funeral," Frost answered.

"Well, what is it then?" Bannard's increased impatience almost created static on the line.

Frost told him the news; there was no more talk about running out the door.

"What have you done about it?" Bannard shouted through the phone.

Frost told him of his meeting with Doyle, or at least the part dealing with Donovan. He also said that Bannard's Executive Committee concurred with what he had done.

Bannard was silent for a long interval. Then he asked, "Reuben, do you think I should come back?"

Of course you should, Reuben thought, if you had any notion of hands-on management of firm affairs. But then again, Bannard was away on important business and there really was little he could do in New York, at least until their suspicions were confirmed. He reviewed the alternatives with Bannard and was not surprised when the latter said he would stay in Chicago.

"I'm here alone, so there's no one who can go to Sussman's board meeting. And it sounds as if there's nothing to be done at the moment in New York. Besides, Reuben, I have complete confidence in you."

How sweet, Reuben thought. How very, very sweet. But he did not chide his former partner. Instead they talked over details—Bannard would return as soon as conditions permitted, but he would be unlikely to get to Donovan's wake. Could Frost represent the firm there? He would call as soon as he got in. And yes, he would meet Frost the next morning to arrange Donovan's funeral service.

"All right, I talked to Bannard," Reuben told Cynthia. "He has so much confidence in me he isn't returning from Chicago until tonight. Isn't that nice?"

"Well, he ought to have confidence in you," Cynthia said, kissing her husband on the forehead as she dashed for the door and the day's appointments.

Wednesday was a difficult day for Frost, Merritt, Tyson and Coxe. They, together with Bannard, were the only members of the firm who knew the terrible secret that some unknown laboratory was undoubtedly in the process of confirming, a secret that led inexorably to the conclusion that Graham Donovan had been murdered. All of them tried to keep as low a profile as possible. It was no accident that all four found a reason not to have lunch at the Training Table.

Circumstances were particularly tricky for Frost. All day Wednesday colleagues from other firms, clients and friends called in to express condolences and, in Bannard's absence, were referred to Frost. Many naturally asked the cause of death; Frost could only respond, most uncomfortably, that Graham was thought to have died from a heart attack.

In the evening, Frost went to be present during visiting hours at Frank Campbell's, the Madison Avenue funeral parlor where Donovan's body had been taken. With Bruce Donovan boycotting all aspects of the funeral ritual, Frost felt that someone had to be present during the wake.

Frost was touched by the sentiments expressed that

evening. A surprisingly large crowd passed through Campbell's, including several successful investment bankers who recalled how Donovan had guided them in their novice years through the intricacies of the securities laws (and, Frost knew, taught them a good bit about investment banking in the process, without ever seeming to overstep the boundaries of the lawyer's role).

An impressive number of Chase & Ward's nonlegal staff members also called to pay their respects—stenographers, file clerks, the office librarian, one or two of the older messengers. This was neither an easy nor a convenient thing for most of them to do, living as they did in the outer boroughs or the suburbs. As he greeted a steady stream of employees, he thought once again how wrong his former partners were who now regarded the firm, which had doubled in size over the past ten years, as a business to be conducted, at least as far as nonlawyers were concerned, like an impersonal corporation. And how wrong George Bannard was to float every idea he read in the *Harvard Business Review* as a potential reform at Chase & Ward; there were times when Frost thought that, if Bannard had his way, the firm would ultimately be run like a Japanese transistor factory.

If the attendance by Chase & Ward employees that evening was any indication, the old feeling so noticeable to him as a younger man, that all were part of a Chase & Ward extended family, still had viability. As an Executive Partner he had done his best to foster that feeling, attending innumerable wakes for deceased employees, a few weddings, even a christening or two. Bannard might better, he thought, devote his time to activities like that than reading those crazy articles about Japanese business.

The evidence of "family" feelings he saw around him made Frost the more uneasy as the evening went on—uneasy because of his inability to share his forebodings about the cause of Donovan's death and uneasy because the Chase & Ward "family" might well be harboring a murderer. He was deeply relieved when the visiting hours were over and he could join Cynthia for supper at Prezzemolo, the latest in the seemingly never-ending succession of chic—and often very good—Italian restaurants opening on the Upper East Side.

Bannard had called Frost late Wednesday evening, after returning from Chicago. Although Frost made it clear that there were no new developments to report, Bannard nonetheless asked Frost if he would come by the next morning to give him an "update" over breakfast. Frost reluctantly agreed, though he hated breakfast and throughout his career had done his best to avoid breakfast meetings. He had undoubtedly become oriented away from an early-morning schedule during the years when his wife had been an active performer. Elaine's late at night was more to his liking than the Regency Dining Room at dawn. For his own part, Frost felt incapable of doing truly productive work early in the day and he secretly doubted that the advocates of breakfast meetings, including George Bannard, were any more capable of it.

But, shortly after eight on Thursday morning, Frost walked up Park Avenue to Bannard's apartment building. He remembered the apartment itself as being stuffed to the point of oppression with antiques; after Bannard had met him at the door and led him through to the dining room, Frost knew his memory had been correct. The rooms were so full that there were several areas where it was actually difficult to navigate.

Whose taste did all this reflect? Eleanor's, he supposed; at least she had full vision. Not that the objects were in bad taste, just that there were so many of them. Frost felt all the prouder of the less-is-more environment he and Cynthia had lovingly created in their townhouse, sparsely furnished with sleek modern furniture of the best design.

Oh well, to each his own, Frost thought as he sat down at the dining room table beside Bannard, who was finishing off a large plate of scrambled eggs with gusto.

"What would you like, Reuben?" Bannard asked.

"Oh, just some toast and coffee."

"No juice?"

"Already had some, thanks."

Bannard rang for the maid and repeated Frost's modest request.

"So we have trouble on our hands, do we?" Bannard asked.

"It certainly looks that way, George. But we won't be entirely sure until we hear from Doyle."

"He didn't call you yesterday?"

"No."

"Damn. I wonder why not? Should I try to get him now?"

"It's a bit early, you know," Frost said, with some satisfaction. "But sure, try him."

Bannard went into the library to place the call. He was back almost at once to report that there was no answer.

"That's what I figured," Frost said.

"Reuben, I still can't believe it. I know, I know what you saw, the muddy water and all. But it doesn't make sense. People like Graham only get murdered in mystery stories or the movies, not in real life. Who the hell could have done it?"

"George, I've thought a lot about that since yesterday noon. When someone's murdered, you're supposed to look for a motive, I believe. What could it be? Jealousy? Greed? Keeping Graham from revealing something? It's hard to speculate."

Bannard looked at his watch. "Well, there's no point in speculating until we're sure. Meanwhile, we'd better get over to the church to see your Dr. Clark."

"Not *my* Dr. Clark, George. I'm making no representations or warranties about him at all, except that he seems willing to bury Graham."

Second Memorial Church was within walking distance of Bannard's apartment. The two men set out together in the bright September sunshine. Both welcomed the chance for fresh air before entering the church, where they knew they would find the stifling smell of funeral bouquets.

Once at the church, Bannard glanced impatiently at his watch once again. Nine-fifteen. Forty-five minutes before Graham Donovan's funeral service was to begin. And here he was in something called the community room of the church, talking with Dr. Clark and Reuben Frost.

Bannard had never met Dr. Clark, but he felt that he had, having read about him so frequently in the *Times*. Dr. Clark, the advocate of unilateral disarmament; Dr. Clark, outspoken foe of the Right To Life lobby; Dr. Clark, East Side reform Democratic leader; Rowland Clark, marathon runner; and, not to be overlooked, Rollo Clark, ragtime pianist and occasional nightclub performer. In fact, Bannard reflected, he had read about the carrot-haired figure before him in virtually every capacity except as spiritual leader of Second Memorial.

The rector was approaching fifty, a fact he attempted to conceal with a modish styling of his red hair, a styling more appropriate to a *Gentleman's Quarterly* model. He was pleasant enough, but Bannard found off-putting what appeared to be his transparently false air of sadness over Donovan's death.

"This must be very difficult for you gentlemen," he said in a grave, stentorian tone. "But we will try to make things as easy as possible for you."

"We appreciate that, Rowland," Frost said.

"Graham Martin Donovan. Was he called Graham by his friends?"

"Yes," Bannard said.

"And he was a partner of yours and Mr. Bannard's?" the minister asked, turning to Frost.

"Yes."

"At Chase & Ward, is it?"

"Yes."

"What kind of law did he practice?"

"He was a corporate lawyer. A lawyer for businesses," Bannard said, a strain of impatience showing in his voice.

"Oh, yes. I read that in the *Times*," Dr. Clark said.

"May I ask why all the questions?" Bannard asked, now with greater impatience.

"The eulogy, Mr. Bannard. After all, your partner was not a member of the Second Memorial community. So asking you questions is the only way I can gather the information I need."

"I see."

"And what about relatives? I take it there are none."

"Well, not quite. There is a son. An archaeology professor at NYU. But he has made it very clear he wants nothing to do with his father's funeral," Bannard explained.

"I'm sorry to hear that."

"I'm not sure you would be if you had ever talked with him," Bannard added.

"Now, what about Graham's favorite songs?" Rev. Clark asked, already calling the deceased by his first name.

Frost, to whom the question had been directed, seemed temporarily nonplussed. Bannard filled the silence. "Favorite songs?" Bannard was incredulous, and his feelings showed. Was this man running a dating service or a church?

Dr. Clark laughed, a bit uneasily. "We have found it very effective to play one or two favorite songs of the deceased. It helps to bring his friends closer to him, to remember him better."

"By songs, what do you mean?" Bannard asked, treading into unknown territory. "Popular songs?"

"Well, yes. Show songs and the like—things that Graham liked to sing or liked to dance to."

"I'm afraid I can't help you. I knew Graham pretty well, but I don't think I ever heard him sing or request a song."

"Too bad. We'll try to make do. Did Graham have a sense of humor?"

"Oh yes. A somewhat cynical one, but a definite sense of humor," Frost said. "Wouldn't you agree, George?"

"Oh, yes. Yes, indeed," replied the man who more than once had been the target of a Donovan barb.

Several of the partners entered the room, including Arthur Tyson and Peter Denny.

"Is this where we're supposed to be, George?" Denny asked.

"That's right. We'll all march in together from here."

"Is there any particular order or anything? I'm too young to have done this before."

"What did you have in mind? The order of the letterhead? No, there is no special order, is there, Reuben? Just line up two by two and try to look presentable going down the aisle." Bannard turned to Tyson, who was combing his hair in front of a mirror at the side of the room. "Arthur, we'd better go." The two of them left Dr. Clark and went out the door to the church proper.

"So that's the running holy man," Tyson observed.

"Yes. Just be glad you didn't have to talk with him for fifteen minutes the way Reuben and I did."

"Difficult?"

"No, just fatuous."

"George, what are we supposed to do here?"

"Just get people to their seats. The first four rows on each side are for us and for Bruce, if he shows up, which I doubt. The spouses sit generally behind us, though there's no assigned seating. As for the rest, just be nice to them—most are clients—and escort them down the aisle."

"How did Chicago go, by the way?" Tyson asked in a low voice.

"Very interesting," Bannard answered. "Sussman's board got a little bit away from him. The board met to rubber-stamp the merger yesterday morning, but so many questions were raised that Sussman had to adjourn the meeting until his financial wizards could get together more information. They approved it in the end, but I'm not sure Bernie Sussman now has much good to say about the merits of having outside directors. Here come some customers. I'll tell you more about it later."

As people began coming into the church, Bannard was disconcerted to hear the organ playing "Just One of Those Things." My God, Bannard thought. I suppose this is meant to be one of Graham's favorite songs. Give Dr. Clark credit for persistence, if not taste.

Harold Knight, president of First Fiduciary, entered and shook Bannard's hand vigorously.

"George, I can't tell you how sorry I was to hear about Graham. I hate to think how many years we go back."

"I know, Harry. Sadly enough, so do I."

"All very sudden, wasn't it, George?"

Bannard agreed that it was, though Knight's question made Bannard realize for the first time the embarrassment and agony the firm would suffer if Donovan had in fact been murdered. He left Knight at a front pew and hurried back to the rear of the church, where more and more people were coming in. In their midst he spotted Dwight Draper of Draper Chemicals. Given his antipathy to Draper, he tried to avoid him, but Draper rushed up to Bannard and clutched him by the arm.

"What an awful thing, George," he whispered confidentially in Bannard's ear, gripping his arm as he did so. "Graham was like a brother to me. He helped me out almost from the first day I went into business. And he never gave me bad advice." Draper poked Bannard's chest for emphasis as he talked.

"I'm sure that's true, Dwight. We're all going to miss him," Bannard replied, coolly and correctly.

"I still don't believe it. Graham was in the best shape recently that I've seen him since Marjorie died. Why, I saw him Monday in fact, and he seemed to be absolutely thriving. Suntan, trim weight—at least trim for him— good spirits. But I guess when your time has come, your time has come."

Bannard inwardly winced at the inane cliché. Then winced again as the organ switched to "Embraceable You."

"You've got the finest law firm in the world, George," Draper continued. "So I know you'll survive. But Graham Donovan is going to be missed, let me tell you. Who can replace him? And who *will* replace him on the Draper Chemicals work?"

Bannard was appalled at Draper's attempt to talk business, but he couldn't break away from the man. "Dwight, we really haven't had time to discuss it."

"We rather like that young fellow, Phelan, who's been helping Graham out."

The jam-up of people waiting for ushers in the back grew. "We'll have to talk about this soon, Dwight. Now I've got to get to work."

"So I see. I'll give you a call." He touched Bannard's arm once more. "Again, George, all my condolences."

"Thank you, Dwight."

Bannard hurried to the back. Somewhat to his surprise the church was getting quite full, with an odd mixture of people ranging from captains of industry to superannuated Chase & Ward messenger "boys" to Donovan's maid. Most of the partners' spouses were present too, including Anne Singer. Bannard was formally correct as he showed her to a seat next to Eleanor.

As ten o'clock approached, Bannard returned to join his partners in the community room. Janet Hudders, one of the two women partners, was wearing a wool dress of an appropriately somber shade of gray. Most of her male counterparts were dressed in keeping with the occasion as well, the most notable exception being Larry Scott, who wore a bright blue shirt with a red and white striped tie. Bannard was not surprised at this lapse of taste. One had come to expect as much from Scott. As another partner had once remarked to Bannard, when God was passing out the goods Scott had stood too long in the ego line and not long enough in the civility line. His lack of taste and general boorishness were only tolerated because he was an extremely competent litigator.

"All right, we'd better line up," Bannard called out to the group. The partners began forming in twos amid a flurry of putting out cigarettes, brushing off lapels and buttoning suit coats.

Reuben Frost approached Bannard. "You should be at the front, George."

"And you should be with me," Bannard answered. They took places at the head of the column. As they walked toward the exit Bannard thought that, by and large, the assembled might of Chase & Ward looked pretty good. Lots of steel gray hair and an occasional paunch, but hardly a collection of the lame, the halt and the blind.

Rev. Clark came into the room, wearing academic robes with a scarlet hood. Harvard? Bannard wondered. Probably.

"Are we ready?" he asked Bannard.

"Whenever you say, Dr. Clark."

"Okay, you go ahead." He opened the door and the procession began filing out.

Much to Bannard's relief, the organist was *not* playing Cole Porter, but Bach's *Sleepers Awake*. Bannard felt the eyes of the crowd on him as those on the aisle turned to view the Chase & Ward procession. When the lawyers were seated, Dr. Clark entered from the side and stood at a lectern.

After a reading, which Bannard guessed to be from *The Prophet* (though he had never read it), and a hymn, Dr. Clark addressed the congregation.

"My dear friends. We are gathered here today to celebrate. To celebrate the passing of our friend, Graham Donovan. Celebrate, you say? How can you use the word *'celebrate'* to describe Graham's untimely death?

"Well, I don't mean that we are celebrating Graham Donovan's death. No, no. We are celebrating Graham Donovan the man. Remembering the wonderful life he led. Remembering him as the friend he was.

"A few moments ago, Mr. Collins, the organist, played a medley of Graham's favorite songs—old songs, good songs. 'Just One of Those Things.' 'Embraceable You.' Cole Porter. Gershwin. Wonderful talent, and talent that Graham Donovan appreciated.

"Graham had a style of living that cheered up those around him. He had spirit. He loved the joys of life, the pleasures of life.

"And that marvelous sense of humor! Not a low comic's sense of humor, not something off the vaudeville stage or the TV screen, but a subtle, vibrant sense of humor that made all of us the happier."

Us! Us! thought Bannard. Where does he get that from? He never met Donovan in his life! Bannard could

barely contain his anger at Dr. Clark's artificial performance. He shifted in his seat and glanced at Frost,
sitting next to him. If Reuben was disturbed, he was not
letting on. Frost was all attention as Dr. Clark continued.

"Yes, Graham Donovan made many of us happier.
Some of us he made better, as a wise counselor and
dedicated lawyer. And some of us—yes, let us not deny
it—some of us he made richer, again through his good
counsel and advice.

"We are all in Graham's debt. He has touched us all
in some way. So it is right that we celebrate him. That
we celebrate this splendid man who walked amongst us.

"Now let us stand for a moment of silence while we
contemplate this good man's life."

The congregation rose. Dr. Clark asked everyone to
join hands as the organ began playing, softly, "When
the Saints Go Marching In." Bannard was beside himself, listening to a Dixieland tune, holding hands with his
seventy-four-year-old colleague and thinking of Graham's
murder.

Fortunately the service soon ended with another po-
etry reading, this time from Emily Dickinson, and, for
reasons totally unfathomable to Bannard, the communal
singing of "America the Beautiful."

The professional Irish pallbearers removed the wooden
casket, and Bannard and Frost led the Chase & Ward
partners out the rear door. Bannard wanted very much
to get away from the church. He could not bear the
thought of anyone telling him what a "beautiful" service
it had been—nor could he bear confronting the preposter-
ous Dr. Clark.

"I've had enough," Bannard muttered to Keith Merritt as he came down the steps. "Let me speak to Eleanor for a minute and then let's get the hell out of here.
The day is bound to pick up after this."

Bannard, so often right, was very wrong about the
rest of that Thursday.

BAD NEWS AND ANOTHER
LUNCHEON

FROST ARRIVED AT CHASE & WARD SHORTLY BEFORE NOON.
Ross Doyle was waiting for him in the firm's reception
room. Doyle, clearly on the lookout for Frost, stood up
to greet him as he came through the glass doors at the
main entrance to the office.

"Good morning, Reuben. Can I see you for a moment?"

"Of course. You have something to report, I hope?"

"Yes."

"Then come on." Frost gently took Doyle by the arm
and propelled him toward his office. He thought he
should probably call Bannard, but then decided he would
hear Doyle out first.

"I've got news on both fronts, Reuben," he said,
once they were inside with the door closed.

"Both fronts?"

"Yes. Donovan and—"

"Oh yes, the Stephens thing," Frost interrupted, as
he remembered the episode he was not supposed to
know about.

"I wish I could use the good news/bad news gambit,
but I can't," Doyle said.

"You mean it's all bad."

"I'm afraid so."

"Then let's hear about the water carafe first."

"Okay. I took it and the used glass to Keller Labora-
tories, a lab I've used from time to time in the past. I

was after them all day yesterday to get a report, but apparently they had a helluva time identifying the substance they found in the residue on both the carafe and the glass. They worked all last night on it and finally reached a conclusion this morning."

"And it was?" Frost asked.

"It was a derivative of digitalis—not digitalis itself, but a chemical distillate from it. A distillate that is the basic ingredient of Pernon, a new heart treatment drug that recently came on the market."

"So it was medicine, not a poison?" Frost interjected.

"I wish I could say that it was, Reuben. But it was not just plain digitalis or this new stuff, Pernon. It was a distillate equivalent to a high concentration of digitalis. A lethal concentration."

"Then why didn't Graham die in his office? He presumably drank the poison there."

"I wondered the same thing, so I asked a pathologist friend of mine about it. He told me that a delayed reaction of two or three hours would not be unusual. And the symptoms are very much those I understand Graham had."

"Convulsions?"

"Convulsions, and all the symptoms of cardiac arrest. Cardiac arrest, induced by the digitalis, is in fact the cause of death. I'm afraid he was murdered, Reuben."

"But how could he drink the water with the poison in it? Wouldn't he know what was happening to him?"

"Have you ever tasted instant iced tea, Reuben? As you learned the other day, Graham drank it every morning with his Danish, or so Miss Appleby said. My guess is you could put almost anything in that powdered stuff and not know the difference."

"But what about the color?" Frost persisted. "Wouldn't he have seen that awful color we saw the other day?"

"Not necessarily. Don't forget you only saw the brownish stain after the liquid had spilled. If you were pouring it into a glass—and one with iced tea powder in it at that—you might not notice."

"It all seems improbable to me. And who put the goddam stuff there in the first place?"

"That, as they used to say, is the sixty-four-thousand-dollar question."

"Let's see if George Bannard is back from the church yet. We'd better give him the bad news right away." Frost dialed Bannard's extension and was told he was in the office.

"Tell him Ross Doyle and Reuben Frost will be right down to see him," Frost said to Bannard's secretary.

In Bannard's office, Doyle repeated the laboratory's findings. Bannard, like Frost before him, tried to reinterpret those findings in some way that did not point to murder, but with no more success than Frost.

"You know, Ross, there's one little fact you haven't been told," Bannard said.

"Which is?"

"Which is that the City Medical Examiner did an autopsy on Donovan and concluded that he died of a heart attack."

"How do you know that?"

"Arthur Tyson. Arthur Tyson was there the whole time and claimed the body once the autopsy was over," Frost said.

"And did Arthur perhaps ride herd on the poor M.E. who did the autopsy? I've worked on enough things with him to know that he can really be tough when he starts leaning heavy."

"Yes, I suspect he did, judging by the way he described it all to me," Frost said. "And he had Donovan's doctor, Stanley Hall, giving the examiner hell as well."

"So perhaps there was a suggestion—just a suggestion—that Donovan had a history of heart attacks?" Doyle asked.

"I suppose so," Frost said.

"But how the hell could Arthur Tyson or Stanley Hall influence an autopsy?" Bannard asked. "An autopsy is a medical procedure, not a public opinion poll."

"George, let me tell you something. You've never been divorced, right?"

"No, certainly not," Bannard said, puzzled by Doyle's question.

"Well, George, if you've ever been divorced and want a license to remarry in New York, you have to present your divorce papers to a lawyer from the corporation counsel's office for approval. Can you imagine what that is like?"

"What do you mean?"

"What it is like, day after day after day, examining divorce papers? Or dealing with those without papers? Liars, cheats, crazies, bigamists, the whole works. Do you know what it's like? What it's like if your mother was proud of you the day you graduated from law school, proud of you the day you passed the bar exam? And maybe proud of you as eighty-fifth assistant corporation counsel in charge of divorce papers?"

"No, Ross, I really don't know what that might be like," the Executive Partner of Chase & Ward said, subdued.

"Well, if you can imagine it, transpose the scene to medicine. Doctor in charge of the day's dead bodies. Big chance for loyalty to the Hippocratic oath, right? Big source of pride to your mother—my son the coroner, right?"

"Um."

"Um, indeed. George, these guys, these assistant M.E.'s, they're not your Columbia Presbyterian teaching faculty, not your Brick Church vestrymen. And not your brilliant pathologists, discovering new diseases and new causes of death. These are ordinary Joes, cutting open stiffs for a civil service living. Now do you understand why one of them says a corpse stuffed full of poison got that way because of a coronary?"

"Ross, you're very eloquent. Maybe I do understand. But under all the circumstances, don't you think we should try and keep them from burying Graham? Shouldn't we let the Medical Examiner have another look?"

"Yes, of course."

"Let me call Campbell's right now," Frost said. "I talked to them yesterday." He had Mrs. Davis place the call and told his story to a very puzzled attendant at the other end.

"Mr. Donovan was to be cremated, right?" the voice said.

"That is absolutely right, and that's why I'm calling you to get the cremation called off. There has to be a new autopsy of Mr. Donovan."

"Well, sir, I'll do my best," the disembodied voice said. "But you ought to know that they do these things pretty fast and Mr. Donovan's body was taken there right after the funeral."

"I know that. But please do your best, as this is very important," Frost said. "And let me know as soon as you can." Frost hung up the phone.

"I'm afraid I have other glad tiding," Doyle said. Bannard looked around uncomfortably; he knew Doyle was referring to the Stephens matter, which he did not think Frost knew about.

"I've had a break in the Stephens stock thing," Doyle went on.

Frost, playing the scene for all it was worth, got up to leave.

"No, no, don't go, Reuben. This is the stolen papers thing that was being hinted at at lunch yesterday. Someone took some papers from the files and tried to bear down on the price of Stephens stock."

"I see," Frost said.

The lawyers' interchange left Doyle totally confused; he did not figure out that he had been conned into telling Frost a good bit more about the incident than Frost then knew.

"Go ahead, Ross. What's the news?" Bannard said.

"Let me tell the story in sequence."

"Have it your way."

"Okay. My sister-in-law works in the back office operation at Bennett Holbrook," Doyle said. (He was going to add, "as I told Reuben the other day," but his instincts—rightly—told him not to.)

"So?" Bannard said.

"The broker who got the big tip from the press release wasn't about to be cooperative. He was downright surly, in fact. So, instead, I sweet-talked my sister-in-law—not an unpleasant task, since I quite like her—into letting me have a peek at a computer printout of the customer records around the time the press release surfaced. My luck was with me. I found a purchase of ten thousand shares on August 9—which is the day after the Bennett Holbrook broker called Donovan—by a name I recognized. No street name, no nominee name, nothing. And working backwards, I found a sale by the same person a week earlier."

"So it was just as we thought—the guy was trying to drive down the price of Stephens so that he could cover his short sale," Bannard said.

"Your analysis is correct. Except that it wasn't a guy."

"Who was it?"

"Grace Appleby."

Frost leaned back in his chair. In its way, the answer that Miss Appleby was the culprit was obvious, given her access to Donovan's office; indeed, Frost had looked her over with suspicion in their encounter two days earlier. But, still, stock market plunging seemed out of character for this prim and cool woman. She was disagreeable—everyone agreed on that—but there was no reason to think she was disloyal. Then Frost remembered her remark about Smith Kline & French, which showed a more than passing interest in business.

"She was an obvious suspect," Bannard said, as if he had known Miss Appleby was the guilty party all along. "But I don't think anyone seriously thought it was she. What's the Stephens stock price? That was a pretty healthy plunge she was making."

"Yes, indeed. At the time the price was around seventeen dollars a share—that's one hundred seventy thousand dollars. You must be paying your secretaries better than I thought, George."

"I don't understand it. That's a lot of money. There

has to be something—or someone—behind this. Can you have her followed?" Bannard asked.

Doyle looked surprised. "Sure. That's easy. But I don't offhand see what that will accomplish."

"I'm not sure either. But I just can't believe one of our loyal secretaries is mixed up in some six-figure stock fiddle unless someone else got her involved."

"Well, it's worth a try, I guess. Tailing her will cost money, though."

"Never mind that. There's more at stake here than a few hundred bucks," Bannard said.

"Or a few thousand?"

"Or a few thousand," Bannard replied.

"Ross, do you suppose the two things are linked?" Frost asked.

"How do you mean?"

"The poisoning and the press release incident."

"I suppose it's possible. From what I understand, she certainly had access to Donovan and the water carafe."

"But where would she get the poison?" Frost interjected.

"Good question," Bannard said. "Ross, we've got to know more about this woman. You've got to have her followed."

"Fine."

Bannard looked at his watch and stood up behind his desk. "I've got to go to . . . an engagement now. I'll call you this afternoon."

"Fine," Doyle said.

"And Reuben, we should talk after lunch," Bannard added.

"Sure, George. Sure," Frost replied. He marveled at Bannard's crude attempt at tact, for Bannard's "engagement" was the weekly partners' lunch from which Frost had been so recently banned. "Call me at your convenience."

Partners' lunch was a ritual that took place every Thursday. All members of the firm were expected to attend unless busy with clients or away. Except for semiannual meetings when new partners were chosen, the weekly get-togethers were the only formal gatherings of the partnership. The principal business each week was usually to review new matters to make sure the firm did not have a conflict. That the firm might find itself on two sides of a controversy—"meeting yourself going around the barn," as Bannard called it—was entirely possible, given the fact that new business could come in to any of the Chase & Ward partners and the further fact that Chase & Ward was involved, one way or another, in almost every industry. Fortunately the review that took place at each Thursday's lunch smoked out most of the potential conflicts so that embarrassing collisions around the barn were very rare.

The Thursday lunches were always of interest to the partners since the status of the firm's financials—and the amounts available to be parceled out to the partners— were reviewed on a weekly basis.

Attendance was generally high at these weekly meetings, but certainly not because of the food. The lunch, served in a private dining room at MacMillan's, would have disgraced a self-respecting roadside diner. Chopped "steak," a purplish, ill-cooked lump of nondescript meat, and a piece of untitled fish cooked in peanut oil were among the regular fare. Old man MacMillan, no fool, knew his financial district customers; prime interest was in the business transacted, not in the quality of the food.

Occasionally over the years there had been rebellion and demands for shifting the locale of the Thursday lunches, particularly from the younger partners, depressed at the thought of facing MacMillan's handiwork week after week, year after year and decade after decade. But no one had been able to come up with an alternative offering a convenient location, privacy and speedy service.

The members of Chase & Ward began arriving at the customary hour of one o'clock, entering MacMillan's ugly private party room with its plain, light brown walls. They ranged themselves around the tables, which were pushed together to form a U. By common consent, Bannard and his Executive Committee sat in the bottom of the U, and the other partners sat wherever they liked along the sides. Some compulsively selected the same seat week after week, but most did not give a thought to where they sat.

Attendance was heavy. Summer vacations were over, so nearly all the members of the firm were in the city. Besides, most had kept the morning free because of Donovan's funeral. (And the imminence of the September 15 quarterly federal income tax payment made many more than a little curious about Chase & Ward's current bank balance.)

Bannard had hurriedly relayed the news of the laboratory's findings to Coxe, Merritt, and Tyson while walking to the restaurant. He also told them about Miss Appleby, but the four agreed that there was probably a limit to the amount of bad news that could be digested by the firm at one sitting. Besides, no one had considered what exactly to do about the Appleby problem. But clearly the partners had to be told about Donovan's poisoning. And, at least in Bannard's view, to decide whether the police should be called in.

The four sat at the head table and tried to avoid telegraphing by their expressions the bad news they possessed until after lunch—chopped steak this time—had been eaten. They joined in the luncheon chitchat, which consisted mostly of a critique of Donovan's funeral service.

"I hadn't realized that the Supreme Court had outlawed prayer in your churches," Marvin Isaacs remarked. Others quickly reacted to disassociate Dr. Clark and his church from their part of Christendom.

"He was nondenominational, all right," Nigel Stewart added. "Or should one say non-nominational? I don't believe he mentioned the Almighty once."

"I wondered about that," Isaacs went on. "And when the saints went marching in, where did they march to?"

"Now, Marvin, there have to be some Christian mysteries that you are not meant to fathom," Merritt said.

"That's for sure. But speaking as a Jew, I must say I

would have preferred a good high church Catholic mass, Peter," Isaacs said, nodding to Peter Denny.

"I of course agree with you, Marvin," Denny said. "Though there are some that say our services these days are more like Dr. Clark's."

"Ladies and gentlemen, can we get started?" Bannard called out over the conversation. "I realize we haven't had dessert, but I've asked the waiters to skip it today as we have a very important matter to discuss."

Many of the partners looked around the room with surprise, hoping to read some meaning into their colleagues' expressions.

"Captain, would you have the waiters leave now? You can clear the tables later," Bannard said, addressing MacMillan's aged functionary standing at the side of the room.

This caused still further glancing around the table; this had never happened before at the partners' luncheon. What was going on?

"Ladies and gentlemen, I have something very serious to report to you today. Very serious and very shocking. Indeed, I suspect what I have to say will be the saddest and most shocking thing that has ever happened in the history of the firm."

The room was totally silent as Bannard spoke.

"We all know Graham Donovan is dead. Several of you were there when he died. But this morning we learned conclusively something else about his death—namely, that he was murdered."

There was audible buzzing in the room. "Murdered?" at least three incredulous voices said aloud. Roger Singer, the partner who had been sitting next to Donovan when he died, was one of them. He repeated the word over and over to himself, as he stared off into space.

"I know you probably don't believe me. But let me tell you what I know, and you be the judge."

Bannard told the group about how he had deputized Reuben Frost to open Donovan's desk and what spilling his water carafe—and the subsequent laboratory findings—had disclosed. "There you have it, my friends. What do you think?"

"I'm not convinced, George," Nigel Stewart said. "Sure, it all looks mighty funny. But you have no proof of the connection between Graham's death and the water carafe. And how do you square it with the autopsy? I'd hate to try and convict anyone on the evidence you have."

"Oh, come on, Nigel," Arthur Tyson replied. "We'd all like to agree with you—my God, would we like to agree with you—but the probability of murder is just too high. We can't hide from it."

"Maybe we can't hide from it, but we don't exactly have to advertise it in *The American Lawyer* either," Stewart answered.

"Why not, Nigel?" Bannard asked. "Here we've got thirty-seven—excuse me, thirty-six—people who know what happened. A secret like that can't be kept for very long. Besides, don't we have some obligation as lawyers to go to the police, to report this crime?"

"Not the way the farmers that run the American Bar Association think," Stewart countered. "Christ, with their notion of 'professional responsibility' as they call it, those yokels wouldn't even discuss the subject. I don't think we have to go to the police unless we want to. And I don't know why in the name of God we would want to in this case."

"Because I think George is right," said Coxe, predictably. "As lawyers, we just can't ignore the existence of a crime, particularly when that crime is murder."

"Listen," Marvin Isaacs interrupted. "We could spend the rest of the day arguing whether we have a duty to go to the police. I say duty or not, we damn well need their help. One of our partners—one of our very own—has been poisoned. And poisoned in his office, at that. There is a murderer loose in our office and I say we should call the police right away. How do we know that the murderer is not some madman who will pick one of us off next? I say we need the police and damn soon."

Isaac's appeal to self-interest turned the tide. Only

one other person spoke up to oppose what he had said. This was Ralph Steele, the partner in charge of hiring new lawyers for Chase & Ward. With the tunnel vision he always displayed, regardless of the subject being discussed, he told the group that publicity about a murder at the firm "would be bad for recruiting." Bannard impatiently cut him off.

"Ralph, the only thing worse for us than publicity about a murder would be a rumor—a rumor that no one could ever put an end to. Chase & Ward would be like a haunted house as far as your dear little law students were concerned."

"I think Marvin is unquestionably right," Bannard went on. "So I propose to call in the police as soon as we leave here. Agreed?"

There was no dissent.

"Very well, then, the meeting is adjourned."

"George, before we go, do you have any idea who might have done it?" Isaacs asked.

"None," Bannard answered. Then, ignoring what he knew about Grace Appleby, he added, "None whatsoever. Neither does Ross Doyle. I just hope to God the person is not sitting in this room or working at this firm."

"Amen," said Coxe. And on that prayerful note the most exciting partners' luncheon in Chase & Ward history came to an end.

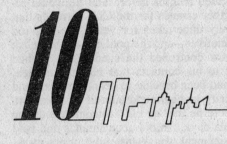

AN OUTSIDER OBSERVING THE PARTNERS OF CHASE & WARD leaving MacMillan's Restaurant would have known that they had just received bad news. It was a subdued group; there was not even the nervous laughter often heard in times of stress.

The partners departed in groups of two and three, each talking quietly, soberly. Roger Singer walked out into the street with Fred Coxe and Keith Merritt. Coxe and Merritt both shook their heads in disbelief as they walked along.

"Fred, who the hell is trying to screw us up?" Merritt asked.

"How would I know? Christ alone knows we're not angels, any of us. Nor are our friends and our clients. But murder? Jesus."

Roger Singer walked side by side with his two colleagues but said nothing. At the next stoplight he left them, saying he had to buy cigarettes. Singer did buy cigarettes—the first pack in more than a year. But how was he expected to endure this latest bit of stress without the help of nicotine? He ripped the pack open and lit up while still standing across the counter from the Iranian who ran the tobacco store.

Smoking as he walked, Singer made his way toward One Metro Plaza. He walked slowly, trying not to jar his shaken psyche by rapid or sudden movement. His mood was one of total despair. Nine months earlier, his whole life had changed as two forces triangulated on his brain, bringing him to a nearly total collapse.

Singer had decided months before that he would refuse to go on further errands for the CIA—errands that he had patriotically undertaken for years. He was too uncertain of the motives—and the politics—of the oafish outsiders who now controlled the agency and he had flatly announced to his contacts that he was through. Subtle pressure had been brought to bear, however, and the previous January he had found himself on a plane to Mexico City, where he met an old acquaintance dating back to Guatemala days. An old acquaintance and paid assassin. The assignment was distasteful, but not markedly more so than others he had executed in the past—to give his old contact instructions for killing a Cuban guerrilla leader, a latter-day Che Guevara, whose clever organizing efforts were interfering with the power elite in the country in which he was operating.

His mission accomplished, Singer had returned to New York, where a week later he learned from the newspaper of the botched assassination. The Cuban revolutionary had escaped without injury, but a crowd of nuns and children had been killed.

Roger Singer had graduated from the University of Chicago imbued, as they said, with the idea of performing public service at some time in his career. As a young man he naively thought this might mean running for Congress; the years had disabused him of that idea. The time required to stroke fund-raisers and party district leaders just was not available to a busy lawyer at Chase & Ward. Then the opportunity to carry out missions for the CIA arose and, while unorthodox, at least partially fulfilled Singer's desire for public service.

But killing nuns for an unclear purpose did not exactly accord with Singer's ideal, and this latest incident had in fact caused him to wake up sweating in the middle of the night.

Then there had been the matter of Anne and Graham Donovan. Singer had noticed a changed pattern to Anne's behavior in midwinter. He himself was devoted to spending weekends at their home in the Hamptons. They had had it winterized several years before so that they could use it in all seasons. To Singer, it was a great relief to spend quiet weekends in the country; he was totally indifferent to the weekend socializing in the City he missed out on by rusticating in Sagaponack. Reading, chopping wood, puttering about their handsome country house meant more to him than theatergoing or cocktail parties. Anne had always accompanied him without complaint when, quite suddenly, she found excuses for coming back to the city early or arriving in the country late or, on occasion, not coming at all.

"Oh, Roger, I know you love the country, so you go ahead," she had said, for example, just before the long Washington's Birthday weekend. "I've got some sort of bug and I think I really need just to stay here and be quiet. But don't let me stop you. Poor darling, I know you don't like to cook for yourself, but you'll be better off there than looking after a croupy invalid here."

Singer had thought little of the evasions until one weekend when Anne had pleaded that she must go and see her maiden aunt in Connecticut. As far as he knew, Anne had never been especially fond of the aunt—Singer in fact had only met her once since their marriage—so he was slightly puzzled by her sudden interest in her Connecticut relative. But it was all plausible; Anne had said that a cousin had called to say the aunt was about to have surgery of an undisclosed kind and that she was very down and needed company. So, in mid-February, Anne had gone to Wilton, Connecticut while Roger had gone to Long Island.

None of this aroused his suspicions until he tried to reach Anne at her aunt's later in the weekend. He had received a call from one of his European clients asking him to come to Brussels on the overnight flight on Sunday, and he had called to tell his wife of his changed plans. To his puzzlement, she was not at her aunt's in Wilton—the old lady was quite confused by his call, claiming that she had not heard from Anne in months—

and he was surprised, on a second call, to find his wife at their apartment in the city. When asked what she was doing there, Anne blithely replied that her aunt did not seem depressed at all but, with her endless complaining, threatened to make Anne so. As a result she had come back early from Connecticut.

Singer did not confront his wife with the obvious contradiction between what his wife and her aunt had told him. The old woman more than likely was addled and had forgotten that her niece had been there. Or perhaps Anne had simply needed a weekend of solitude—he sympathized, as more and more he desired time totally to himself—but had been reluctant to stake it out directly.

Four days later, Singer wound up his business earlier than expected and decided to take the morning Concorde from Paris rather than the regular afternoon flight from Brussels. He had not bothered to call Anne to tell her of the change and, when he arrived at their apartment about ten in the morning, she was not there. The cleaning woman, who had come in at eight-thirty, had not seen her either. He found this very odd, since Anne usually did not go out until late morning. Singer was annoyed, but thought no more about it and went off to the office after changing his clothes.

Singer finally reached his wife late in the afternoon. Where had she been? Oh, back visiting her aunt in Wilton overnight. Singer did not believe her. But again he kept silent, though he became more observant of her behavior.

Then he had found the small book of love poems in the drawer of Anne's desk. He did not as a matter of practice or habit search through his wife's belongings, but one evening, looking for a stamp in her desk, he had come across the slim volume. He opened it out of curiosity, only to find an inscription "For Anne, dearest, dearest Anne, G." in handwriting that he recognized as his partner Donovan's. All of a sudden the reasons for his wife's recent evasions became clear—she and Donovan were without question having an affair.

Singer's discovery made him physically nauseous; he rushed to the bathroom adjoining their bedroom and threw up. Then he tried to collect himself. What could he do? What should he do? Instead of anger, he felt only guilt. He had been remote of late, he knew. The CIA episode had thrown him into a deep depression. His sense of self-esteem had plummeted. Instead of a patriotic hero using his skills to help his country, he saw himself as a conspirator with assassins, with killers of nuns. He also saw his relationships with his rich Latin American and European clients differently. Wasn't he really just a lackey for a bunch of too-rich, tax-evading, socially irresponsible oligarchs? Was this the practice of law and the life the idealistic young Chicago graduate had had in mind?

He knew that his own preoccupations had made him less than an ideal companion for Anne. So in his depressed guilt he had not confronted her with the evidence of her affair. Why wouldn't she have an affair, given the unworthiness of her husband? he thought.

The added weight of Anne's infidelity pressed Singer deeper into depression. By Eastertime he was virtually not functioning—staying in bed until the middle of the day, then going to the office and staring at the harbor out the window.

Suicide was never far from his thoughts. Why not? Who or what was there to live for? There were no children to comfort him and scarcely any friends—certainly no friends to whom he could outline the dimensions of his depression. Only an unfaithful wife.

Finally, with the greatest effort, he started seeing a psychiatrist recommended by his regular doctor. The man turned out to be surprisingly sympathetic. He had written about the psychological effects of war and had also seen countless successful men and women reduced to ineffectuality by depression.

The doctor had told him not to expect instant relief from his mental problems. But gradually Singer felt certain he was getting better, and the black cloud above his head began to lift. But now, he was sure, he would be plunged back into depression. With his wife's lover murdered, he did not think he could bear the inevitable suspicion of his colleagues, who certainly—on the principle that the husband always knows last—must already have known about Anne and Graham.

Singer came up to One Metro Plaza as if approaching a prison, walking so slowly that those around him turned to look as they passed him. He took the elevator up and went immediately to his office without speaking to anyone.

Sitting at his desk, he thought again about suicide. Could one jump through the floor-to ceiling windows in the office? He thought that he recalled an instance where a distraught executive had been able to jump by throwing his attaché case through the window first. But what if the glass didn't break? They would probably commit him to Payne Whitney. Besides, would it be fair to the firm that had nurtured him to create another scandal on its premises?

In a desultory way Singer went through the piled-up correspondence on his desk. A letter from the practising Law Institute asking him to participate in a seminar on foreign investment in the United States; the month's schedule of off-the-record talks at the Council on Foreign Relations (including a speech by the State Department operative Singer was sure knew about his most recent mission entitled "What Should We Do about Terrorism?"); a telex from his client, M. Allard, asking him to get in touch at once with M. Allard's American investment advisor regarding a new real estate investment in the United States. He pondered the telex for several minutes, deciding that the matter could wait despite his client's urgent tone.

Instead, he turned to the appalling pile of form letter appeals for funds received on a daily basis by all affluent professionals. Normally these junk appeals went straight to the wastebasket; today Singer read each one carefully as a way of passing the time and occupying his mind. Cystic Fibrosis; Legal Aid; the Fresh Air Fund; Planned Parenthood; the Museum of the City of New York. But the desperate urgency of these appeals, each one claiming to have isolated a fundamental societal problem in need of solution, only depressed him more.

Then he thought about Anne. Should he call and tell her about Graham Donovan's murder? He could not face the prospect. Nor could he face the inevitable speculation that would surely take place that afternoon in a hundred whispered, closed-door conversations. He had to get out.

"Miss Lawrence, I'm going up to see Mr. DaSilva and won't be back," he told his secretary.

"Can you be reached?"

"No; it's a very confidential meeting and Mr. DaSilva would be very upset if a strange call interrupted. I'll be at home later if anyone needs to reach me."

He had used the DaSilva gambit before when he needed uninterrupted time alone, time to think, time to avoid confrontation with anything or anyone.

Singer bought a copy of the afternoon *Post* at the newsstand in the basement of the building and took the West Side subway to Times Square. On the way he read the *Post's* screaming headlines and breathless coverage of a brutal robbery-murder by a gang of black youths. In his depressed state, the yellow journalism of the city's afternoon daily affected him, though he had no rational connection with either the murder victim or the murderers. The newspaper's sleazy coverage confirmed his then-current view that the world—and New York City—were unhappy, distressing places, for him and for everybody else.

Singer also scanned the movie ads in the *Post;* what he most needed at this moment was the darkness of a large Broadway movie house—not a pornography theater, as many in Times Square were—but an enveloping anonymous cavern that would take him away from the realities of his world and his dark, despairing thoughts.

He would have preferred a cleaner and more decorous theater on the East Side, but there was too great a risk of encountering acquaintances, perhaps the wives of his fellow partners, seeing a matinee. So he made his way to Loew's and took a seat amid the score or so of school dropouts, junkies and bag ladies in the bowels of the old, rococo movie palace.

The movie was one of the comedy hits of the year, but it did not improve Singer's outlook at all. Third-rate actors muttering leaden dialogue—laced with obscenities that the screenwriters undoubtedly thought were witty— did not amuse him, but instead deepened his sense of depression about himself and both the smaller and larger world about him.

Singer left before the movie was over. He had to get away—away from Anne, away from his colleagues, away from the city that had become dirty and hateful to him. He took a taxi home, made a quick call to Air France, packed a bag and headed for Kennedy Airport. The comforting dark of the movie theater had not soothed him; perhaps a visit to old haunts in Europe would.

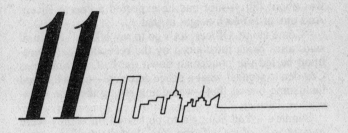

Luis Bautista, detective second class, homicide squad,
New York City Police Department, introduced himself
to Dorothea Cowden, the Chase & Ward receptionist. It
did not take more than a glance for her to conclude that
he was startlingly handsome: dark eyes; long but neat jet
black hair; a thin, sensual mouth; light, copper-colored
skin that gave the impression of a smooth, even and
permanent suntan. And his tall body—he was easily six
feet—was so well muscled that it seemed on the verge of
exploding out of his gray glen plaid suit. Except for a
small nick on the bottom of one front tooth, he was a
near-perfect masculine specimen, or so he seemed to a
woman used to greeting the steady stream of visitors,
more often than not paunchy and balding, who came on
business to Chase & Ward.

When Bautista had stated his business, she called
George Bannard and was surprised when he came out
personally to greet the visitor. The encounter struck her
as funny. Both were tall men, but there was at least one
contrast that amused Miss Cowden—Bannard had an
off-the-rack body in an impeccably tailored and well-
fitting suit, while Bautista clearly had a custom-made
body (the product, she was certain, of careful workouts
at a gym) in an off-the-rack suit that simply did not flow
with his muscular contours.

Bannard, too, was surprised. When he had called the

Police Department less than an hour before, he had assumed that he would be delivered into the hands of an Irish—or possibly Italian—cop. He had not expected someone this young—he correctly guessed that Bautista was about thirty—nor had he expected a Puerto Rican. And one of his own height at that.

"Come along, Officer, let's go to my office," Bannard said, after being introduced by the receptionist. Whereupon he led the policeman down the hall, leaving Miss Cowden to wonder what a police detective—and a damned handsome one at that—was doing seeing the firm's Executive Partner.

Bannard asked Bautista to be seated once they were in Bannard's office with the door shut. Bautista sat down in the burnished antique chair opposite Bannard's desk.

"Thanks very much for coming so promptly," Bannard told his guest. "Needless to say we're pretty upset around here just now, so I'm glad to enlist your support."

"Not at all, sir," Bautista replied, as he pulled a notebook and ballpoint pen from his pocket. "I gather from what you said on the phone that you suspect your partner Graham Donovan was murdered?"

"That, unfortunately, is the case. But before I go further, I'd like to ask my partner—colleague—Reuben Frost to join us. Mr. Frost used to have my job at this firm as Executive Partner, and he's much more familiar with recent developments than I am. Do you mind?"

"Whatever you say, Mr. Bannard. Anything that will clarify the situation is all right with me."

"Good," Bannard answered. He buzzed Mrs. Davis and asked her to tell Frost to join them. Mrs. Davis buzzed him back almost at once. "Mr. Frost will be here right away," Bannard explained. "His office is just down the hall."

"Fine," Bautista replied.

An awkward silence followed as they waited. How did one make small talk with a homicide detective, Bannard wondered.

"Mr. Bautista, how long have you been on the police force?" Bannard finally asked. As he did so, he realized that his question was not unlike the question clients, meeting him for the first time, had asked of him in younger days: "Mr. Bannard, how long have you been at Chase & Ward?" He had resented the question then, and realized that Detective Bautista might resent a similar question now.

"Eight years, sir," Bautista answered, with no visible sign of resentment.

"And are you from New York?" Bannard asked, realizing too late that he was implying that Bautista was some sort of parvenu immigrant.

"More or less, sir," Bautista replied evenly. "I was born in Puerto Rico, but came here with my mother and dad when I was three. I went to Stuyvesant High School and John Jay College before joining the department."

"I see. And murder is your specialty?"

"Yes, I guess you could say that. I've been on the homicide squad for two years."

"Interesting," Bannard responded noncommittally, while thinking that the man across the desk was probably all right, having graduated from a good high school (Bannard thought it was good, on the basis of his dim knowledge of such things) and the city college where (Bannard was almost sure) police officers were trained.

Bannard ran out of conversation at this point and stared impatiently at his door, waiting for Frost to enter.

During the ensuing silence Bautista looked about him and marveled at the contrast Bannard's quarters presented to the usual sort of lawyer's office visited by homicide detectives—dimly lit, dirty-walled warrens with flyspecked windows looking out on air vents. Not aseptically clean offices with breathtaking views of the city's harbor. Bautista reflected too that this was not exactly the type of office he could aspire to once he completed his night law course, now in progress, at St. John's Law School.

Then Reuben Frost entered Bannard's office. Bannard did not stand up but Bautista did.

"Mr. Bautista—do I have that right?" Bannard asked.

"Yes, sir."

"Mr. Bautista, this is Reuben Frost. Mr. Frost is a former partner in this firm, was formerly the head of this firm, and has been involved with this whole Donovan matter."

The two men shook hands, each one sizing up the other.

"Glad to meet you, Mr. Bautista," Frost said. "You're a homicide detective, I assume?"

"That's right, sir."

"Good. I'm awfully afraid that's what we need here right now."

"How do you wish to proceed?" Bannard asked.

"Well, sir, I'd begin from the beginning, or what you think is the beginning," Bautista said. "But before you begin, you gentlemen should understand that the autopsy on Tuesday showed that your Mr. Donovan died of a cardiac arrest. I was at the precinct when the call came in about Donovan and I caught the case. I was upstairs at that club with your partner . . ."

"Arthur Tyson," Bannard prompted.

"Tyson, and was actually present at the autopsy. Cardiac arrest is what the M.E. said. There was no mention of homicide."

"Tell me, Officer, in your experience has the medical examiner always been right?" Bannard asked. Both he and Frost waited intently for the reply.

"Well . . . the fact is I'd rather not answer that one. Why don't you just go ahead with your theory," Bautista said.

"I'm afraid it's more than a theory," Bannard replied. Then, at Bannard's prompting, Frost again told the tale of the poisoned carafe, ending with Doyle's report that morning.

"So you see," Bannard interjected when he thought Frost had finished (or more precisely, when Bannard thought he should be finished), "my partner Graham Donovan didn't have a heart attack but was murdered. Poisoned."

"Mr. Bannard, it sounds plausible to me," Bautista replied. "But just a few questions, sir, if you don't mind."

"Fire away."

"Mr. Frost, what was the name of the private detective you called?"

"Ross Doyle. D-O-Y-L-E. Office at 24 Water Street."

Bautista wrote this information down. "And any particular reason why you gentlemen didn't call the police earlier?"

Both men fumbled for an answer, with Frost finally replying. "Yes. We simply didn't want to get the police involved—or for that matter to bother the police—until we were absolutely sure of what happened."

"I see. Mr. Doyle said death was due to digitalis poisoning?"

"No, he said the water carafe in Donovan's office contained digitalis, or some derivative or concentrate of it," Frost said, with a lawyer's precision. "We inferred the cause of death from that."

"Mr. Donovan was, let's see, fifty-seven, is that right?" Bautista asked, consulting his notebook.

"That's right. Fifty-seven," Bannard said.

"And when is the funeral?"

"It was this morning."

"And what was to happen to the body?"

"It was to be cremated. But I've already called the funeral home to try and stop that," Frost explained.

"Good. We'll probably be too late, but it's worth a try," Bautista said. "I asked Mr. Tyson this, but let me ask you again. Was there any family?"

"Only a son, and he and his father weren't even speaking. His wife died a couple of years ago," Frost said.

"He lived alone?"

Frost hesitated and looked across at Bannard. Did Donovan live alone? He supposed so. Certainly Anne Singer did not live with him—he was almost certain—but considering the possibility caused him to pause before saying yes.

"You are sure of that?" Bautista asked, noting the hesitation.

"Yes, yes. Quite sure." This interrogation was not

going to be easy, Frost thought, and judging by the stern
look on Bannard's face he seemed to agree.

"What about suspects, gentlemen? Any idea who might
have done it?"

"None whatsoever," Bannard replied quickly.

"I don't," Frost echoed.

"None at all? Your partner was poisoned in the same
office as you and you don't suspect anybody?"

"To be frank with you, Mr. Bautista, the last few
days have been so upsetting that I don't think anyone
around here has really thought about suspects," Bannard
said.

"No one? You haven't thought of anyone who might
have killed your partner?"

"Well, there is one person. But I find it absolutely
impossible to believe she is guilty," Bannard said.

"She?"

"Graham Donovan's secretary, Grace Appleby."

"Why do you suspect her?"

Bannard told the detective what he knew about Miss
Appleby's stock market activity, adding his own personal judgment that she was not acting alone and de-
scribing his instructions to Doyle to have her followed.

"I think you did right," Bautista said. "She sounds
like a prime suspect to me. Motive? Maybe Donovan
had caught on to what she was up to. Access to the
victim? Couldn't be easier."

"But where would she get the poison?"

"Sir, you'd be surprised how easy that is. Not as easy
as dope, probably, but getting poison is easy, easy, easy."

"I still say I can't believe she committed murder,"
Bannard said.

"And I suppose you didn't believe she was playing
around in the stock market either?"

"You have me there," Bannard answered.

"But if it isn't Miss Appleby, who else might it be?
Any of your partners? Did any of them have any reason
to kill Donovan?"

Bannard was not going to be caught hesitating again.
Distasteful as it was, he told Bautista about Anne Singer.

"And I'm sure you're going to tell me that there's no way you'd believe that this woman's husband would commit murder," Bautista said.

"Damn right," Bannard answered with some heat. "I've worked with Roger Singer on an almost daily basis since he returned ten years ago from his tour of duty with the CIA—"

"CIA? What was he doing in the CIA?"

"I don't know; none of us does. In the late sixties—isn't that right, Reuben?" Bannard asked.

"I think that's about right, yes."

"About fifteen years ago, Roger Singer went to work for the CIA. He had been working on a number of South American matters for us and he told us that he was going to be involved in some long-range planning and study projects for the agency. He took a leave of absence and was gone for about fourteen months. He's been a fulltime partner since then, though everybody suspects he's kept his hand in at the agency. He often goes off for a week or two on mysterious trips that we never learn anything about."

"It sounds to me like he's on the black side of the CIA, the undercover part."

"I've never thought of it that way, but I expect you're right," Bannard replied.

"The part where murder and poisoning are sometimes real important."

"Are you suggesting that Roger—," Bannard started to ask, again with some anger.

"I'm suggesting nothing. I just point out that your Mr. Singer had a motive to kill your Mr. Donovan and that he's probably encountered murder before."

"I refuse to believe it."

"Mr. Bannard, I'm not asking you to believe anything. I'm only trying to figure out who the suspects may be. You mentioned a son. What about him?"

"I don't know him, though I've met him several times over the years," Bannard said. "He's an archaeology professor at NYU and would appear to be a complete shit, if you'll pardon the expression."

"I've heard the word."

"I was the one who told him his father died," Bannard continued. "For my trouble, I had to listen to a not very coherent story of how cruel Graham Donovan had been to his wife before she died and how bitter the son was about it. He said he had no intention of coming to the funeral—and he didn't—and that there was 'nothing in it for him,' meaning, presumably, that his father didn't leave him anything. Which was in fact the case."

"You've seen the will?"

"I have," Frost said. "Everything is left to Columbia University—except for twenty-five thousand dollars to Miss Appleby."

"What's the son's name?"

"Bruce. His number is in the book."

"Fine. Now, is there anyone else who might be a suspect? Any other partner?" Bautista emphasized the *other*, but Bannard let it pass.

"Or retired partner?" Bautista pressed, looking squarely at Frost.

"Absolutely not," Bannard said, this time without hesitation. Frost, meanwhile, could barely suppress a smile at the idea of one of his retired colleagues being a murderer.

"How about the young lawyers? Associates, don't you call them? Any of them have a reason to do in the deceased?"

Again Bannard was nonplussed. The thought that one of Chase & Ward's "best and brightest" might commit murder had simply not occurred to him. But now that it was suggested, it certainly was well known that Donovan had been hard, harder than most, on his associates. He had demanded a great deal of the young lawyers who worked for him and, as he had more than once admitted to Bannard, he was not always as appreciative as he might have been of their work. Nor had he been interested over the years in being a kingmaker, sponsoring the candidacies of associates for partnership. Quite the opposite, in fact; Donovan's critical judgment had sunk more than one otherwise promising candidacy. But had any of this driven an associate to murder? It was a possibility, though to Bannard's mind a remote one.

"I'm hesitating because I would have thought the possibility ridiculous," Bannard said, taking the hesitation bull by the horns, "but I certainly can't think of anyone remotely capable of committing a murder. We've got a lot of very ambitious young lawyers here, perhaps some that are even ruthlessly ambitious, but I don't think any of them would murder to get ahead."

"Why do you assume that it would be murder 'to get ahead'?"

"Well, you got me to thinking about Donovan's relations with the associates, which were not always the best. He did not always push the careers of the lawyers who worked for him."

"Anyone in particular?"

"I would have to think about that. But as I said, I can't believe . . ."

The conversation was interrupted by a buzz from Mrs. Davis. Frank Campbell's was on the phone to report that Donovan's body had, in fact, been cremated. Bannard cursed quietly and relayed the information to Bautista.

"Damn. Well, nothing we can do about it now. But getting back to what I said earlier, please, gentlemen, give some more thought—a great deal of thought, in fact—to the question of who killed your partner."

"Mr. Bautista, we certainly will. We want to find Graham Donovan's murderer and are prepared to let the chips fall where they may. So how do you want to proceed? I assume you'll want to question everyone around here that might know something?" Bannard asked.

"Let me think about that," Bautista said.

"We can have anybody you want here at any time," Bannard said, warming to the subject. "Do you want us to set up a schedule for you?"

"Not just yet, Mr. Bannard. I want to think this one through before we go all out."

"You're not doubting that a murder took place, are you, Officer?" Bannard asked.

"No, I'm not. But I do want to talk to that medical

examiner and to the laboratory people your detective hired. Just precautions, but I want to take them."

"Up to you, of course," Bannard answered. "But I must say that seems like an unduly cautious approach. We've had a murder here and we may all be in danger. I frankly don't think this is a time for caution."

"I hear what you're saying, sir, but there are certain rules by the book that must be followed."

"Mr. Bautista, I perhaps have seen too many movies, but I thought when a murder occurred an investigation started," Bannard said, in his best WASPish voice. "And I would have thought that the not inconsiderable taxes the partners of this firm pay to this city would have entitled us to police attention when we need it."

"I'm sorry if you disagree, Mr. Bannard, but this is my case and I will just have to handle it in my own way," Bautista said. "Let me follow up on the things I mentioned and get back to you, but I assure you, Mr. Bannard, that the investigation has already begun," Bautista said. Frost followed the verbal dueling between the two men with interest, realizing from Bannard's demeanor that the detective had managed to infuriate the Executive Partner.

"You speak of procedures, Mr. Bautista," Bannard continued. "I would have thought the first 'procedure' would be to question everyone that might be able to shed some light on what happened." There was no stopping Bannard now. "I might add that several of us, myself included, are good friends of the Mayor. And I can assure you he will hear about this if the police screw around with this investigation."

"Mr. Bannard, I realize you're upset," Bautista replied, carefully and without any show of temper. "And if you want to take this up with the Mayor, that's your prerogative. We're always glad to have the Mayor reminded that the Police Department does exist. But as I said before, I'm afraid I've got to handle this case in my own way. Okay?"

Bautista remained calm as he finished speaking, but it was clear he expected a compliant response.

Bannard, angry as he was, realized this too, and acknowledged the officer's query with a reluctant nod of his head. Frost, who had been silently agonizing at Bannard's imperious manner—just because lawyers knew how to lean hard did not necessarily make it wise to do so—admired the young policeman's calm in standing up to the bullying; he was nonetheless glad that the confrontation now seemed at an end.

"By the way, could I see the deceased's office before I leave?" Bautista asked.

"Of course. Come with me," Bannard said.

"And will Miss Appleby be nearby?"

"If she's there at all, she'll be sitting at the desk directly outside Donovan's office," Bannard said.

"She's a severe but nice-looking woman with gray hair," Frost added, bringing up the rear as they left Bannard's office.

The visit to the site of the poisoning was not enlightening or, if it was, Bautista did not let on. And to his disappointment Miss Appleby was not at her desk. When the detective had finished looking around, Bannard asked him to return briefly to the corner office, though, as far as Bautista was concerned, there was nothing more to be discussed at the moment. Frost did not know what Bannard had in mind either, but whatever it was it made the Executive Partner palpably nervous. Back behind a closed door, Bannard told Bautista and Frost what was troubling him.

"Detective, is there any chance of keeping this out of the newspapers?"

"Until we find the murderer, yes," Bautista answered. "I don't think it is in anyone's interest to broadcast the fact that your partner was murdered; the chances of catching the killer are going to be greater if he—or she—does not know that murder is suspected. We don't need one of those *Post* headlines—'Wall Street Biggie Poisoned at Posh Club'—to complicate things. I don't think you have to worry though, given the way the newspaper business works in this town."

"What do you mean?"

"Well, unless the Police Department chooses to make a big announcement about this case, the only way the press will get the story is by looking at the police blotter. Yesterday, the only thing the blotter showed was that your partner died of cardiac arrest. And the new entry, with more intriguing information, will not be made until late this afternoon, long after the hardworking police reporters have taken their daily look at it. To get press attention for your murder in this town, Mr. Bannard, you have to be a careful planner, timing your crime so that the tigers of the press can discover it on the blotter and blow it up for the afternoon headlines. You could be done in by a one-man nuclear bomb and it would never make the news if it happened at the wrong time of day."

"I hope you're right, Mr. Bautista," Bannard said. "The whole question of publicity is of course secondary; the important thing is to find Graham Donovan's murderer. But if it can all be done quietly, so much the better."

Reuben Frost wondered whether Bannard saw the inconsistency in the positions he had taken with the police officer—wanting an all-flags-flying investigation on the one hand, yet the utmost secrecy on the other. Frost thought he might just have a word with Detective Bautista; he liked the man's ability to withstand Bannard's inconsistent outbursts and thought perhaps the two of them could communicate in a less contentious way.

"Is that all, Mr. Bannard?" Bautista asked.

"Yes, I guess so," Bannard said. "Just let us know what we should do next."

"Fine," Bautista said.

"George, I'll show Mr. Bautista out," Frost said.

As Frost and Bautista walked down the hall, Frost asked the detective to stop off at his office. Bautista was puzzled, but he followed the older man inside Frost's modest quarters.

"Come in, Detective," Frost said. "I'm sorry I can't give you the panoramic view anymore, but make yourself comfortable anyway."

"Anymore, sir? I don't think I understand."

"Oh, nothing," Frost said, suddenly appalled that he was apologizing—complaining?—about the size of his office. "I'm pretty much retired, you see, so I really don't take an active part in what goes on in the firm. I used to run it, after a fashion, but that was a while back."

"Then how did you get involved with this Donovan thing?" Bautista asked.

"I happened to have the good luck to be around, I guess. George—Bannard—had to go to Chicago on Tuesday, so he left me in charge of things. It was supposed to be only annoying details about the funeral until the incident with the water carafe occurred.

"I hope, by the way, that you applied some discount to Mr. Bannard's remarks," Frost continued. "He gets carried away at times and this nastiness has put him under pressure—one doesn't like to have a scandal occur on one's watch. He *is* a friend of the Mayor's, by the way—there's some resemblance in their temperaments—but I don't think he's quite ready to make trouble yet."

"I understand," Bautista said, grinning broadly. "I'm used to heat from above, below and sideways."

"I'm sure you are," Frost replied, a slight if sympathetic smile on his face as well. "And I'm also sure you'll somehow reconcile George's desires for both a full-blown investigation and total secrecy."

Bautista grinned again. "That may be harder. But we'll try."

"How *do* you think the investigation should proceed?" Frost asked.

"Let's consider one other alternative first," Bautista said, looking straight at Frost. "I couldn't really raise it with Mr. Bannard, after the things he said, but let me try it on you."

Implicit in Bautista's statement were the conclusion that Frost had struck him as an eminently more reasonable man than Bannard and the shrewd hunch, dimly recognized, that perhaps both he and Frost, each in his

own way, had been somewhat abused by the Executive
Partner.

"Mr. Frost, one approach would be to forget this
whole thing. You and your firm have discharged your
responsibility by notifying the police of the alleged murder. The murder was probably a personal thing, fester-
ing out of some grievance against the deceased. So it's
not likely to recur. And even if we found the murderer,
you'd have a hard time proving that your cremated Mr.
Donovan had been poisoned. You'd have to discredit
the autopsy to do it. As you may have guessed from my
response in Mr. Bannard's office, that is probably not
the hardest thing in the world to do. But it wouldn't help
when you're trying to convict somebody beyond a reasonable doubt.' Besides, there's no one around demanding vengeance; the son is the only relative, and from all
you have told me about him he may well be a suspect.
So let's forget the whole thing. No publicity, no public
scandal. Everything will just be forgotten."

"That is unthinkable," Frost replied. "Sure, all of us
would like to avoid scandal and publicity, as Bannard so
clearly indicated. But I don't see how we could live with
the possibility that there may be someone among us who
has committed murder. We've got to solve this thing."

"I was hoping you would say that," Bautista said.
"But I did want to get on the table that the path to a
triumph of justice may be a little slippery."

"I know all that," Frost replied. "But I repeat, where
do we go from here?"

"Well, despite what Mr. Bannard says, I'm going to
try and keep things low-key for a couple of days. Sure,
we could interview everybody in sight, but I've got a
hunch the information we need to start working on can
be gotten more quietly."

"Such as?"

"Such as trying to narrow down who had access to
Donovan's office. Who was in a position to poison the
water in his carafe? He apparently made his iced tea
with water from that carafe every morning. And from
what you tell me, the poison that was put in his water

could remain potent for up to twenty-four hours. So we only need to check on the time from Monday morning through Tuesday morning."

"Oh, I think we can cut it even finer than that. Unless I am mistaken, the water in the partners' carafes is changed every night. So we only really have to worry about Tuesday," Frost said.

Bautista grinned again. "Mr. Frost, you sound like a detective." Then, after a pause, he asked, "Do I get the impression you want to be involved with this investigation?"

Frost was embarrassed, embarrassed because his eagerness had apparently shown through.

"Of course I do. Graham Donovan was my friend. This firm was my life for almost half a century. I want to do whatever I can, Officer."

"Perfect. Well, as I say, you can inquire around about the access thing. And maybe try to find out if you're right about the water carafes being emptied at night. And I'd keep an eye on your Miss Appleby. Bannard said she's going to be followed?"

"That's what Bannard decided. So something may come of that."

"Yes."

"And what else?"

"Just keep your eyes and ears open. And here's my direct number if you need to call me in a hurry," the detective said as he handed Frost his card. "And I'll check in with you tomorrow. Something is sure to turn up."

"I hope you're right, Mr. Bautista. I hope you're right," Frost replied.

EXECUTIVE COMMITTEE MEETING

12

THE MEMBERS OF GEORGE BANNARD'S EXECUTIVE COMMIT-
tee, except for Keith Merritt, were not drinkers of the
Perrier and white wine school. Arthur Tyson favored
bourbon, and Fred Coxe and Bannard martinis—the drier
the better. Merritt nearly always drank Campari or something equally light. Coxe unashamedly drank his martinis like Coca-Cola, consuming twice as many drinks as
his colleagues, who overlooked his slight but nonetheless visible shaking and the occasional slur in his speech.
Bannard usually confined himself to a single martini at
these cocktail hour get-togethers unless the agenda was
a full one, in which case he would extend himself to
two.

Bannard knew before he left his office that this Thursday evening would be a two-martini night. He would
need the two drinks to unwind and there was enough to
talk about over two drinks.

Like clockwork, Bannard's colleagues appeared at the
Hexagon Club bar at six o'clock. They sat down at their
usual table in the corner of the room, a table affording a
magnificent view of midtown Manhattan and beyond (a
view that they seldom, if ever, noticed), and called Arturo,
the bar waiter.

After ordering drinks—Bannard always signed for them,
which the others took to mean (but never asked) that the
bill would be paid by Chase & Ward as a business

118

expense—the foursome conversed nervously in unusually quiet voices. (Merritt, as the expert on firm operations and finances, knew that in fact Bannard put in chits for their committee drinks, but he had never raised the subject with Bannard or his colleagues.)

The four men realized that one fact made this Thursday's meeting different from all of those that had gone before—the irretrievable absence of Graham Donovan, the fifth member of the Executive Committee. This fact and the now undeniable cause of their partner's death subtly altered their usual behavior. Tyson was extremely subdued, and Merritt rather more manic. And Coxe began drinking even more rapidly than usual, if such was possible.

Bannard, who often complained vocally about the burdens of being the Executive Partner in the best of times, did not complain, but did act as if the weight of the whole world were on his shoulders.

"What a day," he told his confederates. "First that joke funeral, then the lab report, then our exciting lunch, then the NYPD. Let me tell you about *that*." Bannard recounted the meeting with Officer Bautista, and the policeman's seeming unwillingness to proceed immediately with a full-dress investigation.

"The whole meeting was completely unreal," Bannard said. "No respectful Irish cop ready and eager to bring a killer to justice, but a *tall* Puerto Rican—a matinee idol at that—acting supercautious."

"Goddam," Tyson exploded. "He sounds like the jerks at the medical examiner's office." Still seething about their behavior two days earlier, he recounted again for the benefit of the group the runaround he had gotten, though considerably deemphasizing any role he may have had in bringing about the erroneous autopsy result.

"It certainly is extraordinary," Coxe said. "And where does all this leave us?"

"Way up a muddy river, I'd say," Merritt observed.

"I'm afraid you're right," Bannard agreed glumly.

"George, it sounds to me like you're going to have to

add playing Sherlock Holmes to your executive responsibilities,'' Coxe said.

"No, Fred, you're wrong. We are *all* going to play Sherlock Holmes," Bannard said, signaling Arturo for another round as he did so. (Coxe had already summoned the waiter back with a second martini, which was almost gone.)

"Well, if that's the case, let's begin," Merritt said. He took his engagement calendar and a pen from his suit coat pocket and opened the calendar to the pad of paper affixed to the inside cover. "Let's make a list of every possible suspect we can think of."

"Oh, for heaven's sake, Keith," Tyson exploded. "We're never going to be able to solve this thing. Besides, there are no suspects."

"Oh no?" Merritt said petulantly. "How about Grace Appleby?"

"Unlikely," Bannard said, "as I tried to tell Bautista."

"But a suspect just the same, right?" said Merritt, as he started to write down her name. "With all that funny business about Stephens stock, she may well have had a motive."

"But, as I said to Bautista, where did she get the poison?" Bannard interjected.

"What did he say?" Coxe asked.

"He had no idea, but said there were a hundred ways you could get it."

"Doesn't she do volunteer work at some hospital?" Tyson asked. "I seem to recall one day at lunch when someone was complaining to Graham about how disagreeable his secretary had been that Graham said she was really Florence Nightingale in disguise."

"By God, I think you're right, Arthur," Bannard said, his voice shaking slightly. "I do remember Graham telling us that."

"So I'll put an asterisk after her name, for access to the poison," Merritt said. "Now who else do we have? What other Chase & Ward employees?"

"I can't think of any," Coxe said. "Everybody liked

Graham. And rightly so. There was just no reason to kill him.''

''Well, Fred, there you are obviously wrong—I was about to say dead wrong. Do you think someone poisoned Graham's water carafe by mistake? Maybe they were really after you and just goofed it up,'' Bannard said.

''That's not especially funny, George,'' Coxe shot back, pouting slightly.

''All right, who else? No employees? How about clients?'' Merritt pressed.

''Let's see,'' Bannard said. ''Whose work was Graham doing recently?''

''Well, Stephens Industries, obviously, as we know only too well,'' said Tyson.

''Who did he deal with there?'' George asked.

''I think only Joe Mather. Donovan never had any respect for Stephens' general counsel, what's-his-name Peck, and Mather didn't like him either. Mather was always going around him and dealing directly with Graham,'' Tyson said. ''I know, because I do the Stephens litigation.''

''Maybe Peck killed Donovan,'' Coxe said.

''Don't be silly, Fred,'' Bannard barked at him. ''If we're going to play Keith's little game, let's play it out.''

''Graham was doing the corporate work for First Fiduciary,'' Merritt said.

''Not much help there,'' Tyson said. ''Harry Knight is too old and too feeble to murder anybody, and most of the vice presidents over there are too *feebleminded* to commit murder.''

''You're right, Arthur. I suppose it's worth a little digging to see if there's anyone over there who had it in for Graham, but I would guess you're not going to find much,'' said Bannard.

''Then of course there's Dwight Draper,'' Merritt said. ''I know Graham's been involved with him recently because his chemical company is about to go public. He's been around pestering me incessantly for tax advice.''

"No good," Bannard said. "I don't like him much, but he and Graham go way, way back. I saw Draper at the funeral and he said he and Graham were like 'brothers.' Draper as the murderer—it just doesn't wash."

"So, gentlemen, thus far I have one name on my list, poor Grace Appleby," Merritt said. "Is that the best we can do? How about the associates? Any prospects there?"

"I can think of about four that are probably capable of anything, but I don't think any of them ever had anything to do with Donovan," Tyson said.

"And I can think of four too—probably different from your four—but again, I don't know of any link to Graham," Bannard said. "You remember that Donovan was never very enthusiastic about the young lawyers who worked for him, and certainly never pushed any that I remember for partnership. But did he have blood enemies among the associates? I doubt it."

"Look, it may just be possible," Tyson said. "For the associates, becoming a partner in Chase & Ward is more often than not the biggest thing in their lives. They get divorced for it, they become workaholics for it, they develop a psychosis about it. To be denied a partnership after working your behind off for seven or eight or nine years can be pretty devastating. Maybe somebody was just twisted enough to take it out on Donovan."

"What about that fellow Donovan spoke out against at our last two election meetings?" Tyson asked.

"You mean Perry Griffith?" Bannard answered.

"That's the one," Tyson said.

"Well, Donovan certainly didn't like him," Bannard said. "I remember it well. All the partners were sitting around at the meeting and Griffith seemed like a pretty good bet to become a partner, either this year or next, when Donovan spoke out. Remember? He said that Perry Griffith was a fine lawyer, that he had a fine mind, but that there was just some 'missing element' that made Donovan hesitant."

"Yes, and when some of us tried to pin Graham down, all he could say was that he thought Griffith was just too ambitious for his own good," Coxe said.

"And that was enough to sway the vote against Griffith," Bannard added. "Maybe you should put him down, Keith."

"With an asterisk?"

"What do you mean?" Bannard asked.

"Remember, an asterisk means reason to think the person could have had access to poison," Merritt answered.

"No reason for an asterisk as far as I know," Bannard said.

"Aren't we being a bit hasty?" Coxe asked. "Sure, Donovan spoke out against Griffith—twice, in fact. But our partnership election meetings are secret. Nobody knows what goes on—"

"Oh, Fred, how naive can you be?" Tyson broke in. "Sure our meetings are secret. So are the meetings to select a pope, but eventually the world knows what politicking went on among the cardinals. Besides, Graham Donovan was such an open person that he himself probably told Griffith what he had done."

"Even if he hadn't," Merritt said, "Griffith has to have known that someone was against him, and it shouldn't have been too hard to figure out that Graham was the one."

"Who does he work for now?" Tyson asked.

"Austin Culin," Bannard said.

"Was he ever told he would not be a partner?" Merritt asked.

"No, he wasn't," Bannard said. "You remember we decided he should have another chance because of the divided opinion about him. Culin is supposed to be giving him really close scrutiny this year. But he has to have known that things aren't going too well, since his law school classmate, Artie Dawes, became a partner this year."

"And you're right, George, he must have known what Graham felt about him. So, knowing he realistically only had one more shot at becoming a partner, perhaps he thought with Graham out of the way . . ." Merritt's voice trailed off; he was appalled at his own logic.

"You're much too suspicious, Keith, but put him down," Bannard said.

Merritt did so, as Tyson asked the group if they shouldn't have another drink. "I know we're going over our limit, but this is a special occasion of sorts."

"Hell, why not," Bannard said, signaling Arturo.

"I'm going to switch to white wine," Bannard said. "If I keep on with gin, I'll be putting everyone I know on Keith's list."

"Which isn't getting much longer," Merritt noted. "Who else? Who else joins the elect?"

"What about Donovan's son?" Tyson asked.

"Bruce. Yes, I suppose he could be a suspect. God knows he seems to have hated his father enough," Bannard said. "But how could he have gotten into the office?"

"I should think that would have been pretty easy," Tyson said. "He must have known his way around there pretty well from times past; surely he used to come and see his father when they were on better terms. And you know as well as I do that Dorothea Cowden isn't efficient enough to log in everybody that comes in here, even though it's her job to do so."

"All right, put him down," Bannard directed. "Without an asterisk, right?" The others nodded.

"Anyone else? Or are we down to the last group we haven't considered?" Merritt asked.

"Which is?" Coxe asked back.

"Ourselves, dear Fred, ourselves. Which one of us, which of our brethren here at Chase & Ward might have killed Graham?"

"I suppose there is the obvious," Bannard said with a sigh.

"You mean Roger Singer?" Merritt asked. "I'll put him down."

"Let's remember that this is all hypothetical," Bannard said. "But having said that, I think you'd better add an asterisk, Keith."

"Why?" Coxe asked, a puzzled look on his face.

"CIA, Fred," Bannard replied. "It never would have

occurred to me, but Officer Bautista pointed out that Roger may well be familiar with poisons—and murder—from his CIA days.''

"Good God, George, I never thought of that,'' Coxe said.

"Okay, who else?'' Merritt asked. Then, when there was silence and no more nominees emerged, Merritt, smiling, asked, "What about me?''

"Oh, Keith, I doubt it,'' Bannard said. "You couldn't hurt a fly—I don't think.''

In some odd way, Merritt seemed relieved at this reassurance. "So are we through with the list?'' he asked.

Again there was silence, which was finally interrupted by Fred Coxe, now on his fourth martini.

"What the hell, Keith, if we really want to play your game, don't you think we should add Arthur's name?''

"What the hell did you say?'' Tyson shouted back, his face twisted in fury. "What the hell did you say, you son of a bitch?''

Coxe, who had been grinning at his own drunken jest, abruptly stopped when he saw—as even a drunk could see—Tyson's rage.

"Only a joke, Arthur,'' Coxe said lamely. "Don't get excited.''

"Well, I am excited, you miserable little souse. How dare you insinuate such a thing!''

"Arthur, Arthur. Forget it,'' Merritt interjected nervously.

"Keith, you stay out of this,'' Tyson barked. "I goddam well want to know what's on Fred's pickled brain.'' He started to lunge toward Coxe, but Bannard restrained him.

Coxe was breathing heavily, a look of great hurt on his face. Then he spoke, slowly and deliberately. "Okay, Arthur. What I said was a joke. But let's face it, everybody knows you want George's job when he retires. And the biggest obstacle standing in your way was Graham Donovan.''

Tyson stood up and addressed the group. "I'm not

going to stay here and put up with this crap. If the rest of you want to listen to this silly little drunk, go ahead. Be my guest. But I don't. Goodnight, gentlemen.''

Tyson was out of the room before his stunned colleagues could respond.

"George, should we go and bring him back?" Merritt asked.

"No. I think enough damage has been done for one day. Let him go," Bannard answered. "And as for you, Fred, whatever possessed you to bait Arthur like that?"

"I'm sorry, George. But it does us all good to see the old brute jock in Arthur occasionally."

The remaining group continued to drink in silence. Merritt sat with his pen poised over his handwritten list. "Shall we review the bidding?" he asked. "Here's the list," he said, turning it around for all to see:

> *Grace Appleby**
> *Perry Griffith*
> *Bruce Donovan*
> *Roger Singer**

Coxe and Bannard stared at the list of names.

"And what about Arthur? Should we add his name?" Merritt asked.

"Yes, Keith, put it down," Bannard said after a lengthy pause. "And on that note, let's all go home."

A SIMPLIFICATION AND A COMPLICATION

13

Bannard was both disturbed and depressed as he re-
turned to the Chase & Ward offices to pick up his
briefcase. A new stack of papers had arrived that afternoon from Bernard Sussman's army of MBAs in Chicago and had to be reviewed that evening, even though
Bannard's thoughts were of his murdered partner and
the disarray within his Executive Committee—disarray
he saw spreading to the firm as a whole if Donovan's
homicide was not solved promptly.

As he went down the hall, he was surprised to see a
light still on in Reuben Frost's office. It was after seven
o'clock and Frost, however active he remained in the
firm's practice, was rarely around after five. Bannard
poked his head inside Frost's office. Frost was sitting at
his desk with a voluminous typewritten document and
an open Securities Law handbook in front of him.

"Reuben, what the hell are you doing here at this
hour?" Bannard asked.

"Oh, just catching up," Frost answered. "Austin Culin
asked me to look over a draft of a revised Frontier
Utilities mortgage that young Perry Griffith got up."

"Why?"

Frost ignored the implication of Bannard's question—
why was a gone-to-pasture retired partner being asked
to do active work?

"I guess, George, because I am thought to possess

127

some drafting ability,'' Frost replied evenly, concealing his real reason for staying late—to talk to the night maintenance crew about Graham Donovan's water carafe. ''The mortgage is one of Charlie Chase's dinosaurs, so archaic it should have been laid to rest long ago. Run-on sentences, endless subclauses, unwieldy cross-references—all the curses of nineteenth-century scrivening. But the damn thing's open-ended, so Frontier still issues bonds under it. But now they want to sell bonds to the public, so they decided it was time to do a little modernizing.''

''How is Griffith's draft?''

''Not bad, but it's discouraging, George. To go public, as you know, the mortgage has to be qualified under the Trust Indenture Act.'' Frost took a small delight in belaboring what he knew was obvious to Bannard, giving him a small dollop of his own medicine.

''Yes, of course,'' Bannard said, taking the chair in front of Frost's desk.

''How long has Griffith been here? Seven years?'' Frost asked.

''Something like that.''

''Well, he's screwed up the Trust Indenture Act provisions that have to be in a public mortgage. Wouldn't you think he could get that straight?''

''Of course. But times are changing, Reuben. Getting the Trust Indenture provisions into a mortgage is strictly a mechanical job, copying out what the Act requires word-for-word. That's now done by paralegals and proofreaders.''

''I know, George, but isn't somebody ultimately responsible for seeing that it's done right?''

''Sure. The partner in charge.''

''How about Mr. Griffith? How much does he make?''

''I suppose around eighty thousand.''

''So he's too high-priced to bother about such petty details?''

Bannard sighed. ''I know what you're saying, Reuben. But you're bucking the trend of the times. Word processors, paralegals, Xeroxing. They're all wonderful—and too often used as substitutes for thought.''

"In my younger days, when I was making about five percent of what Mr. Griffith makes, I would probably have been fired if I had done what he did.''

"Everything's changing, Reuben. And not for the better either. Look at that diffident cop we talked to today.''

"I know. I do think you were a bit harsh with him, though. He was cautious, sure, but he seemed to be thorough and to know what he's doing. I'm sure he'll swing into action when he's satisfied that a murder actually occurred.''

"I hope so. We've got to get this thing solved or this whole firm will burst apart," Bannard said. He then recounted the events that had occurred over cocktails, the making up of Keith Merritt's list and Arthur Tyson's tirade.

"Tyson really does have a vile temper, doesn't he?'' Frost said. "I've often wondered why he hasn't gotten into more trouble because of it.''

"I know. But if suspicions get more wild, everybody will be at each other's throats, not just Fred Coxe and Tyson.''

"Agreed. Let me know if nothing happens on the police front tomorrow and I'll give our friend Bautista a call. After your outburst, it might be better if I called him.''

"Sure, Reuben. Whatever you think. I guess I was a little rough with the fellow.''

"Yes.''

"George, you mentioned Keith Merritt's list. Who is on it?''

Bannard picked up a pad of paper and reconstructed it, asterisks and all.

"What do the asterisks mean?'' Frost asked.

Bannard explained what they stood for.

"Well, all I can say is that it's interesting.''

"I guess. Well, goodnight, Reuben. Don't work too late.''

"I'll try.''

* * *

With Bannard gone, Frost set about the business he had stayed late to accomplish. He was almost certain that the partners' water carafes were filled up every night; he recalled from times past that one of the maintenance staff would come around late each night, tug at his forelock, and take away the water carafe to be refilled. But he had to confirm this.

Frost had tried the water in his own carafe—one of the perquisites of partnership that Bannard had not taken away (presumably because it had not occurred to him, Frost thought bitterly). It had seemed fresh, but his question about the refilling procedure still needed to be confirmed.

After searching the halls, he found the superintendent of the night custodial crew assigned to the office. She was an amiable woman, with whom Frost had developed a nodding acquaintance over the years. The acquaintanceship was indeed "nodding," since Frost did not know her name and had never before spoken to her long enough to determine that she spoke in a heavy Eastern European accent and was, in fact, barely comprehensible in English.

Communicating with the woman about Donovan's water carafe was not easy. She first thought Frost wanted a drink of water and acted properly puzzled as to why he was making the request of her. Then she thought he wanted the water carafe in his own office refilled, whereupon she promised to send the boy in charge of such matters around to him.

Frost decided not to undo the second misunderstanding, having all but exhausted his rudimentary knowledge of German, which had seemed to help in establishing contact. Instead he bided his time at his desk with Griffith's draft of mortgage until a young Hispanic entered his office, excused himself, and announced that he would refill Frost's water carafe right away. Unlike Detective Bautista, who was all cool and dignity, this boy was charged with nervous energy and made his explanation and his move for the water receptacle into a rhythmic dance; he almost appeared to be responding to the beat of an invisible Sony Walkman.

"No, don't take that," Frost said. "Sit down for a minute. I want to talk to you."

The youth was confused by this—in his line of work one did not often sit down and confer with the clientele—and more than a little nervous. Frost was silent for a moment as he surveyed the youth opposite him—very slight, probably in his early twenties, and rather attractive, but with his looks marred by some lingering adolescent acne.

"I just wanted to ask you a couple of questions," Frost said, in a manner designed to be soothing but which did not seem to have that effect. The boy visibly squirmed in his chair and a look of wariness came into his eyes.

"Yeah? Okay. Shoot."

"You work here every night?"

"Yeah. Except Saturdays and Sundays."

"But Mondays? You do work Mondays?"

"Yeah."

"And every night you refill the water carafes in the partners' offices?"

"Yeah, that's right," the youth answered. "Right after I finish vacuuming the halls and the offices, I go around and put fresh water in the . . . what did you call them?"

"Carafes."

"Carafes. It's the last thing I do before I go home."

"And what time is that?" Frost asked.

"About eleven, eleven-thirty," the youth replied. He was properly respectful in answering Frost's questions, but his attitude betrayed something of what he was feeling—namely, why was this old guy asking him these crazy questions? Was he trying to flirt? Why did he want to know when he went home? Was he going to ask him out? He'd been through this pickup routine before, didn't like it, and was prepared to bash Frost's head in if that was what he had in mind.

Frost was oblivious to the thoughts he was generating,

though he did realize the questions he was posing probably seemed inane to one who did not know the reason for them.

"Were you working here on Monday this week?" Frost pressed.

The boy did not respond immediately, then answered quickly, "Yes. Yes, I was."

"And did you refill all the water carafes Monday night?"

"Sure. I tell you, I always do that before I go home. So if I worked Monday, I did that," the boy answered.

"Did you know Mr. Donovan?"

"Donovan? No, man, I don't think so."

"He had the big corner office over on the other side of the building."

"Oh, yeah. Is he the old guy that died the other day?" Frost nodded, wincing slightly at the description of his dead and younger colleague as an "old guy." "I didn't know him, but I know which one is his office, yeah."

"And last Monday you refilled his water carafe?" Frost asked.

"Look, man, what's your game? I told you I worked Monday night and I did my job. I always do my job. So, sure, I refilled his water . . . thing." The boy was agitated and seemed to take offense at the suggestion that he might not have done his job; he was also defensive about his wrestling with the new word *carafe*.

"No offense, young man. I'm sure you did your job. I was just checking."

"Is that all? Can I split now?"

"Yes."

The youth got up and headed for the door. As he was about to leave Frost asked, "Oh, one more thing. What is your name?"

"Carlos."

"Carlos what?"

"Carlos Faghater," the boy shot back just before slamming the door.

Frost was taken aback by the reply, then laughed to himself when he realized the false impression he had created. Given the circle of friends he shared with his wife, homosexuals were hardly unknown to him, so he was doubly amused at the inadvertent reaction he had stirred up in young Carlos. All in all, the Hispanics he had encountered had certainly added *salsa* to his day.

Frost was just switching the light off in his office when Keith Merritt called to him from down the hall. "Reuben, wait a minute," he said. "I've got to talk to you."

As he came nearer to Frost, it was evident that he was in some distress. He seemed to be sweating slightly, though it was a cool evening.

"Reuben, let's have a drink," Merritt said as he reached Frost's side.

Frost was surprised by the request. He of course knew Merritt well, indeed had worked with him since the latter's earliest days at Chase & Ward. But he had never, as far as he could now recall, had an after-hours drink with Merritt.

"I was just going home, in fact. There'll be some time before Cynthia has dinner ready, so why don't you come with me?" Frost said.

"No, Reuben. Let's go someplace down here; I've got to see you alone," Merritt said, the words flowing desperately fast.

"Well, can't we talk right here?" Frost asked.

"No, no, I won't be able to say what I have to say without a drink."

Frost had never seen Merritt, a modest imbiber as far as Frost knew, so insistent on drinking. What on earth was bothering him? There was only one way to find out, so Frost agreed, reluctantly, to his odd request.

"Where shall we go?" Frost said. "The club is closed by now."

"I don't know. I seldom go to bars down here. Isn't there one up on Hanover Square?"

"I think there is. Shall we go there?" Frost asked.

"Yes."

"And can I have at least a hint about what this is all about?"

"Wait till we get there," Merritt said.

Harry's Bar was crowded with a noisy, rowdy group of what Frost took to be stockbrokers. Did their roisterous drinking mean that the market was up or down? Frost never could remember which reaction was supposed to trigger marathon imbibing and in fact had the suspicion that there was a breed of stockbroker that ended the day with fraternity-style boozing no matter how the market had performed. The raucous group at Harry's looked the same as the crowd he had often seen in the Wall Street bars in his associate days, when the dignified premises of the Hexagon Club had not been open to him. The only difference seemed to be the substitution of women brokers in their dressed-for-success suitlets for the secretaries who used to hang out in the bars after working hours.

"Great place you've got here, Keith," Frost said over the din.

Merritt smiled weakly. "It's all right, Reuben. If we go over there in the back, I think we can be alone."

They edged their way through the noisy crowd and found a quiet table in the next room. Merritt called the waiter and, quite out of character for him, ordered a double Scotch. Frost asked for a single.

"Now, Keith, will you please tell me what this is all about?"

"Reuben, I've known you almost since the day I walked in Chase & Ward's front door. I've always respected you and felt that you were one of my backers when I made partner.

Frost grunted noncommittally, though Merritt's surmise was in fact correct.

"When I saw your light on tonight, I decided I had to talk to you—talk to you or somebody. What I'm about to tell you isn't going to be easy. It would have been bad enough without Graham's death, but his death in some ways makes it worse," Merritt said. He paused and looked down at the table.

"Keith, please. What the hell are you talking about?"

"Reuben, just give me time. I'll get to the point."

"Please do. I really want to get this over with," Frost said.

"Do you remember the leveraged lease deal we did for Maxwell Foundries two years ago?"

"Vaguely. I guess I saw it on the list of new client matters. What about it?"

"Well, you're not keyed into leasing, so it probably doesn't mean that much to you. But for those of us in the leasing field, the deal is quite well known. At the time it was completed, it was the largest leasing transaction ever done and, if inflation hadn't sent up prices, it would probably still be the biggest."

"What do you mean by biggest?" Frost asked.

"I mean the biggest goddam lease ever written in the history of the world. Literally. A twenty-year lease of a billion-dollar heavy machinery plant, calling for total rent payments of one-point-six billion dollars."

"I'm impressed. But what's the problem?" Frost said.

"It's a placed in service problem," Merritt answered.

"Placed in service problem? What are you talking about? Is that tax jargon?" Frost asked. "If so, please keep in mind that my tax knowledge, such as it is, all but ended with the '39 Code. The Code of 1954 was, and is, a great mystery to me."

"And you always avoided learning anything about leasing," Merritt said.

"You're right. I was too old a dog to be taught the leasing tricks when they came along."

"Okay, okay. I won't give you a complete course in leasing, but there are a couple of things you have to know so that you can understand the mess I'm talking about."

"Fire away," Frost said with resignation.

"All right. Well, you know that there are three basic parties to a leveraged lease—the lessee, the lessor and the lender. The lessee, Maxwell Foundries in our case, wanted to buy an asset, the new Ohio plant, but because of its depressed earnings could not use the tax benefits from owning the plant—that is, the investment credit and the depreciation deductions. Are you with me so far?"

"Yes, yes, go ahead," Frost answered impatiently.

"So, it went out and found Global Leasing, one of the companies in the Multibank Group. Multibank is very profitable, as you know, and was eager to get the tax benefits on the plant. So Global Leasing agreed to buy the plant and, as is usual in these transactions, borrowed a big part of the purchase price from a group of insurance companies, headed by Equitable as I recall. It then leased the plant to Maxwell for the one-point-six-billion-dollar rent I referred to—rent that is enough to pay off the debt to the insurance companies and to give Global Leasing a profit as well. In addition, Global gets the benefits of owning the plant by taking the investment credit against its federal tax bill and taking depreciation deductions on the plant in computing its taxable income."

"Yes, Keith, I understand that much. I'm not quite as complete an ignoramus about these things as I made out," Frost said. "But I still don't see where there's a problem."

"Reuben, be patient," Merritt went on. "As you also know, this shifting of tax benefits is not very popular in Washington, outside the Reagan White House anyway. Except for the Reaganites, the Federal Government in general has been very hostile to leasing for tax purposes and the Internal Revenue Service has erected a lot of roadblocks to make leasing more difficult. Like the question of placed in service."

"Which means what?" Frost asked.

"The asset in question—our plant—cannot have been placed in service before Global bought it. Otherwise, Global would not have been entitled to take the investment credit on the transaction—which in this case was big bucks, ten percent of the billion-dollar purchase price or one hundred million dollars. And one hundred million that goes straight to the bottom line as a credit against the Multibank Group's tax bill."

"So I suppose the IRS is now saying that Maxwell's

plant was placed in service before Global bought it and has disallowed the credit?''

"Precisely," Merritt said. "The agents are now auditing the transaction and that is the position they are taking."

"But can there be any argument? Isn't it easy enough to tell whether the plant was placed in service or not?" Frost asked.

"Unfortunately, like most IRS questions, it's not so simple. It's not a black-and-white proposition, but one that depends on all the facts. For example, if material was put through the plant assembly line just to test it out, that would probably not mean it was placed in service. But when does testing end? When is the plant ready to go, once you turn the switch? These are terribly complicated questions, Reuben, and even though they provide grist for the mill of tax lawyers, most of us wish they would go away."

Merritt paused and took another large gulp of his drink, draining the glass. Almost simultaneously he commandeered another—Frost passed—and continued his lecture.

"So, to get down to the Maxwell case. We gave a Chase & Ward opinion in the Maxwell transaction that the plant had not, for tax purposes, been placed in service when Global put up its money in 1979," Merritt explained.

"And what did you base that opinion on?" Frost asked.

"Lots of things, Reuben. A visit to the plant, talks with Maxwell personnel and engineers for the contractor. We did a very careful job, because it was a complicated matter and a lot of money was at stake," Merritt said.

"But the IRS says you were wrong," Frost said.

"Worse than that, Reuben. In conducting their audit they came across a memorandum from the chief engineer of the plant division to the division president saying that the plant was ready to go. And that memo was dated *six weeks* before we gave our opinion saying it had not been placed in service.''

"But the two aren't necessarily inconsistent, are they?" Frost said. "Being ready to go doesn't mean you've gone.''

"Not necessarily, but the lecture on that subject—the difference between being placed in service and being *ready* to be placed in service—could go on all night. That isn't the problem. The problem is the engineer's memo shows that I got a copy. Which, if true, means that our opinion was not only wrong but probably negligent as well.''

Frost was stunned. Lawyers, like doctors, constantly fear malpractice cases. Financial lawyers, like those at Chase & Ward, working on multimillion- and multibillion-dollar transactions, have particular nightmares about their potential liabilities. Nowhere is this more acute than in the tax area, where advice is not bad, mediocre or good but right or wrong. Frost suddenly reassessed his long-held belief that tax lawyers—including his former partner Merritt—were a generally quirky and eccentric lot. He had always thought it was somehow related to the particularly bookish nature of the practice, dependent as it was on the Internal Revenue Code and countless regulations, rulings, procedures, and the like on such esoteric and not entirely real questions as "placed in service." But perhaps there was another cause for the eccentricity, that cause being the highly dangerous tightrope walking that tax lawyers have to do day in and day out in advising their clients. But there was no time for ruminations of this sort now. Frost had to get out of Merritt all the facts about the Maxwell problem.

"Well, Keith, did you get the memorandum?" Frost asked, in as even a voice as possible.

"Reuben, I swear I didn't. Obviously if I had, the opinion never would have been given unless I'd been fully satisfied that the engineer was wrong in what he said in his memo. Life is too short to cut corners like that," Merritt said with conviction.

Frost believed him. Merritt might be eccentric and

flighty at times, but he was a complete straight arrow in terms of his professional conduct.

"I've searched the office's files and my personal file on the matter and there is nothing. I've talked to Bill Roy, who worked on the Maxwell matter while he was still an associate, and he has no recollection of it either."

"How do you explain your name on the memo then?" Frost asked.

"Look, none of the engineering or business types at Maxwell had ever done a transaction anything like the Global lease. And since its success depended so much on tax matters, I was sort of a guru for them. Everybody fed me information; I scratched my belly and gave them back answers. So they were all instructed to send me every interoffice communication that had any bearing on the tax issues. My guess is Mr. Engineer dutifully told his secretary to send me a copy, secretary dutifully typed my name on the bottom of the memo, and then secretary forgot to send it. I was the only outside addressee; she probably didn't know where to reach me."

"What does the guy say who got the memo? Why did he never raise the issue with you?" Frost asked.

"Get ready for a good one," Merritt said. "The fact is the fellow who got the memo wouldn't recognize the issues it raised if they bit him. Of course, he now says that he realized the memo cast doubt on the placed-in-service conclusion. But since I was shown as a recipient of the memo, he just assumed that I had gotten it and had taken it into account in reaching the result."

"Good God," Frost said. "Good God in heaven." Frost reflected that through some combination of skill and luck—in the case of Chase & Ward, most people who knew the firm well would have said skill—no real threat of malpractice liability had ever occurred. Now, on top of everything else, Keith Merritt was telling him that the firm might face a malpractice claim of staggering proportions. And even though he no longer shared in the partnership profits, Frost was nonetheless concerned for his former partners and the reputation of the firm where he had spent his working life.

"Keith, I assume that Maxwell has to pay up if Global loses the investment credit," Frost said.

"That's right. Maxwell gave a typical indemnity agreement to Global, saying that if Global ever lost any of the tax benefits it expected in the transaction, Maxwell would make Global whole on an after-tax basis."

"After tax?"

"Right."

"What are the dollars involved, Keith?" Frost asked, constricting his stomach as he did so.

"Well, the plant cost just under a billion, nine hundred ninety million as I recall. Th investment credit on that is ten percent, or ninety-nine million. So, if Global has to pay Uncle Sam ninety-nine million, Maxwell has to pay Global ninety-nine million, which is income to Global for tax purposes. So Maxwell also has to pay Global enough additional to pay its taxes on the first ninety-nine million. All told, Reuben, with interest and penalties and everything else, we're talking close to two hundred million dollars."

"Keith, do you really think this will ever happen?" Frost asked.

"When all is said and done, I don't. But it may take a trial and an appeal from the trial to protect Global—and ourselves."

"Even if they made Global pay up, is it clear that we are at fault?"

"Of course not. But somebody is going to have to decide whether or not I am lying when I say I never saw the Maxwell memo," Merritt said.

The combination of Merritt's grim news and the Scotch made both men silent for more than a minute. Then Merritt blurted out, "Of course Graham Donovan's death doesn't help at all."

"How do you mean?" Frost asked, alarmed and puzzled at this new tack in the conversation.

"Graham was the partner in charge of Maxwell. So when I had all the facts together I went to tell him about this last Tuesday morning. I must have been one of the

last people to see him in his office before he died,"
Merritt said, a desolate look on his face.

"You mean you think people are going to think you
poisoned Graham?"

"Well, aren't they, Reuben?" Merritt asked, his voice
quavering. "The fact is, Graham was not very pleasant
about the whole thing. There was an edge to his voice
that made me think he thought somehow I had seen the
Maxwell memo. I told him so and he denied it. But it
was not a pleasant meeting. Once people know what we
talked about, they're sure to be suspicious."

"But no one needs to know what you talked about,
Keith," Frost said.

"Oh, that's easy to say, Reuben. What do you do
when the police come around to question you? What do
you say when they ask if you have any new leads, any
new suspicions?"

"I don't have any suspicions, Keith," Frost said.
"None at all. But right now it's time to go home."

As they waited for their check, Frost realized sadly
that Merritt's name would now have to be added to his
own list of suspects. Had his intention been to divert
attention to others? Or perhaps to get some pathetic
reassurance when the others did not include his name?
Frost sighed inwardly as he thought over this newest
complication.

Merritt, who lived in Brooklyn Heights, and Frost
hailed separate cabs after leaving Harry's. As they parted,
Frost put his hand on Merritt's shoulder. "Keith, did
you kill Graham?" he asked in a calm, steady voice.

Merritt smiled a sad smile. "No, Reuben, I didn't,"
he responded, also in a calm, if resigned, voice. "Killing
Graham wouldn't have solved my—the firm's—problem."

14

Despite the bombshells that had burst about him on Thursday, Frost slept soundly when he finally got to bed after leaving Keith Merritt and did not wake up until nine o'clock Friday morning, an hour later than usual. He woke up relatively well rested, if slightly hung over from Thursday's drinking with Merritt.

Cynthia had already left for ballet class when Frost got up. He was just as glad. She was a patient, shrewd and understanding woman, not an empty-headed showgirl; she had been a valued confidante over the years. But he could barely get the facts of recent events straight in his own mind, let alone sort them out with sufficient coherence to enable his wife to understand them.

Drinking the orange juice and coffee she had left for him, he quickly discarded the *Times* and reviewed Thursday's events once again in his mind: the god-awful funeral service for Donovan; Doyle's report of the laboratory findings; Detective Bautista; and then, just to complicate everything, Tyson's irrational outburst at Fred Coxe and Merritt's tax problem.

Frost also recalled Merritt's suspect list, asterisks and all:

> *Grace Appleby**
> *Perry Griffith*
> *Bruce Donovan*
> *Roger Singer**

* * *

Since Tyson wasn't around to berate him, Frost mentally added Tyson's name. And, with a good deal more reluctance, Keith Merritt's as well. Confronting this unpleasant reality, he broke off his speculating and left the apartment for the office.

Once he had arrived at Chase & Ward, Frost decided to call in Perry Griffith, in part to discuss the Frontier Utilities mortgage, but more importantly to look him over in a new light—as possible murder suspect.

Griffith was a source of wonderment to many at the firm. Since one could not be admitted to the bar in New York before age twenty-one, Griffith had to be at least twenty-eight years old. Yet he looked barely sixteen (within the past year he had been asked in a midtown bar for proof that he was of drinking age). A blue-eyed towhead, he had caused more than his share of sighs among the firm's female employees—sighs because he was so youthfully handsome and sighs because it was known that he was happily married.

Griffith's looks were deceiving, however. Many an adversary across the bargaining table, sure that the open-faced Griffith must be inexperienced, had ended up, if smart, with new respect for him, and if not smart, taken to the cleaners. He was both tough and stubborn—qualities that, when taken together with his appearance, formed a disconcerting combination.

Frost had "borrowed" Griffith to work on a hurry-up merger transaction just before his own retirement as a partner but otherwise knew him, except for his recent contact with the youth's mortgage draft, only by reputation. His earlier brief encounter—the whole transaction had been signed up over the course of a long weekend—had led Frost to respect Griffith's abilities, if not necessarily to like him. There was just a bit too much of the blood lust for Frost's taste, just a shade too much competitiveness and desire to devour an adversary.

Of course, the name of the game was to represent one's client to the fullest, but as he had grown older, Frost came more and more to the view that there was a real difference between the hand-to-hand combat of court-room litigation and the negotiating process that charac-terized most of the corporate department's work. The litigator was trained to stall and delay, to conduct a war of attrition against an opponent; the corporate lawyer was normally subject to quite opposite demands—to do a deal in a hurry, to get an agreement drafted, negotiated and signed before circumstances shifted or a party changed his mind. Many corporate lawyers—and not all of them in Kokomo, either—never learned this basic distinction. More often than not in any transaction there would be a lawyer less concerned with getting the deal done (chances are the same lawyer would use the word *finalize*) than with scoring largely unimportant points for his client.

Griffith had some of this aggressive, win-all-the-points quality and Frost had had to act as the peacemaker more than once in the transaction Griffith had worked on for him. Yet Griffith was smart, there was no question about that.

Griffith, when he entered Frost's office, had just been to the Chase & Ward cafeteria and was carrying a cup of coffee.

"Perry, do you have a minute?" Frost asked.

"Sure," Griffith replied noncommittally.

"Then sit down. Here's your draft of the Frontier mortgage with my marks on it. I'll be right back, once I get a cup of coffee myself."

Minutes later Frost returned and found Griffith sipping his coffee and looking over the marked-up mortgage.

"Reuben, I'm sorry about the screwup on those Trust Indenture provisions. Austin said I should get my draft to you right away and I did not have a chance to recheck them before I gave it to you."

"My boy, never complain, never explain," Frost said.

"I beg your pardon?"

Frost laughed. "Just an old office expression Charlie Chase, the original author of that mortgage, was fond of. I'll accept your explanation, but he never would. He probably would have ripped up your draft right before your eyes—all three hundred pages of it. And in the days before the Xerox, that might have been the end of it—and the end of you.''

"Well, then I'm glad it's you and not Charles Chase honchoing this one,'' Griffith said.

"Anyway, except for the Trust Indenture glitch, your draft looks pretty good. At least it reads as if written in this century—perhaps not in the 1980s, but certainly 1910.''

"Thanks.''

"Why don't you look over my comments and let's talk about them on Monday. Feedback, I believe it's called.''

"Feedback?''

"Yes, feedback. Someone told me that that's what all young lawyers want. Feedback. Criticism of their work by their skilled and senior mentors—as long as the criticism isn't too severe.''

"Oh, yes. Of course. I guess I was just surprised that *you* knew the term. No, I look forward to feedback. Not everybody can have their work vetted by Reuben Frost.''

"Quite true. So, as far as the mortgage goes, let's talk Monday. You'll also see that I outlined some redrafting for you on the release provisions. I think we can streamline the procedures for getting property out from under the mortgage in the future.''

Griffith started to get up.

"Don't go, Perry. I have something else very serious to talk over with you.''

Frost had made up his mind to bring Griffith into the Donovan case. Ambitious associates were great information gatherers, sifting every morsel of gossip and rumor for nuggets that might enrich their status. It was just such gossip and rumor that might prove useful to Frost if he was going to continue to pursue the Donovan investigation, as he had known he would since talking with Detective Bautista the day before. Bannard, eager as he was for a solution—and right he was about that—was probably temperamentally unable to conduct a discreet inquiry, and surely his crippled Executive Committee was not. Besides, Frost secretly acknowledged to himself, cracking the mystery would be sweet revenge for Bannard's post-retirement slights.

"What I have to say is extremely confidential," Frost said. "I must ask you not to tell anyone—anyone, including your wife—what I am about to say to you. Is that understood?"

"Of course," Griffith replied evenly, looking straight at Frost.

"It's about Graham Donovan's death," Frost continued. "Contrary to what you have heard, it appears that Donovan was murdered."

"Murdered?" Griffith repeated, an incredulous look on his face. "Didn't he die while he was having lunch? How could he be murdered?"

"A fair question. But just listen and I'll tell you," Frost said. He then went on to retell the story of the poisoned carafe; as he did so, Griffith's expression continued to reflect his incredulity. "Now, having heard the story, what do you think?" Frost concluded.

"What do I think? I'm too shocked to think anything. It's absolutely incredible that Graham Donovan was murdered. It doesn't make any sense," Griffith said.

"I certainly agree with you there," Frost said. "But now that you know what happened, do you have any ideas who might have done it?"

Griffith shrugged. "Absolutely none," he said. "I just can't imagine such a thing happening."

"Well, the police officer in charge of the case said it will only be solved if people keep their eyes and ears open. Perry, that is what I want you to do. As an associate who knows his way around here, you're much more likely to hear things than any of us partners."

"I'll certainly do my best," Griffith said. "But right now I'm afraid I haven't got even a suspicion to go on."

"That's all right. Just keep your eyes and ears open. And your mouth shut." Frost stared directly at the young lawyer. Griffith returned his stare, then got up and tossed his coffee cup in the wastebasket beside Frost's desk.

"You never liked Graham, did you?" Frost said, as

Griffith was turning toward the door. Frost's question made him turn back.

"Correction. Graham Donovan didn't like me," Griffith said.

"How do you know that?" Frost asked.

"He told me. I'd been working for Graham for almost two years—working for him hard, I might add—when we had our little annual chat at raise time. He told me how much he appreciated my work—my 'very excellent' work, he called it—but said that in all candor he had to tell me that he could not recommend me for partnership in the firm."

Griffith paused; recounting what must have been an unpleasant conversation was clearly a strain. "I felt like a knocked-over bowling pin," Griffith continued, his voice picking up both speed and animation. "This was the first time in five years at Chase & Ward that anyone had ever said a negative thing about my work."

"And you didn't hate him for that?" Frost asked.

"No . . . no, I don't think I hated him. I was just sorry things turned out the way they did. I think he was wrong and I don't think he was fair to me, but I didn't hate him." Griffith was choosing his words carefully, as if he had not considered the question of his feelings toward Donovan before. Then, suddenly, he seemed for the first time to realize the import of Frost's question. "And if you mean did I dislike him enough to kill him, the answer is no. There may be many ways to a partnership, Reuben, but murder isn't one of them, thank you very much."

"I wasn't accusing you, Perry. I wasn't accusing you," Frost said with a sigh. Seemingly mollified, Griffith left the office. But accusation or no, Frost did not cross Griffith's name off the list of suspects.

Frost turned to the problem of finding out from Grace Appleby who had visited Donovan's office Tuesday morning. He had all but given up on the possibility of concealing Donovan's murder from her—assuming she did not, for the obvious reason, already know about it. Appleby had seen the stain made by the poisoned water from Donovan's carafe during the desk-opening episode. It simply was not now possible to ask her who had had access to Donovan's office and the water carafe just before his death without leading her to the inevitable conclusion of murder.

A week earlier, Frost would have had no hesitation in enlisting Appleby's help in finding Donovan's killer; a trusted, loyal employee, completely devoted to her boss, she would in fact have been one of the first people he would have turned to. But Doyle's revelations about her stock trading had changed all that. She had not only engaged in activity for which she would have to be fired, once the murder investigation was out of the way, but had become a prime suspect in that investigation.

Frost would have preferred not to reveal to Appleby that Donovan had been murdered—or, more precisely, that he knew Donovan had been murdered. If the woman had in fact done the poisoning, his inquiries would accomplish nothing and merely alert her to his knowledge. And even if she hadn't, he instinctively did not want to share confidences of any kind with a woman that the firm would soon have to fire. But there seemed no way out and perhaps, Frost thought, her behavior will be revealing when she finds out what I know.

Appleby looked drawn and slightly haggard when she came to Frost's office. Urged by the stenographic supervisor to take some time off, she had refused, saying that she preferred to remain at work just for the present, clearing out files and otherwise disposing of Donovan's presence at Chase & Ward. But the strain of the end of her "marriage" showed in her puffy eyes and pale face.

"Good morning, Mr. Frost," she said as she came into the office. She took a seat without being asked, seeming to know that her encounter with Frost would be more than a few words on the run.

"Grace, I'm afraid I've got some bad news for you once again," Frost said. She did not respond, so he continued, having decided to tell her directly about the murder. "All evidence is that Graham Donovan was murdered."

Again the woman did not respond, but began crying silently. She took a handkerchief from inside her sleeve, wiped her eyes and blew her nose. "It's awful," she said. "Just awful." She continued to cry, but finally seemed to get control of herself.

"I knew it. I knew it as soon as I saw that terrible brown water on Mr. Donovan's desk. He was poisoned, wasn't he?"

"It appears so, Miss Appleby. The laboratory test on that brown water showed the presence of poison."

"He was such a good man, Mr. Frost. Who would have done such a horrible thing?" she asked, her voice distorted with seemingly genuine grief. If she was dissembling, she had Frost fooled.

"That's what we have to find out, Miss Appleby," Frost said. "I'm at a total loss myself to know who might have done it."

"How can I help, Mr. Frost? What can I do?" she asked.

"Well, the first thing is to try and recall who saw Donovan in his office Tuesday morning—or more precisely, who went into his office that morning. You would have seen anyone who went in there, I assume?"

"In general, yes. I'm not there all the time of course. One steps away to use the copier or to go to the ladies' room, things like that. But when Mr. Donovan is there—was there—I was usually sitting outside to answer his call."

"Do you remember who came in Tuesday morning?" Frost pressed.

"I'm trying to think. It was not a very busy morning, as I remember. Mr. Merritt came in to see him for quite a long time, I'm pretty sure of that. And Mr. Griffith, I remember him coming in too."

"Do you know what they talked about?" Frost asked.

"No. He had the door shut," she answered.

"Are you sure they were the only two? How about anyone from outside?"

"No, I don't think so on Tuesday morning. Mr. Draper had been in on Monday, I remember, but I don't think Mr. Donovan had any visitors from outside the office on Tuesday. But I can check my records."

"Records?" Frost said, puzzled as to what she meant.

"Yes. To help Mr. Donovan write up drafts of his time charges every morning for the day before, I kept a list of the people he saw and of his telephone calls. He never saw the list I started for Tuesday, of course, but I think it is probably still in the papers on my desk."

"Could you check, please?" Frost asked. Appleby got up and went out, returning in moments with her typed notes for Tuesday.

"I was right, Mr. Frost. The only two people I have down for Tuesday morning are Mr. Merritt and Mr. Griffith. And there are only two telephone calls."

"To whom?"

"Mr. Draper."

"And?"

"Mrs. Singer," Appleby answered after a slight hesitation.

"Did you place all of Donovan's calls?"

"Yes. He was quite helpless about remembering numbers."

"Well, I don't know whether what you've told me is helpful or not. But do you have any ideas, Miss Appleby? Any suspicion, any notion of who the killer might be?"

"I'm afraid not, Mr. Frost. No notions at all," she answered.

"Well, if you get any, let me know, will you please?"

"Of course, Mr. Frost. We must find the killer. We absolutely must," she said.

"Thank you, Grace, I appreciate your help," Frost said as he rose, terminating the visit.

After she left, Frost was about to take a drink of water from the carafe beside his desk when he thought better of it. Instead he walked to the drinking fountain down the hall. As he came back, he thought about the information he had learned. Only Merritt and Griffith had apparently had access to the fatal carafe. And, of course, Grace Appleby.

Shortly after lunch Bannard called Frost to report that the Police Department had not been heard from.

"Let me call Bautista and I'll get back to you," Frost told Bannard. Frost was anxious to forestall another confrontation between Bannard and the officer, since he personally did not see how the investigation would be advanced by the grilling of the office staff, which Bannard was still determined was the way to proceed.

Frost called Bautista's direct number and was relieved when the detective answered.

"Mr. Bautista, this is Reuben Frost."

"Yes, sir. How are you doing today?"

"Fine, thank you. I'm calling, needless to say, about the Donovan case. You remember my colleague George Bannard?"

"Yes, of course I do," Bautista replied.

"Well, he still seems determined to have you fellows come in here and question everyone about the murder."

"And what do you think?"

"I think it would be a mistake; I've been making a little progress along the lines we discussed yesterday. I can't say I've had any great insight into the matter or scored any big breakthrough, but I think we're moving in the right direction. Is there a chance we could talk today? I'd like to tell you what's been going on."

"Sure thing. Should I come down there?"

"No, that would be a mistake. Bannard might demand that you start questioning the staff immediately. How about the Gotham Club? I often stop there for a drink on the way home. Would that be convenient?"

"Whatever you say. Where is it?"

"Fifth Avenue and Fifty-sixth Street. One West Fifty-sixth."

"What time?"

"Five?"

"Done. And as for your Mr. Bannard, it's now mid-afternoon on Friday, so the chances of setting up interrogations with people for today are practically gone. And I don't see that we gain anything by running around to people's homes over the weekend. So tell your Mr. Bannard that I've checked out the laboratory report and I'm satisfied a homicide has taken place. Tell him further that we've got some leads we're checking out—I assume that statement will be more true after we talk this afternoon—and I'll report back on Monday."

"Fine."

"Oh, and one more thing. Give Mr. Bannard my regards."

"See you at five o'clock."

Bautista and Frost met as they approached the Gotham Club front door promptly at five.

"Come this way," Frost said. "I expect the bar will be deserted on a nice September Friday afternoon like this." He was right. Except for a pair of members who looked comfortably like fixtures, the bar was deserted. Frost led the way to a corner table, out of earshot of the bartender and the members.

"You know, it's a rule of this place that one can't discuss business here. But I'm sure the house committee would make an exception for an ongoing murder investigation," Frost said.

Bautista laughed easily as he pulled his notebook from his pocket.

"Oh God, I forgot that you will probably want to take notes. Papers and notebooks are out-of-bounds here too."

Bautista put the notebook back in his pocket. "That's all right," he said. "My mother always told me I had a good memory. It's good to exercise it once in a while."

"I'm sorry, I never thought of your notebook."

"No problem."

"Let's have a drink and I'll tell you what I've learned."

Frost ordered a vermouth and soda. Bautista, apologizing, said that he was still on duty and asked for a Coca-Cola.

"How inconsiderate of me to bring you to a bar. Of course you can't drink on duty," Frost said.

"Think nothing of it, Mr. Frost. It happens all the time. So give me an update."

Frost told the officer what he had learned about re-filling the water carafes—omitting the homosexual mis-understanding—and gave as good a secondhand account of the Executive Committee meeting as he could. He also told him of his conversations with Keith Merritt—swearing him to secrecy about the tax problem—and with Perry Griffith and Grace Appleby.

Bautista was silent until Frost had finished.

"Let me ask you some questions," he began. "First off, I assume that the Appleby woman doesn't know that you know about her stock manipulations?"

"That's right."

"And nothing will be done about firing her until this thing is over?"

"I'm sure that's right. But I'll make sure of that with Bannard."

"Good. And your private detective fellow is still tail-ing her?"

"As far as I know."

"Now what about this man Griffith? Do you know what he saw Donovan about Tuesday morning?"

"No idea."

"And he didn't volunteer that he'd seen Donovan just before he was poisoned?"

"Not a word."

"I wonder what should be done about him?"

"I wanted to ask you that. My first instinct was to call him back to my office and confront him with it. But then I thought it might be better to leave him on the loose for a little bit."

"I think you did the right thing. Give him a little rope to play around with."

"I'm glad you agree."

"Now let's see. Tyson. He's a tough customer, as I found out on Tuesday. But would you say his temper tantrum was typical or not?"

"He has a terrible temper, certainly. But I think the episode yesterday shows that he is very nervous."

"Guilt perhaps?"

"I hope not."

"And this Keith fellow—"

"Merritt."

"Yeah. He's under a lot of strain too. Right?"

"Definitely."

"That leaves, if my fine memory is correct, Bruce Donovan and Roger Singer," Bautista said.

"Yes. I can't tell you any more about them. I haven't seen or talked to young Donovan at all. And come to think of it, I haven't seen Singer since the funeral."

"Is that unusual?"

"No, not at all. Weeks sometimes go by when I don't see some of my partners. Former partners, I mean."

"Anybody else who belongs on that list?"

"Not that I've thought of. I'd say it's plenty long enough as it is."

"Mr. Frost, I think you've done a good job. And, in the process, you've probably learned just about as much as I would have by asking questions around your office myself."

"Glad to hear it," Frost replied, finding himself more than a little pleased at the detective's praise.

"One other thing. When I visited Donovan's office yesterday, I concluded that Miss Appleby was the only one who would have had a direct view of those going in and out of his office. I'll recheck that the next time I'm there, but is that your impression?"

"Yes, that's right. Some offices face a bank of secretarial stations. But Donovan's faces only Miss Appleby's desk."

"Okay." Bautista drummed his fingers on the cocktail table in front of him, momentarily lost in thought. "A couple more questions, Mr. Frost. I assume at this point you don't have a theory as to who did it?"

"No, I don't. I know all the people we've talked about, except Donovan's son."

"Okay, then. If you don't have a prime suspect, can you tell me which ones you think might be capable of murder?"

Frost sighed and sipped slowly from his drink. "I would have said that none of them was. But maybe I'm just not a good enough judge of human nature."

"That I doubt, sir," Bautista said.

"Maybe all of them are capable of having done it. As to which ones might be more likely . . ." Frost's voice dropped.

"Yes?"

"No. No. I really can't say one is more likely than another. I'm sorry."

"Well, keep pondering it," Bautista advised. "Meanwhile, here's what I'm thinking. We've got the Appleby woman under surveillance, or so we think. I think I'm going to try and see Mr. Bruce Donovan sometime over the weekend. Otherwise, let's just wait until Monday and see what happens. If one of the suspects is really guilty, maybe he—or she—will do something to show it. I think that's all we can do. Do you agree?"

"Yes."

"On Monday I've got to testify in court in the morning," Bautista continued. "So I think I'll come by your office right after lunch. To make an appearance for Mr. Bannard's benefit so he doesn't get me in trouble with the Mayor, if nothing else. Meanwhile let's keep thinking and watching and see what we can come up with."

"Fine."

Consciously or unconsciously, Bautista had slipped into the first person plural as the conversation ended. Reuben Frost found himself secretly pleased at the new but unspoken bond this evidenced and was pleased too when the detective gave him a vigorous two-handed handshake as they parted company on Fifth Avenue.

IF A PUBLIC OPINION POLL WERE TAKEN AMONG THE AS-
sociates at Chase & Ward and their wives, the result
would probably show about half wholeheartedly in favor
of the firm's annual lawyers' dinner dance and the other
half dead set against. The tradition had started before
any of Chase & Ward's present lawyers came to work
there, making it a truly venerable one. As the firm had
grown, what had begun as a relatively intimate social
affair had taken on the dimensions of a charity ball—
indeed, only the largest public rooms in the city's hotels
could now accommodate its partners and associates and
their wives and guests.

The partners of the firm, and most of their spouses,
were in general positive about the dance. For those
curious about the young lawyers, the dance was an
opportunity to meet, talk and socialize with some of
them and guests. Support for the dance was not quite as
enthusiastic as it had once been, however, since changing sexual mores had introduced an element of social
confusion daunting to even the most socially accomplished. In times gone by, the charming, sweet young
thing at one's left at dinner was the wife or girlfriend of
an associate (wife if the name was the same, girlfriend if
different). Today, the sweet young thing was just as
likely to be a lawyer employed by the firm. And the
difference in surname with her escort meant nothing:

she could be a genuine date, in the old-fashioned sense of the term; a woman asserting her feminism by retaining her maiden name after marriage; or an unmarried live-in companion. Ice-breaking conversations had become perilous, with the initiator often falling through the ice. Some of the more seriously wounded in these skating exercises were less than happy with the dance.

Among the younger lawyers and their wives, opinions were divided. There were many, but by no means a majority, that regarded the event as an invasion of privacy, a surreptitious attempt by the partners to assess the social graces of their associates—and their spouses. Others, children of the sixties in fact or in spirit, deplored what they perceived as the ostentation of the affair. Donate the cost to a worthy charity, they would say; don't spend good money on needless bread and circuses.

The more prevalent view was that the dance was a fine occasion to dress up in black-tie—not a common occurrence in the lives of most of the hardworking young lawyers—drink some good wine, smoke a decent cigar, and in general spend an opulent evening at Chase & Ward's expense.

Frost, when he had been the Executive Partner, had never been a great enthusiast of the dance, but he had been required to attend by virtue of his position. And to be polite to the likes of the young lawyer, emboldened with drink, who had told him how to run the firm, and the embittered young wife who had blurted out to him that Chase & Ward's demands on her husband's time and energies were wrecking their marriage.

This year, under police instructions to keep his eyes open, he actually looked forward to the dance, although he conveyed some forebodings to Cynthia while they dressed for the evening.

"Don't forget," Frost said to his wife, "not one word about the murder business. The partners of course know about it, plus that associate I told you about, Perry Griffith."

Frost had in fact brought his wife fully up to date on

developments, including the Merritt-inspired list of suspects.

"I wish I could carry Keith Merritt's list with me," she said. "I could use it like a dance card and keep track of the culprits."

"Very funny, my dear," Frost said. "I'm sure you can keep track of everything without a list."

"By the way, will the Singers be there tonight?" Cynthia inquired.

"Why do you ask?"

"Well, under all the circumstances and given Anne's situation and all . . ."

"I'm sure they'll be there. The last thing I should think either of them would want would be to call attention to themselves by staying away," Frost said. "Now, are you ready? It's time to go."

"Yes, I'm ready. And just a little bit excited. After all, how often do we go to dances where a murderer may show up? *That* ought to liven up the old dinner dance for once!"

There was no receiving line at the dinner dance. Several years before, a very stuffy wife of one of the older partners had suggested that there be one. It would add a properly formal tone to the evening, she said, and underscore to the young lawyers just who was underwriting the affair. Frost, then still the Executive Partner, had vetoed the idea outright. The young lawyers were perfectly well aware of the dance's sponsorship and what it needed, if anything, was less formality rather than more. Nonetheless, Cynthia and Reuben Frost, among the first arrivals at the Manhattan Room of the Standish Hotel, stood near the entrance and informally welcomed many of the guests as they arrived.

The black-tie requirement for the dance was meant to add a touch of elegance to the proceedings but did not entirely accomplish its purpose. As Frost observed the entering guests, he saw several outfits that he, at least, would not classify as black-tie—a powder blue tuxedo on one, a blue lace dress shirt on another, a shiny velvet dinner jacket on a third (this one a partner). They looked, Frost thought, like refugees from an ethnic wedding.

The women fared somewhat better. Many, mostly thrifty wives of the older partners, wore dresses that had been seen at least once, and in some cases many times, at previous affairs. At least a few designer dresses were evident, usually on the backs of the firm's women lawyers or working wives. And, true to form, there was one girl, a date of a brand-new lawyer, whose breathtaking décolletage was the cause of much comment.

As Frost mingled in the crowd, he found that when the partners mentioned the murder at all, it was in such a guarded way that no one overhearing them could catch their meaning. And if the wives had been told (as he was almost certain most of them had been) they certainly did not let on, showing, in the case of one or two of the more burbling spouses, either admirable restraint or ignorance. In the best Chase & Ward tradition, he kissed each of them as they met. (Kissing of partners' wives and the firm's women partners was permitted, and indeed expected in most cases. Kissing by partners of associates' wives and women associates was neither permitted nor expected. Kissing of male associates by partners' wives was optional with the wives. Kissing of male guests by other male guests, commonplace enough in ballet circles, as Frost well knew, was not even for a moment contemplated.)

Frost was grateful when the signal was sounded for dinner. Retrieving Cynthia from a nearby conversational knot ("noose" she would have called it, had she been asked to describe it), he passed into the Standish's main ballroom, which was decked out for the evening with beflowered tables for eight.

The tables were numbered, since it had been decided some years before that assigned seating was the only way to mix up the crowd; otherwise the dance would in effect be a series of small cliques of those who worked together at Chase & Ward on a regular basis. And the partners—and retired partners—would not be evenly distributed around the room. Individual place cards made

the seating even more precise, separating spouses to
avoid the huddling together of bashful couples, an exception being made for the unmarried and newlyweds,
who were permitted to sit side by side.

Frost usually reviewed the seating list for the dance
when it was circulated at the office. By comparing it
with the file of associates' biographies provided to all
the lawyers, he could mentally scratch out small talk for
use at the dinner table. (A remark like "I understand
you clerked for Judge DuBois" could be a lifeline for
rescuing a sinking conversation.) But his day on Friday
had been sufficiently full that he had not had time to do
his homework, so he picked up a seating list from a pile
at the ballroom entrance. He quickly discovered that he
and Cynthia would have as dinner companions that evening Harold Collins, a fiftyish permanent associate in the
firm's real estate department, and his wife Marcie (decent but bland, Frost thought); Laura Acheson, a new
associate in trusts and estates that Frost had not met,
and her date, Martin Daniels (unknown quantities); and
the Griffiths, Perry and Alice (potential trouble, though
Frost remembered Alice Griffith from previous encounters as both pretty and bright and, he seemed to recall, a
student at Cornell Medical School).

Examining the place cards at the assigned table, Frost
discovered that he was to be seated between Alice Griffith and Laura Acheson. Cynthia was across the way,
between Griffith and Harold Collins.

The society band had already begun playing a bouncy
fox-trot from a current Broadway show and had attracted a number of guests to the dance floor. The Frosts
waited patiently at their table, but eventually the whole
group assembled, necessary introductions were made,
and all sat down to eat the rather soggy seafood crepes
(crêpes de fruits de mer maître d'hôtel, the souvenir
menu for the evening called them) that began the meal.

Frost groaned inwardly when he tasted the white wine
being served—not because of its quality, which was
excellent, but because of what he was sure was its
healthy price. Every year the cost of the dance in-

creased, not geometrically but certainly substantially. The event was planned entirely by a committee of associates and neither Frost nor Bannard nor the managing partner in charge of associates ever quite had the courage to lean on the committee to exercise restraint. Hence the *grand cru* Chablis that he was now drinking.

Making the best of adversity, he turned to Miss Acheson, a tall, open-faced brunette with swept-back hair sitting at his left, and pronounced the wine "excellent."

"It's very nice," she replied. "Do you know a great deal about wines, Mr. Frost?" she asked, looking him directly (flirtatiously?) in the eye.

"Not a great deal, Miss Acheson."

"Laura."

"Laura. But I can tell this is very good."

"I went to Stanford, and we had some wonderful wines in California," Acheson said.

Oh my God, a California wine bore, Frost thought. He did not express his long-held view that all California wines were made in one of two (red or white) tinny vats and tasted almost precisely alike.

"Have you ever been to the wine country in California?" the girl continued.

"No, I can't say as I have," Frost said.

"It's fabulous, it really is," Acheson said with great conviction. "We used to go for weekends up into the mountains and visit the wineries. The wines were really super, and the country was nice too."

"No, the closest I've ever gotten to the California vineyards was the Loire Valley. That's pretty nice as well." Frost would have looked pointedly at Laura Acheson as he said this, but his view was blocked by the burly waiter yanking away plates from the first course.

Dancing started in earnest again between the courses. Frost, eager to terminate the California wine conversation, asked Cynthia to dance.

"How's it going?" he asked.

"Lovely, Reuben, lovely. I'm hearing all about Harry Collins's garden."

"Oh, God," Frost murmured. With the possible exception of descriptions of car trips—and California wines—gardening conversations were at the top of Frost's boredom list.

"He's had a vegetable garden for the first time this year," Cynthia said. "He's only had flowers before. Want to know what he raised?"

"No," Frost said, twirling his wife around hard to emphasize his feelings. "Shut up and dance."

"You sound like Jerry Robbins, dear," she replied.

Back at the dinner table, Frost turned from left side to right and struck up a conversation with Alice Griffith.

"Alice,"—he was not about to be reprimanded for formality again—"do I recall correctly that you are at Cornell Medical School?"

"Well, Mr. Frost—"

"Reuben." He could play the game too.

"Reuben, I am actually now doing my residency there. I've finished medical school and my internship," she answered.

"At New York Hospital?"

"Yes."

"What is your residency in?"

"Geriatrics."

"Geriatrics? Hmm. That means you'll be able to take care of me," Frost said.

"Maybe. But lawyers live so long and remain so healthy they're not really ideal patients for us," she answered, a warm, teasing smile breaking over her face.

"I guess that's so, isn't it?" Frost said. He thought of Dorrance Ward, who had died at the age of 101—in a car accident.

"Yes, I think it is. Just look at all the healthy old men at Chase & Ward," she said.

"What about Graham Donovan?" Frost asked, embarking on a voyage that he hoped would be one of discovery.

"Oh, that was a terrible surprise," the young doctor said. "My husband used to work for him, you know."

"Yes, I did," Frost replied.

"I can't say we were ever very close to Mr. Donovan," she said, but without any apparent animosity. "It seemed quite odd for a man in his late fifties, who I guess was in good health, to die so suddenly."

Was she referring to the murder or wasn't she? Frost could not tell.

"But I guess I of all people shouldn't be surprised when a healthy person has a heart attack," Dr. Griffith went on. "Only the other day I had just left the room of a patient that I had examined very carefully—everything was fine with her—when I got called back. In the thirty seconds since I'd left her, she had had a massive heart attack. There was nothing we could do, mouth-to-mouth, electroshock, nothing."

Frost now proceeded with caution. "That's very interesting. God knows I'm no doctor, but isn't there a new drug on the market that you people use in heart attack cases?" Frost asked, looking carefully at his dinner companion.

"There probably is, but I don't think I know the one you're referring to," she answered.

"I believe it's a refined form of digitalis of some sort," Frost continued. "As I recall, it has an odd name— Pernod, Penrod, no, Pernon."

As he spoke the name, his companion gestured and overturned the glass of red wine in front of her plate. She sprang back in her chair to protect her dress, but the effort was unnecessary. Only part of the wine had spilled by the time Frost had reached over to upend the fallen glass. The spilled wine flowed mostly onto Alice Griffith's plate, leaving her dress unscathed.

"Let's get you another plate," Frost said. He summoned a waiter and soon the damage was fully repaired, and Dr. Griffith had a new serving of the entree (*mignonette de boeuf farci*, the menu said).

"That was really clumsy of me," she said, blushing as she spoke. "A doctor shouldn't be so clumsy. But I always have been."

"I'm sure that's not true," Frost said.

"Oh, but it is," she answered. The woman then recalled in some detail—and in what Frost thought was a

hurried, nervous voice—an incident that had occurred at
Lasserre in Paris on her honeymoon with Perry.

Frost's mind was racing and he paid scant attention to
Dr. Griffith's frantically related anecdote. Had she deliberately overturned her wine to avoid answering his question about Pernon? And was this nervous tale-telling
now going on merely an instinctive reaction to a social
gaffe or a filibuster to distract him from pursuing his
questions? Frost did not know the woman well, but in
previous contacts he had never found her either clumsy
or loquacious, the qualities that had come to the fore
coincidentally with—or as the result of—his mention of
Pernon.

More questions came into Frost's head as the mono-
logue continued. Ross Doyle had told him that the distillate of digitalis used to make Pernon had been the cause
of Donovan's death. But could the distillate be *derived*
from it as well? Could someone with access to Pernon
reconcoct a fatal poison from it?

Alice Griffith came to the end of her story as Frost
thought through the implications of what he had seen
and heard. ". . . and there were three waiters, a busboy
and a captain crawling around the floor looking for the
wedding ring of a very embarrassed young bride."

"Did they find it?" Frost asked, picking up the conversation again.

"Yes, thank God. It had rolled an unbelievable distance and was under the table of a very surprised Japanese couple. Everyone was very nice, though, and the
restaurant gave us champagne to celebrate."

"That's an amusing story," Frost said. "It's nice to
know that Lasserre has a human side."

Frost did not pursue his questioning about Pernon; he
saw no point in it. Instead he escaped to the dance floor.
The dances between courses had proved to be a god-
send, though ironically his escape route this time was a
dance with Laura Acheson, the girl he had tried to get
away from earlier. She had clearly done her homework,
as she asked Frost about his interest in the ballet while
moving about the floor. Frost was still distracted, sort-

ing out the implications of his conversation with Dr. Griffith, and paid less than full attention to his dancing partner. Besides, it soon developed that her sketchy knowledge of the subject was confined to the San Francisco Ballet. Ever the elitist in dance matters, Frost found serious conversation about that company just not possible.

Frost returned to his table, sighing inwardly. One more course to go. (Two years earlier in a rare exercise of authority, Bannard, after some prompting from his partners, had ordered the dinner committee to cut the number of courses from four to three in the interest of reducing the time spent at the dinner table. No more salad and cheese.)

He looked across the table at Perry Griffith. Could this boyish innocent be a murderer? At the moment he was being terribly polite to Marcie Collins, who was regaling him with a long tale about something. Gardening? Frost knew that Griffith, despite his appearance, could be a tiger of a lawyer. But could he be a cold-blooded murderer as well?

As soon as the dessert course (*bombe glacée portemanteau*, the menu said) was over, Frost signaled to Cynthia that it was time to go. He was suddenly overwhelmed with the realization that Graham Donovan's murder was no closer to solution and that Alice Griffith's "accident" had certainly not shortened the list of suspects. His spirits were not aided in the least by the spectacle he and Cynthia encountered as they were leaving the hotel— Keith Merritt, dead drunk, totally out of character, being all but carried out by his wife and Irwin Johnson, a young associate who worked for Merritt in the tax department.

Drunk as he was, Merritt spotted Frost and called out to him, "There's light at the end of the tunnel, Reuben, there's light at the end of the tunnel!"

Frost wished he were listening to drunken wisdom. But if there was even a glimmer of light, he certainly did not see it.

A DISTRAUGHT WIFE

16

"YOU LOOK AWFUL," CYNTHIA FROST SAID, *STARING ACROSS* the breakfast table at her husband.

"I can't help it. I slept very badly."

"Too much party."

"No. Too much murder."

"Only one that I'm aware of."

"I've got to call Doyle," Reuben Frost said, more to himself than to his wife.

"Doyle? Why?" his wife asked, unable to follow his disjointed train of thought.

"He's got to find out more about the poison that killed Graham. He told me it was a distillate of digitalis used in this new drug they call Pernon. What I now need to know is if you can do something to Pernon to reduce it down to a distillate."

"What are you talking about?" Cynthia said, still perplexed.

"Remember when Alice Griffith spilled her wine at the dinner table last night? She did it just as I was asking her about Pernon. She's specializing in geriatrics, after all, so I'm damn sure she knows about it. But as soon as I'd mentioned the name, she spilled her wine and embarked on an endless story about losing her wedding ring at Lasserre."

"Oh, Reuben, that was just nerves," Cynthia said.

"I hope to God you're right. But it could mean, if

Pernon can be cooked down into the poison that killed Graham, that we have a nice, neat little scenario: loyal wife steals Pernon from hospital; she and/or husband turn it into a lethal distillate of digitalis; husband kills Donovan with the poison. Okay?''

"Or, for that matter, your Miss Appleby steals Pernon from *her* hospital and does the same thing.''

"Yes, you're right. That's possible too. But all the more reason why I need to know about this goddam Pernon. And by the way, what did you think of Mr. Griffith? You were talking to him most of the time during dinner.''

"Correction. I spent most of the evening talking about Harry Collins's garden. Reuben, he has to be the most boring man at Chase & Ward. *Tomatoes! Rhododendrons! Rosebushes!* I heard it all.''

"Well, I can't feel sorry for you, with the shock I got from Dr. Griffith. Not to mention California's preeminence in the wine and dance worlds. Besides, if you recall, I hold the Chase & Ward endurance record for boredom.''

"You mean Edna—''

"Yes, Edna Merritt's tale of how to get from Manhattan to Kent, Connecticut, with a horse trailer hitched to the car. The most truly bone-crushingly boring story I have ever heard.''

"I know, dear, but Harry Collins would give her a run for her money. And what did I think of your Mr. Griffith? An ambitious and smarmy young man. But a murderer? I don't think so.''

"But on the other hand, how many murderers have you ever met?''

They were interrupted by the ring of the telephone. Cynthia reached behind her chair in the kitchen to answer it, then turned the receiver over to Reuben. "It's Anne Singer and she wants to talk to you,'' Cynthia said.

As he picked up the receiver he realized that he had not seen the Singers at the dance. Had he simply missed them or had his prediction that they would be there been wrong?

"Hello, Anne. We missed you last night," he said.

Anne acknowledged at once that she had not been at the dance, then hurried on to convey the purpose of her call. Would Reuben meet her for lunch?

"Of course, my dear. We're free, I think." He whispered to Cynthia, who nodded her assent. Then a puzzled look came over his face as Anne asked that he have lunch with her alone.

"It is vitally important," she said, leaving Frost without a choice. He accepted, agreeing to meet her at Mortimer's at one.

"Well, how do you explain that?" Frost asked his wife when he had told her.

"I guess we'll have to wait and see," she answered.

"I hope you don't mind, dear. By the way she put things, I think I have to see her on her terms. She sounded faintly desperate."

"No, I don't mind, Reuben. You could probably become as fascinated by her flowing red hair as Graham did. But I think you'll be safe at Mortimer's."

"Thanks."

Cynthia was right, Frost thought, as he saw Anne Singer come in the door of the restaurant. Her distinctive, bright red hair was indeed striking. And as usual she had offset it with a smashing outfit, black pants with a black silk shirt. Heads turned as she strode to Frost's table and kissed him on the cheek.

"Drink?" he said, as they sat down.

"What are you having?"

"A mimosa."

"Good. That's what I want too."

"You're looking splendid as usual, my dear," Frost said, as their drinks were served.

"Thanks. I don't feel it," Anne Singer said.

"Reason?"

"I'll get to that in a minute. But first let me say how

grateful I am that you agreed to see me on such short notice.''

"Not at all. It was just a quiet Sunday for us.''

"By rights I should have called George Bannard. But somehow I've never found him very sympathetic. And you always seemed to be very understanding of Roger's complicated life.''

"Well, I appreciate the compliment, Anne. But what's the trouble?''

"Roger has disappeared. I haven't seen him since Graham's funeral Thursday morning. He left me after the service and said he was going to the office.''

"I saw him at the funeral, but come to think of it I haven't seen him since,'' Frost said.

"No, he went off somewhere Thursday. I had been out Thursday afternoon, but called the office when I got home about five because we hadn't made any dinner plans. His secretary said he had gone for the day. When he hadn't gotten home by nine, I took a look around. A suitcase and his passport were gone.''

"And he didn't leave any indication of where he was off to?''

"None,'' she said, as she finished her drink. The waiter, as if on cue, appeared and asked if they wanted another round.

"What do you think, Anne? I'd just as soon order lunch and a bottle of wine.''

"Sounds fine.''

Ordering accomplished—chicken hash for both—they returned to the case of the missing person.

"Look,'' Anne said, "with Roger's crazy European clients, I'm used to his taking off on a moment's notice for strange places. But he always tells me where he's going. Do you know where he is, Reuben?''

"No, I don't. He certainly didn't say anything to me about going away on firm business. And I don't believe he was on the absence list circulated on Friday.''

"I'm sure not,'' Anne said. "His secretary hadn't heard a word from him on Friday.''

"Could he be doing work for the . . . agency?'' Frost

asked hesitantly. Singer's CIA involvement was not normally a subject discussed so directly, but this did not seem a time for discretion.

"Reuben, I thought of that. But even when Roger was on agency business, he always used to make up some sort of excuse before going away. Besides, I'm not sure but what he hasn't severed his connections there. God knows I've been trying to get him to give up the spy stuff for years without success."

"What makes you think he's given it up on his own?" Frost asked.

"Remember when he was away for two weeks in January? That was an agency trip, though I've never found out to where. Shortly after he got back, he seemed to lapse into a perpetually dark mood. It was the only time he ever opened up about the CIA at all."

"What did he say?"

"He said he was fed up with dirty tricks. That they were for younger and stronger people than he. I gathered he had somehow been involved in a plot that he didn't approve of. I assume to murder or assassinate someone, but I don't know who or what country, or anything else."

"I thought dirty tricks were a thing of the past."

"I said the same thing to Roger. All he said was that old habits are hard to break."

"But you had the idea he was going to cut his connection with the agency?"

"That's what he said. But he is very loyal too, Reuben, so his vow to quit may have been only temporary."

The couple were silent as they began eating their lunch. Looking around while they were being served, Frost was amused to see one of Cynthia's old friends looking over in their direction. But given the seriousness of the business at hand, he did not share his amusement with Anne.

Anne resumed the conversation. "Unfortunately, there's another possibility. Another reason why Roger may have disappeared."

"What's that?"

"Oh, Reuben, dear, don't be so naive. I don't think it's any great secret that Graham Donovan and I were, shall we say—

"Good friends?"

"Thanks. Yes. Good friends. I don't know whether Roger knew about us or not. I was terrified to tell him, but Graham and I were getting more reckless and Roger just may have found out, though I can't imagine he wouldn't have confronted me if he really knew the truth. But what I'm afraid of is that Graham's death may have affected Roger in some way, some irrational way."

"Let me ask you a frank question, Anne. Has Roger been completely well lately?"

"You mean mentally?"

"Yes."

"Why do you ask?"

"Well, he's been acting rather strange at the office. Completely silent whenever he's in a group and just generally taciturn and sometimes irascible."

"You've got it. Ever since the trip in January, he's been gloriously depressed. I don't know whether you've noticed, but some days he doesn't even go to work until lunchtime."

"I hadn't," Frost said. "Was he doing anything about his depression?"

"Yes. He was seeing a psychiatrist uptown. Strange name. Lygian, I believe."

"Sure. Adrian Lygian, psychiatrist to the stars."

"You know him?"

"I've met him. Someone once said that half the famous people in New York go to him and the other half should."

"Well, I don't know about that, but I was sure he was doing Roger some good. But now Roger has gone and disappeared. I'm worried, Reuben. Roger, mysterious Roger, has never done this before. I'm so afraid he'll harm himself—afraid that the agency, or Graham and me, or Graham's death, or some other demon will push him over the edge."

Anne began crying softly as she got more worked up.

Frost offered her a handkerchief and held her by the wrist (presumably witnessed by Cynthia's nearby friend, but he didn't care).

"Has there been any threat of . . . harm? Of harming himself?" Frost said.

"No. Roger never talked that way or made threats like that. But depression can bring on suicide and I can't help but think about it."

"I wouldn't worry about that just yet. I'm going to do some checking this afternoon to see if Roger's off with one of his mysterious clients or off on spook business. Until we've ruled that out, I wouldn't worry. Roger may have been gloomy of late, but I don't think of him as being self-destructive."

"Reuben, I can't thank you enough," Anne said. "Obviously I've got to make a new start on things now that Graham is dead. I just want to have the chance to make things right with Roger."

"I'll keep you posted and you do the same," Frost said.

Frost decided to go to the Chase & Ward office, where with help he might be able to find the home telephone numbers of Singer's European contacts. He arrived, surprising the Pinkerton guard at the desk, who had not seen Reuben Frost in the office on a Sunday in many years.

Frost was amazed at the activity he found. He knew that the office was busy—every client seemed to have come back from the summer with an idea for a new project—but he didn't know business was so good that many associates and some partners were working on Sunday. As he walked down the hall he had a slight twinge of regret that he was not still sharing in the firm's profits.

Once at his desk, Frost called Merritt at home. Merritt was the tax partner who worked with Singer most closely in advising the Europeans and he indeed was able to give Frost a list of names to call and instructions for getting their telephone numbers from Merritt's Rolodex.

The effort proved futile. Frost was lucky in reaching all but one name on the list. But none knew of any plans Singer may have had to be in Europe. He also called Ross Doyle and asked him to find out from his laboratory friends whether the poison that had killed Donovan could be derived from Pernon.

Frost then decided to call Dawson Evans in Washington. Evans had been a contemporary of Frost at Chase & Ward, and in fact had flown up from Washington for Donovan's funeral. He had left Chase & Ward shortly after becoming a partner to work in the Justice Department as an Assistant Attorney General. By the time his tour of duty was over, he had been sufficiently blinded by the bright lights of Washington that he wanted to stay there rather than return to what had then seemed to him Chase & Ward's mundane, apolitical practice. He had stayed and had become a leading Washington lawyer, well-connected and well-heeled, and, most recently, a patriarch of the Democratic Party.

Frost was lucky again, and caught up with Evans as he was coming off the golf course at Burning Tree Country Club.

"Damn, Frost, you're almost as clever as a White House telephone operator," Evans told him. "What can I do for my old partner in crime?"

Frost explained about Singer's disappearance (but not about Donovan's murder) and asked if there was any way Evans could discreetly check whether Singer was off on CIA business.

"That's a tall order, Reuben, but I'll see what I can do. If it will help to relieve Anne's mind, I'll make it top priority first thing in the morning," Evans told him. Anne Singer's red hair had apparently made another conquest.

As he hung up, Frost realized that he had not told Cynthia he was going to the office, so she presumably thought he was still with Anne. He quickly picked up the receiver and told her he would be right home.

"How was the tryst?" Cynthia asked her husband sardonically once he had arrived.

"Very public. Your friend Irene Morgan was watching us the whole time."

"Good."

"Anne Singer is a very distraught woman."

"Why?"

"Roger has disappeared. No message, nothing. And I've been spending the afternoon trying to track him down in Europe. No luck. He's been depressed ever since getting back from some dirty tricks mission last January."

"Dirty tricks?"

"You know, CIA dirty tricks."

"Murder, perhaps?"

"Oh, Cynthia, let's not even think about it—or about its implications. But yes, murder it could have been."

"So Roger is good at it, is he?"

"Cynthia, come on. We can't go on with these wild speculations. Let's just leave it that Roger Singer has been in a depression for several months and that now he has disappeared. All right?"

"Yes, dear. I wasn't trying to bait you," Cynthia said. "What you need is a good, relaxing movie."

"What did you have in mind?"

"There's a Hitchcock revival at the Beekman. I forget which one."

"Let's go. It doesn't matter. Busman's holiday."

NEW INFORMATION

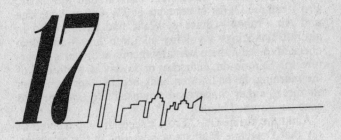

WHEN FROST GOT TO HIS OFFICE MONDAY MORNING, DAWSON Evans had already called and left a message. Frost returned the call and was not surprised to find that Evans had drawn a blank with his contacts at the CIA. As far as they could determine—or as far as they would admit— Roger Singer was not traveling on an agency mission.

Finding Singer was Frost's first priority. Anne's warning about the possibility of suicide, however improbable, had scared him. And though Frost really refused to believe it and could not explain how it might have come about, there was always the possibility that by locating Singer one would locate Donovan's killer as well.

Frost managed to reach Jean Albert, the remaining person on the list Merritt had furnished him the day before, after a series of calls to Paris and London. M. Albert, a shy French multimillionaire who invested quietly in various projects in the United States, relied on Singer as a listening post and as a guide to the complexities of the American laws that might trap an unwary foreigner—disclosure requirements, tax withholding and all the rest. When a new fancy struck him, it was not unusual for M. Albert to summon Singer to Paris, or wherever M. Albert might happen to be, to discuss it. But that was not the case this time. M. Albert told Frost he had not spoken with Singer in three weeks and had no current plans for a personal meeting with him.

A check with Chase & Ward's petty cash window was also unavailing. Frost was assured that Mr. Singer had not recently cashed a check in any unusually large amount.

Through a series of discreet calls around the office, Frost gathered a list of contacts at TWA, Pan American and Air France—Chase & Ward had participated in aircraft financings involving all three lines—and then checked to see if there was any record of Singer's departure for Europe on Thursday or Friday. By the end of the morning, he had gotten back negative answers from all three; either Singer had not used the lines or had used an assumed name.

Amid the airline calls, Frost's secretary interrupted to say that Detective Bautista was waiting in the reception room. Frost told her to send him down.

"What's new, Officer?" Frost asked, preemptively.

"You tell me."

"Well, there are a couple of things to tell. They're things I should not only be telling you but George Bannard as well. Do you mind if the three of us meet together?"

"Of course not," Bautista said, then adding, "You know, Mr. Frost, I think that you think I resent Mr. Bannard's tongue-lashing the other day. And maybe I do. But compared with some of the verbal abuse you get in my job, it really was nothing."

"Good. There was nothing personal about it, I assure you."

"Usually there is. The accusation most often involves having sexual relations with my mother."

"I don't think that's part of George's vocabulary. Not usually, at any rate."

The two men smiled and went down the hall to Bannard's office.

"Good morning, Reuben. Good morning, Mr. Baptista," Bannard said.

"Bautista," the detective corrected him.

"I'm sorry. Bautista. To what do I owe the pleasure?"

"George, I thought you should be kept up to date on

what's going on, not that there's very much," Frost said.

"Well, tell me what there is."

"As far as I'm concerned, the big news is that Roger Singer has apparently disappeared," Frost said.

Both his listeners showed interest.

"How do you know that?" Bannard asked.

Frost told of his lunch with Anne Singer and his continuing efforts to locate her husband. References to the CIA and Anne's relationship with Graham Donovan inevitably formed a part of the account. Bannard kept looking uneasily at Bautista.

"Incidentally, I assume, Mr. Bautista, that all this scandalous information you are learning about us will be kept in confidence?"

"To the extent it's not relevant to my investigation, of course," the detective replied. "I'm interested in finding the murderer, Mr. Bannard, not writing an exposé of your firm."

Bannard grunted, then said, "Well, Reuben, it sounds like you've become a transcontinental detective. How do you feel about Mr. Frost taking over your job, Officer?"

Frost could not tell whether Bannard was sticking the knife into Bautista or not. In any event it didn't seem to cause a wound, and Frost was pleased to hear the detective say that Frost's efforts had been "very helpful."

Bautista then went on to relate the results of a meeting with Bruce Donovan on Saturday morning. He said that he had learned little that was new, except that the son was divorced, lived alone, and was profoundly bitter about his father. As for being on the premises of Chase & Ward, he said that he had not been there since his mother's death.

"So there's nothing promising there?" Bannard asked.

"It doesn't appear so, sir," Bautista answered.

Frost was about to relate his other bit of information—the access of Alice Griffith to Pernon—when Bannard's secretary interrupted to say that Ross Doyle wanted very badly to speak to Mr. Frost. The call was transferred and Frost took it as the other men looked on. Putting down the telephone, he said that Doyle had what he described as some "interesting new information" and wanted to come over and relay it.

"Damn," Bannard said. "I'm late now for a Fidelity board meeting that I promised to attend. Can you gentlemen see him? I'll be back later and you can tell me what's happened."

"Of course, George. We'll take care of it."

While they waited in Bannard's office for Doyle, Frost told Bautista about Alice Griffith.

"I think we're going to have to talk to that young man," Bautista said.

"I agree," Frost replied, as Doyle arrived.

Frost introduced the private detective to the public one and both were introduced to a stolid young Irishman, named Sean Ryan, accompanying Doyle. Although Doyle did not say so, Frost guessed that Ryan, a red-faced youth in his early twenties, was probably a moonlighting policeman. Unlike Detective Bautista, he fitted Frost's stereotype of the typical New York cop. Frost's impression of moonlighting was reinforced when Ryan seemed distinctly uneasy as Bautista was introduced as a city detective.

Doyle told Frost that he had consulted his laboratory friends and that, indeed, the distillate that had killed Donovan could have been derived from Pernon. The process was not at all difficult and could be carried out by anyone with the most rudimentary knowledge of laboratory techniques.

But Doyle said the main purpose of his call was not to pass on this information but rather the information obtained by his helper Ryan. He said that Ryan had been following Grace Appleby since the decision had been made the previous Thursday to keep her under surveillence. Ryan reported that neither he nor another colleague who spelled him had observed anything unusual until the previous evening, when a young man had visited Appleby's apartment in Chelsea, stayed for about fifteen minutes, and left, seemingly very angry.

On the assumption that the young man may have been a Chase & Ward employee, Doyle asked if there was available a file of employees' pictures. Frost said there was. Nonlawyers had always been asked to submit photos when they started work. And in recent years newly employed lawyers had been too, since someone along the line had decided that the biographies of new lawyers circulated around the firm should include photographs.

"What did this fellow look like?" Frost asked of Ryan.

"He was tall, very blond, and quite young-looking," Ryan answered.

Frost did not need to know more. Appleby's visitor was more likely than not Perry Griffith. But it would be best to establish this through an orderly process.

"Let's start with my file of associates' biographies, which include pictures," Frost said. "If that doesn't work, the individual personnel files of the other employees have photographs and you can search through them."

Frost asked his secretary to bring his associates' file into the conference room next door to his office, where he left Doyle and Ryan to study the pictures.

He was sure Ryan would pick out Griffith as the Sunday caller. But what did that mean? Had they perhaps plotted together in the Stephens Industries scheme? Or planned Graham Donovan's murder? Or both? It was all distasteful, although Frost, after almost a week's stress, was willing to accept an unhappy resolution to Donovan's murder rather than no resolution.

Frost and Bautista went to the cafeteria for coffee while Doyle and Ryan studied the pictures in Frost's file.

"I'm sure Grace Appleby's vsitor was the young man we've been talking about," Frost said.

"In that case, we've really got to talk to him," Bautista replied.

Twenty-five minutes after beginning their examination, Doyle and Ryan returned to Frost's office. Ryan carried the notebook full of associates' biographies, open to Griffith's page.

"This is the guy," Ryan said.

"You're sure?" Frost asked.

"Yes. He wasn't wearing a hat, so his face and blond hair were perfectly visible. It was a clear night and I could see him easily from across the street," Ryan said.

"Where does Miss Appleby live? An apartment house?" Bautista asked.

"Yes. Four twenty-two West Twentieth Street," Ryan answered.

"How did you know Griffith went to her apartment?" Bautista asked.

"Two ways. I had memorized the location of the downstairs buzzer to her apartment—easy, since it was the bottom one on the panel—and could see from across the street when her buzzer was pushed. Second, I could see into the large front window of her apartment. The curtains weren't drawn and I saw Griffith through the window before he sat down."

"What time was this?" Bautista asked.

"About eight-ten, eight-fifteen."

"And the visit lasted about fifteen minutes?"

"Yes. He was back on the street by eight-thirty."

"And you didn't follow him?" Bautista asked.

"No, sir. My orders were to stake out Appleby," Ryan answered, somewhat dejected at the suggestion that perhaps he should have followed the young man.

"Okay," Bautista said. "Unless you disagree, Mr. Frost, I think you should talk to Perry Griffith. You said you've been working with him recently?"

"That's right."

"Then my hunch is you may get more out of him talking to him alone. But I'll be right here, in that conference room next door if you want me to join in—or if there's any funny business. If there's any trouble, just press the buzzer on your telephone to your secretary and she can come and get me."

"Do you fellows want to stay around?" Frost inquired of Doyle and Ryan.

"Not unless you need us," Doyle said. "I don't think there's any reason, do you, Officer?"

"No," Bautista answered.

The four men went out, and Doyle and Ryan left. Frost explained the signal arrangement to a puzzled Miss O'Hara and asked her to summon Griffith to his office.

Perry Griffith came into Frost's office carrying the marked-up copy of the Frontier Utilities mortgage.

"Good morning, Reuben." He put the mortgage down on Frost's worktable, assuming they were about to go through a side-by-side review of the text.

"No, no, come sit over here," Frost said, indicating the chair on the other side of his desk. Griffith picked up the mortgage and held it in his lap after seating himself in the designated chair.

"I enjoyed sitting next to your wife Saturday night," Frost began. "I don't know how she does it—raising two children and finishing her residency at the same time."

"I don't either," Griffith said, grinning. "I think of myself as a hard worker, but I haven't got a thing on Alice. She's superorganized and she's got more energy than I'll ever have. She enjoyed talking with you, by the way."

"I'm glad," Frost said, then looked at Griffith silently for a moment as if deliberately to change the mood

"Perry, I'm afraid I didn't ask you in here to talk about Frontier Utilities," Frost began. Griffith looked puzzled but said nothing.

"I've got a very important question to ask you, Perry," Frost said. "And let me say in advance that I think it would be in your very best interests to give me a full, complete and truthful answer."

Griffith remained impassive, but bobbed his head affirmatively and nervously several times.

"What were you doing at Grace Appleby's apartment last night?" Frost asked calmly but harshly.

Griffith looked dumbfounded, his eyes popping slightly. "What do you mean?" he asked angrily.

"Perry, you were seen in Grace Appleby's apartment shortly after eight o'clock last night. You were there roughly fifteen minutes. *What were you doing there?*"

"What is this, some sort of police state? What the hell kind of question is that?" Griffith was both agitated and angry, but he did not stir from his chair. "Reuben, I've worked here for almost eight years," Griffith went on. "During that time nobody has ever questioned either my work or my honesty, and you're not going to start now!"

"Perry, Perry, calm down please. Let's take this thing slowly and quietly," Frost said, emphasizing his words. "Now. Is it not true that you went to Miss Appleby's apartment last night?"

"What if it is?" Griffith shot back.

"Let me repeat. Is it not true that you went to Grace Appleby's apartment last night?"

Again there was silence as Griffith seemed to reflect on the question. Then he said yes, very quietly.

"And what were you doing there?" Frost said.

Silence. Frost could all but see the inner works of Griffith's brilliant mind whirring, searching for a safe answer. Then Griffith slightly but visibly slumped in his chair. The mental computer had not produced a suitably evasive answer.

"Reuben, I'll give it to you straight. I went to see Grace Appleby to ask her not to tell you that I had been in Graham Donovan's office the morning he died. It's as simple as that."

"And why were you concerned about that?"

"Listen, when you talked to me on Friday, you were pretty desperate—you must have been, or you wouldn't have told me about the water carafe, the poisoning. When I thought about it, I knew you didn't have a suspect, but would love to have one—"

"And it occurred to you that you might be one?"

"Right. Graham was standing in the way of my becoming a partner. No question about that, as you yourself indicated. I had a motive, and I didn't need Grace Appleby putting me anywhere near that water carafe."

"I assume she let you know that she had already told me that you had seen Graham Tuesday morning."

"Yes. Yes, she did."

"What else did she say?" Frost asked.

"She wanted to know if I had poisoned Graham."

"And what did you say?"

"I said the same thing I said to you last week. Maybe I had my grievances against Graham, maybe he was blocking the way to my becoming a partner, but that wasn't reason enough to kill." Griffith was shouting by now.

"Perry, if you are innocent, why did you try to silence Miss Appleby?"

"Just like I said. I could see you were looking for a suspect, and I didn't want that suspect to be me."

Frost was now silent, swiveling slightly in his desk chair, so that he looked not at Griffith but at the picture of his wife as Odette at the side of the desk. Then he turned and faced Griffith directly once again.

"Perry, let me ask you one more question."

Griffith did not respond.

"Do you know what drug it was that killed Graham?"

"No. You didn't tell me," Griffith answered. ("And I didn't put it there, so I really don't know," his expression seemed to say as well.)

"It was a highly concentrated derivative of digitalis," Frost said. "One that's used to make a new wonder drug for the heart called Pernon. Ever heard of it?"

"No, I don't believe I have."

"And do you suppose your doctor wife has?"

Griffith sprang out of his chair and brought his fist down on Frost's desk. "Goddammit, Reuben, what the hell does that remark mean? It's bad enough that I have to sit here and listen to your insinuations about me, but you can goddam well leave Alice out of this!

"Of course she knows about Pernon!" Griffith shouted. "She knows about every goddam drug in the pharmacopoeia! She's a doctor, for Christ's sake! So no, it wouldn't surprise me if Alice had heard of Pernon, or cortisone, or boric acid, for that matter. Don't be an idiot, Reuben. I didn't kill Graham Donovan and Alice didn't help me do it!''

Griffith stormed out of the office and slammed the door.

Frost felt sheepish as he sat alone in the office. He had not handled things well. Griffith was undoubtedly right about his acting like an idiot. Frost was pushing too hard to nail a suspect, trying too hard to be an amateur gumshoe. And provoking the young man with the question about his wife was clumsy and gave him cause for anger—or, just possibly, a plausible chance to break off an uncomfortable encounter.

Bautista emerged from the adjoining conference room when he heard Frost's door slam.

"Well?" Bautista asked.

"Totally predictable. Griffith says he went to ask Grace Appleby not to reveal that he had visited Graham Donovan in his office the morning of Graham's death. And he got progressively more angry as we talked and finally walked out.''

"Does he protest too much?" Bautista asked.

"I wish I knew . . . Luis, I wish I knew.''

ANOTHER COUNTRY

CLAUDIO, THE GENIAL MAITRE D' AT THE HOTEL CIPRIANI, showed Roger Singer to a table beside the hotel pool. It was, in fact, Singer's favorite table, facing out into the brilliant sunshine of Venice and commanding a view of San Giorgio.

Ruskin had found San Giorgio an abomination and many felt the same about the Cipriani. Singer emphatically disagreed. He and Anne had made it a point to stay at the hotel whenever they were within striking distance of Venice. Of course many of the guests at "Chips" had more money than manners, but both Roger and Anne loved its sybaritic ambience, its (generally) impeccable service, the excellent food, the linen sheets, the beautiful gardens, the comfortable pool. And lunch at poolside, with here a French millionairess and her retinue of pretty faces, all male; there an Italian fashion designer with his retinue, also pretty, also male; the British conglomerateur and his family; the London art historian and his dowdy wife; the unfashionable but undoubtedly rich American, wearing a polyester shirt and street shoes with his shorts, and his wife, wearing diamonds with her bathing suit and vigorously chewing gum. Something was always happening, and more often than not something interesting, or at least amusing.

"It's been a long time, Signor Singer," Claudio said. (No fool, Claudio inspected the list of arrivals daily to

185

refresh his memory as to the names of returning guests.
The guests, of course, assumed that he remembered
their distinctive and vibrant personalities without any
prompting and, as a consequence, tipped him hand-
somely.)

"Yes, Claudio, it has. Spring last year."

"You coming from New York?"

"Yes. I stopped in Paris first, but took the midday
flight from Paris yesterday."

"And la signora? She is well?" (Claudio gambled
slightly on this one, but the Singers had always appeared
so devoted that he felt reasonably safe in risking the
question.)

"She's fine, Claudio, just fine. Unfortunately there
were things to hold her in New York, so she couldn't
join me."

"I'm sorry."

"So is she," Singer said, laughing. "I came in a
terrible hurry. I needed to get away for a few days'
rest."

Singer took only a minute to look at the menu, then
ordered Parma ham and melon and grilled scampi. And a
full carafe of the hotel's house red wine.

Singer went over in his mind the lies he had just told.
"Fine, just fine." Sure, with her lover murdered and her
husband missing. "Things to hold her in New York."
Like what? With Graham's death, that was no longer
true. "Sorry not to be here with me." A little difficult to
say, since she doesn't know where I am.

But what the hell, Singer thought. The fact that he had
perhaps screwed up his life irrevocably in New York
was no reason for destroying his image at his favorite
hotel.

A waiter brought his wine. It was delicious, just as he
had remembered it, a most acceptable Valpolicella. He
drank two glasses rapidly and eagerly and continued his
idle ruminating about his situation.

Why had he run away? Deep in his own conscious-
ness he knew the reason—he could not face full-time
life with Anne. Anne's arrangement with Graham Dono-

van had, in fact, suited him perfectly. Anne was, whether she knew it or not, emotionally demanding. Like so many of his colleagues—too many, probably—Singer was analytical, unemotional and remote in his practice. Clients paid a fancy price for his cool rationality; they took comfort in having a lawyer who was not emotionally involved in the problem at hand. His colleagues at the CIA felt the same way. Roger was ever the calm, detached observer; political emotions did not cloud his reason.

Unfortunately, Singer brought his remoteness home with him. He knew this, and also knew Anne's almost unlimited need for emotional stroking—a need so great and so demanding that he had often considered divorce as the only way out, the only way to remove the emotional shackles that he felt bound him. Singer was not altogether surprised when Anne's reaching out to Graham Donovan, the new widower, met a reciprocal emotional response of just the sort she was seeking.

Now the brand-new thought suddenly dawned that he really had wanted the affair to continue, freeing him as it did from demands of the spirit he felt incapable of fulfilling. Until this very minute he had not come to the self-realization that Anne's liaison with Donovan was of vital importance to *his* emotional stability.

How could he ever justify his flight to Anne or his partners, explaining to them that he was unprepared to face the prospect of living with a woman no longer emotionally tied to someone else? How could he believably describe the twisted feelings he had about Anne's affair with Graham?

And of course, by running away, he had probably made himself a real suspect in Graham's murder. To the outside, conventional world, he certainly had a motive, the atavistic desire of the cuckold for revenge. And wasn't it possible, if there were an intensive and prolonged investigation, that his past association with CIA "dirty tricks" involving poison would become known? Put these facts together with his precipitate departure from New York, and the carabinieri might yet return him in handcuffs. (*That* would provide lunch and dinner conversation at the Cipriani for several days.)

Singer's dilemma did not come into any clearer focus as luncheon, and his own wine consumption, progressed. Why couldn't his current problem be a simple one, like those he assumed his neighbors around the pool had—whether to seek uplift at the Accademia or new linen towels at Jesurum; where to buy American chewing gum; whether to take boy A or boy B—or C or D or E—to bed that evening. Singer reflected, as he often had, that boy watching was often more rewarding at the Cipriani pool than girl watching. Though the boys were unquestionably beautiful, he would have preferred a higher female ratio.

"How long will you be with us, Signor Singer?" Claudio asked as luncheon was ending.

"I'm not sure, Claudio. Another two or three days, I suppose."

"Shall I save table twenty-two for you tomorrow?"

"Please. *Mille grazie.*"

After lunch, Singer changed his clothes and took the hotel's private launch across to the Piazza San Marco, studiously shunning the American gent with the polyester shirt and his wife. Singer was determined to lose himself in the beauties of Venice, to forget his problems by revisiting favorite old haunts.

Leaving the launch, he strode briskly to the Scuola San Giorgio degli Schiavoni to look at his favorite Carpaccios—*St. Jerome and the Lion* and *St. Augustine in His Study*. Unlike the typical tourist, he did not spend precious time locating the winding route to the Scuola; from past experience he knew precisely how to get there. The visit was a pleasure as always; St. Augustine's dog and the terrified expressions on the faces of St. Jerome's colleagues as the saint's lion friend approached delighted anew. Then to the Campo SS. Giovanni e Paolo and the heroic statue of Colleoni, the fearsome fifteenth-century condottiere. Then back along the canals to the Piazza San Marco, and a long stop at Florian's where Singer drank in again the details of the facade of the basilica, surely one of the world's most extraordinary sights.

By this time Singer was tired and slightly drunk, a condition he improved upon by stopping for one of the very special martinis served at Harry's Bar. Then he took the Cipriani launch back and had a short nap.

That evening Singer attempted more restorative therapy, going to his favorite restaurant in all of Venice, the Antica Besseta at the Riva San Biasio. Again he felt on familiar ground. Anne and he had been there several times, and he was greeted warmly by Signor Volpe, the owner. Singer even remembered what he wanted—spaghetti nero (with a salty sauce of ground anchovies) and fresh, impeccably grilled sole.

Singer was not alone in the restaurant. A multigenerational birthday party was going on in the center of the dining room, honoring, it appeared, the grandmother of the party. Singer watched with admiration the truly prodigious amounts of food consumed by all concerned, from the eight- or nine-year-old youngsters to the aged grandfather. Even Singer—cold, unemotional Roger Singer— was caught up in the festivities, and gladly accepted the glass of prosecco and the slice of birthday cake proffered by the celebrants.

Family was the theme of the evening. He had always known that Signora Volpe ran the kitchen, but he now realized that the slightly awkward young teenager waiting on table was the owner's son.

Flush with even more wine, Singer realized what a fool he had been. He genuinely missed Anne, who had been with him at the restaurant so often. And the family obbligato being played out in Signor Volpe's trattoria brought home to him that a solitary life, or a life without Anne, was really unthinkable. So what if she was emotionally demanding? Was that such a terrible thing? Wasn't it something he could cope with if he half tried? And wouldn't life without Anne in fact be quite awful?

This sudden rush of insight made Singer, at least by his lights, positively exuberant. He spoke volubly to all three of the Volpes in adequate, if ungrammatical, Italian and embraced the father, Italian-style, as he left the restaurant. Impatiently he waited for the vaporetto back to San Marco. He had to return to the Cipriani; he had to call Anne.

Eventually he got back to his room and called New York at once. When the hotel operator rang through with the call, he heard his wife's voice at the other end.

"Anne! Anne! I'm coming back!"

SOME BREAKS

19

REUBEN FROST ARRIVED AT CHASE & WARD TUESDAY MORN-
ing feeling discouraged; the murder of Graham Donovan
simply did not seem, a week after the event, closer to
solution. It was true that he had received a call at
dinnertime the night before from Anne Singer, telling
him of Roger's impending return from Venice.

But this news, while a relief as far as Roger's disappearance went, did not solve the crime. Detective Bautista,
faced with the stalemate, had begun interrogating Chase
& Ward personnel Monday afternoon, but by the time
the two men left the office at seven, Bautista could only
report that nothing new had been uncovered. Dorothea
Cowden, the firm's receptionist, had not seen anyone
suspicious or unaccounted for the morning of the murder, and her record of visitors to the office yielded no
surprises. Grace Appleby repeated her story that only
Perry Griffith and Keith Merritt had been in Donovan's
office on the fatal morning.

Bautista had not questioned Griffith but did talk to
Merritt. He found Merritt in a dreadful nervous state,
but the man said nothing that linked him to the murder
beyond his proximity at the right moment to Donovan's
water carafe.

Bautista had also wanted to question Arthur Tyson,
but Tyson had been out of the office for the afternoon,

and the detective postponed a meeting with him until
Tuesday.

Frost had not been able to do much more. He had
been intrigued by Bruce Donovan's statement to Bautista over the weekend that he had not been in Chase &
Ward's offices since his mother's death. Frost knew that
the firm ran a legal-aid operation of sorts for partners'
relatives, including the preparation of wills for them.
On speculation, Frost had called the firm's files, and in
short order a file was served up that contained a will
executed by Bruce Donovan within the past year, well
after his mother's death.

Frost was reasonably sure the document had been
executed in the office, though it was conceivable that it
had been sent to him for signature. But the witnesses to
the will were Grace Appleby and a young associate in
the trust and estates department, neither of whom under
the firm's strict practice would have been permitted to
sign the witness's declarations unless Bruce Donovan
had personally been present.

It seemed clear that young Donovan had lied to the
police officer. But did that make him a murderer? And
did lying about his presence in the office a year earlier
mean that he was lying about his presence the previous
Tuesday? Frost thought not, and Bautista agreed, though
noting Frost's discovery in his notebook for possible
future reference.

Bautista and Frost had coffee together in the cafeteria
Tuesday morning. Was this becoming a ritual? Frost
recalled all the rough and tough gangster movies he had
seen as a young man, where the good guys seemed to
drink coffee incessantly as they plotted their war against
crime. But he did not see Luis Bautista as Pat O'Brien,
jacket off and gun in its shoulder holster, sipping coffee
from a mug and raging against injustice. And, in such a
scenario, who would Frost be? The whole image was as
ridiculous as Siegfried and Benno getting ready for the
hunt in *Swan Lake*.

Bautista outlined his plan for the morning. He had
already checked with Norman Perry, the firm's head

messenger, to determine which members of the messenger's staff had worked the previous Tuesday within the office. It was possible—just barely possible—that one of them, while making intraoffice deliveries, had seen something of interest. Bautista, operating from the conference room next to Frost's office, was going to question them, along with Arthur Tyson. He was not hopeful about uncovering anything new; nor was Reuben Frost.

Frost, after Monday's encounter with Perry Griffith, really did not feel like talking to Griffith again, even on such a nonexplosive subject as the Frontier Utilities mortgage. In fact, he sat in his office doing what he hated, reading magazines and legal periodicals. One could, and should, justify such reading as keeping up with the latest developments in the law. But he knew, and anyone coming into his office would know, that such reading was a clear signal that he had nothing else (that is, paying work for a client) to do.

Frost was thus doubly grateful for a visit from Keith Merritt and the message he brought—grateful because it distracted him and grateful because Merritt had the first good news he had heard in a week, except of course for Anne Singer's announcement about her husband.

The Keith Merritt who burst into his office was a totally different person from the pathetic, heavy-drinking figure who had poured out his troubles to Frost the previous Thursday night.

"Reuben, we're saved!" he all but shouted as he came toward Frost's desk. Frost motioned him to a seat, but he was too excited to sit down. "We're in the clear on Maxwell Industries," he said.

"Wonderful, Keith. What happened?" Frost asked.

"You remember the engineer's memo I told you about the other night?"

"Of course."

"Well, the IRS has been investigating the matter up and down. They've talked to the jerk who wrote it, looked at all the engineering data and the operating logs, and concluded that he simply didn't know what he was talking about when he wrote that the Maxwell foundry was ready to go. So they've agreed that the facts Maxwell presented to us were correct—and therefore our opinion was correct."

Frost rose and shook Merritt's hand. "Keith, that's splendid, absolutely splendid. So Global Leasing gets its tax break, Maxwell doesn't have to pay an indemnity, and thirty-six heads at Chase & Ward can sleep soundly at night once again. Along with the members of the Lloyds' syndicate insuring Chase & Ward. Right?"

"Absolutely right, Reuben. Absolutely." The two men grinned at each other.

"I'm very glad. I was afraid a big judgment would wipe out Chase & Ward's ability to make my retirement payments."

"Oh no, Reuben. That would never happen."

"Hmm. I'd hate to count on them, if the partners had to cough up for your incompetence." The two men grinned again.

"Yours is the second bit of good news, for a change," Frost said.

"What else?" Merritt asked.

"Roger Singer has been found. He's sitting around Venice somewhere, 'resting' from all the tension he's been under."

"How do you know? Did he call?"

"No, he called Anne yesterday."

"Well, thank God. But that still doesn't solve Problem Number One, does it?"

"No, I'm afraid not," Frost said.

"Anything new?" Merritt asked.

"Nope," Frost answered, running it through mentally. "You're still a suspect."

Merritt smiled weakly, his exuberance now deflated.

"But something is bound to happen soon," Frost added. "I hope."

Frost's wish for a new development was rapidly fulfilled. No sooner had Merritt left his office than Perry Griffith—a much chastened Perry Griffith—appeared.

"Reuben, I want to apologize for getting so angry

yesterday," he said. "But I'm afraid all the pressures and feelings about Graham and his death just got the better of me."

"I understand," Frost replied. "Don't worry about it."

"Do you remember what you asked me last week, when you told me about Graham?"

"What?"

" 'Keep your eyes and ears open,' you said."

"That's right. And do I take it you have something to report?" Frost was excited. His hunch had been that the ambitious young Griffith would move heaven and earth to finger a suspect other than himself. Was it now going to prove correct?

"I'm not certain, Reuben. But I think you should talk to Michael Phelan."

"Phelan?"

"Yes. He's an associate who's been around a couple of years now and most recently worked for Graham," Griffith answered.

Phelan, Phelan . . . After some thought, Frost recalled him—a bespectacled, freckle-faced fellow who appeared to be a cross between Ichabod Crane and Alfred E. Newman. But he had been assured by several colleagues that the packaging was deceiving; Phelan was in fact super-bright and had been first in his class at Columbia Law School.

"I remember now," Frost said. "What about him?"

"Well, as you probably know, Donovan was working with Dwight Draper on taking his company public. Everything was all set, I understand—the registration statement for a stock offering was going to be filed with the SEC this week, and Drake, Monroe was going to head the underwriters. Then a snag developed. But I'll let Phelan tell you about it."

"I'll call him in. Do you want to stay?"

"No. He'd better talk to you alone. But don't say I didn't keep my ears open."

Frost called Phelan immediately, and within not more

than a minute, the tall, gawky associate was in Frost's office, peering through his Coke-bottle glasses.

"Sit down, Phelan. I understand you were working on the Draper public offering with Graham Donovan?"

"That's right, sir."

"And you were about to file?"

"Yes, sir. We were scheduled to file with the Securities and Exchange Commission today, in fact," Phelan answered.

"So what happened?"

"Well, sir, Mr. Donovan sent me out to the Draper plant early last week to do 'due diligence.' I was supposed to read the minute books, read all of Draper's material contracts, et cetera, to make sure everything was disclosed properly in the registration statement."

Phelan was clearly the product of a Catholic school, Frost thought. He had that precise way of speaking associated with Irish monsignors, the underlying urban accent smoothed out, but not completely. And he was didactically explaining to Frost, who had been practising law for fifty years, what a "due diligence" search was!

"So I take it you found something?" Frost asked.

"Yes, sir, I did. Draper Chemicals has a long-term loan agreement with Freedom Mutual Insurance which contains a negative pledge. Under the negative pledge, Draper Chemicals has promised not to mortgage any of its property to anyone else—"

"Mr. Phelan, I am quite aware of what a negative pledge is. Please go on," Frost said with some impatience.

"Sorry, sir. Well, anyway, I later found a credit agreement with Multibank under which Draper had pledged all its accounts receivable as security."

"And this agreement was after the Freedom Mutual agreement?"

"Yes, sir."

"And Freedom Mutual never gave its consent to the Multibank agreement?"

"Not that I could find. And nobody in the treasurer's office over there knew of any consent either."

"When did you tell Graham about this?"

"As soon as I found it, sir. I knew it looked pretty serious, so I told him right away," Phelan said.

"But when, precisely?"

Phelan took a pocket calendar from his pocket and examined it. "The week before last, sir. I think on Thursday, September seventh."

"And what did Donovan do? Did he confront Draper with what you found?"

"Oh yes indeed, sir. Mr. Draper had been in the office a lot getting the registration statement ready. He and Mr. Donovan worked on it almost every day that week. But he wasn't due in that Friday. Mr. Donovan insisted that he come in anyway."

"This was Friday, September eighth?"

"Yes, that's right."

"Were you present when they talked?" Frost asked.

"No. Mr. Donovan felt he should see Draper alone. But I heard about it afterwards," Phelan said, grinning. "Mr. Donovan said there were real fireworks."

"So it was true? Draper Chemicals was in violation of its Freedom Mutual agreement?"

"I don't know that for sure. All Mr. Donovan said to me was that Mr. Draper was fit to be tied and the offering was going to be postponed. He also said I'd done a good job."

"Michael, I would agree. That's what due diligence is all about—trying to find out the truth, no matter how different it is from what people tell you or how inconvenient it is to face. So the offering has been withdrawn?"

"Yes. Mr. Draper came in to see Mr. Donovan again Monday—"

"Are you sure of that?" Frost interrupted.

"Yes. At least Mr. Donovan told me so . . ."

"Monday the eleventh?"

"Yes."

"What time?"

"Right after lunch, I think. Miss Appleby called me about two o'clock to find out where Mr. Donovan was. She said that Mr. Draper was waiting in the office. Mr. Donovan told me later that Mr. Draper had been in and

tried to talk him into letting the offering go forward.
Again he had gotten very angry, or so Mr. Donovan
said. Mr. Donovan said it was an awful mess and he
hadn't decided who he would have to tell if Mr. Draper
didn't straighten things out himself. It is a Federal crime,
you know, to give false information when you apply for
credit from a bank.''

"Mr. Phelan, I have the feeling you keep forgetting
that I, too, am a lawyer.''

"Sorry, sir.''

"Were we counsel for Draper Chemicals on either of
the loan transactions, by the way?'' Frost asked.

"Yes, we represented the company in the Freedom
deal. But the Multibank transaction was done entirely
in-house,'' Phelan said.

"How did you know the offering was called off?''

"Mr. Donovan sent me a note to that effect Tuesday
morning. The day he died.''

"Phelan—Michael—thank you very much for this
information.''

"No problem, sir,'' the young man replied, oblivious
to the unpinned hand grenade he had lobbed onto Frost's
desk.

"Oh, and Phelan, would you send me a copy of the
latest proof of the Draper registration statement?''

After Phelan had gone, Frost decided that he should
double-check the information about Draper Chemicals.
Not that he doubted Phelan, but with homicide the issue, Frost wanted to be absolutely sure of his footing as
he proceeded. But after checking his mental Rolodex, he
sadly realized that his contacts at both Freedom Mutual
and Multibank were rusty and somewhat out-of-date; all
the names he could recall were of those who had retired
or died. Bannard will surely know people to call, he
thought, as he got up and headed toward Bannard's
office. It's about time he did something useful anyway,
Frost thought.

Frost explained the new developments to Bannard. At
once Bannard placed calls on a highly confidential basis

to a Freedom Mutual staff lawyer he had worked with on several financings and to a college classmate who was a senior vice president of Multibank. Within the hour they had both called back with the expected answers: Freedm Mutual was unaware of any secured bank financing, and Multibank was unaware of the existence of an outstanding negative pledge binding on Draper Chemicals.

Meanwhile the Draper registration statement arrived from Phelan in the intraoffice distribution. The printed proof did indeed appear to Frost to be almost ready to file. He started to read it through but stopped in mid-sentence, frozen, when he got to the following passage in the description of the company's business: "Among other products manufactured by the Pharmaceutical Division of the Company are: Validon, a cortisone-based salve used to treat various skin conditions; Pernon, a digitalis-based liquid used . . ."

Frost did not even bother to finish the sentence. He rushed next door to the conference room where Bautista was working and told him he had to see him at once. Somewhat to his embarrassment, he found the policeman questioning Arthur Tyson. By the looks on their faces, it was not a happy meeting.

"I'm just finishing up here, Mr. Frost, I'll be with you in a minute," Bautista said. Tyson looked startled, then angry. Frost quickly shut the door and returned to his office.

Bautista came into Frost's office with a look of relief, presumably from being free of Arthur Tyson. Frost related the new information about Draper and his company. Bautista, sensing that they might be about to have a break, took meticulous notes. When Frost had finished, Bautista flipped back through his notebook.

"Mr. Frost, didn't you tell me that the lab said the poison that killed the deceased had a life of up to twenty-four hours? That it could have been put in his drinking water up to twenty-four hours before he died?"

"Yes, I did. But we decided it was put there the same morning when Donovan died," Frost said.

"And we did so because . . ."

"Because the maintenance man refills the partners' water carafes every night," Frost said.

"And we know that because . . . ?" Bautista asked.

"Because the maintenance man told me so," Frost answered.

"In other words, we have the hottest lead so far, except for the one detail about refilling the water carafes."

"That's the way I see it."

"Tell me again about the maintenance man," Bautista said.

"Well, as I told you, he's very young. Hispanic. Named Carlos, as I recall," Frost said. Once again he saw no reason to bring up the "Faghater" remark. "He told me that the last thing he does before leaving every night is refill the water carafes. And he assured me he had done so the night before Donovan died."

"I think I'd better have a word with Don Carlos," Bautista said. "Do you know how to reach maintenance?"

Frost did not, but through his secretary's efforts he was shortly connected to the basement headquarters of the cleaning contractor responsible for the building. After much checking around, this office reported that one Carlos Garcia was going to be working that night but that he was not due in until three-thirty. Frost relayed this information to Bautista.

"That's all right. I'll go back to what I was doing, except for seeing Mr. Tyson. No help there, but I got another good lecture about police meddling and so forth. Your guys are pretty good at beating up on cops," Bautista said. "Have them send Mr. Garcia up here as soon as he comes in," he added.

"Sure."

"And can I see this registration statement for Draper Chemicals?" Bautista asked. "If Garcia changes his story—and I bet you he will—I have an idea that I may be visiting their plant real soon."

Frost handed the proof to Bautista, who went back into the adjoining room.

*   *   *

Carlos Garcia appeared at Frost's door about twenty minutes before four. Frost's secretary had apparently stepped away, so the youth came directly into the office where his earlier questioning had taken place.

"You Frost?" he asked.

"That's right."

"The boss says I got to see you."

"That's also right."

"What for?"

Bautista entered the office.

"Mr. Garcia—it is Garcia, is it not?" Frost asked.

"Yeah. So what?"

"Mr. Garcia, this is Detective Bautista of the Police Department."

"A cop! What the hell do you want with me?" Garcia yelled.

"Calm down, amigo," Bautista said. "You're not in any trouble. We just need a couple of fast answers. Will you come with me?"

"Where? I ain't going nowhere!"

"Look, amigo, I told you you're not in any trouble with me. Just step next door so I can ask you a couple of questions in private," Bautista said.

The pair left, and Bautista shut the door to the conference room. Frost waited at his desk. He heard voices being raised, loud enough for him to hear that Spanish was being spoken. Then the door opened and Bautista shook hands with Garcia, who then left.

"Well, Mr. Frost," Bautista said, grinning, "you only got part of the story. Our friend, my amigo Garcia, did indeed work last Monday night. However, he's been having some girl trouble and he left a little early—"

"—before changing the water in the carafes," Frost interjected.

"Exactly right. He lied to you because he was scared for his job. But I think I've got the truth now, and it sure makes your friend Draper a hot prospect."

"So what do we do now?"

"Let me make a call, and then I'll tell you."

Bautista went back into the conference room, returning about five minutes later.

"I've got a buddy who's an investigator for the Food and Drug Administration. He owes me a professional favor—a big favor, in fact—and it turns out he happens to be free tomorrow. So I think the two of us just may do some scouting at Draper Chemicals. Very discreet-like. I'll let you know what we turn up, if anything."

"I'll be waiting," Frost said. "Believe me, I'll be waiting."

AN EVENING AT HOME

AS WAS THEIR CUSTOM WHEN EATING AT HOME, CYNTHIA AND Reuben Frost sat in their living room having a preprandial drink. Cynthia kept getting up to look in on dinner; the Frosts did not have a cook. They had tried various expedients over the years—haughty cooks with impeccable credentials, part-time music and dance students who cooked in exchange for board. Nothing had worked out.

The fact was the Frosts enjoyed eating out, and on many evenings were compelled to, not because of Reuben's life but because of Cynthia's. Art openings, plays (on, off and far off Broadway), and of course the ballet, often meant late suppers in a handful of favorite spots ranging from the celebrity camaraderie of Elaine's and the quieter elegance of the Four Seasons to some all-American hamburger spots, with a select list of *haute* Italian, Japanese, and occasional French, Mexican, or Chinese restaurants in between.

Reuben always believed that Cynthia secretly enjoyed cooking for the two of them. It certainly proved her status as super-woman and, if she disliked preparing the occasional meal at home, she certainly did not show it. (In fact she did quite enjoy it, as long as it didn't happen too often.)

This particular Tuesday Reuben was fairly bursting with the news about the day's developments in the Donovan matter. But he had long ago learned—as some of his Chase & Ward colleagues never had—that listening as well as talking was an essential part of marital discourse. Besides, leaving the best for last would add a nice element of surprise.

Cynthia's news was of a grant the Brigham Foundation was making to a Harlem art group for expanded afterschool activities. Impressed with the organizers, whose enthusiasm made up for a great deal of naiveté and lack of practical business sense, she had helped them develop their grant proposal and had gently, but firmly, made them put it on a businesslike basis. The Foundation's trustees had approved the grant that afternoon, with a minimum of the carping that could have been expected from some quarters of the board because of the past failures of a few community-based programs the Foundation had backed.

"I really think this one is going to work, Reuben," she told her husband. "If the people running it are rip-off artists or incompetents, I will be very surprised."

"Well, with all the accountants and lawyers you've brought into the thing, it ought to be fiscally responsible, anyway."

"*One* lawyer and *one* accountant," she said. "And how was your day?"

"Very interesting."

"Keep talking, I've just got to check the stove."

"I think weve cracked the Donovan case."

"Oh good God, wait till I get back!" came the cry from the kitchen. Instead, Reuben went into the kitchen and began his narrative of the day's events, opening a bottle of wine as he did so.

Reuben continued the story over dinner, with an occasional question from his wife.

"Do I know Draper?" she asked.

"Probably not. He's been craving WASP respectability for years, and now he's got a new blonde-bombshell wife who I suspect craves it even more. They've been at a couple of charity things we've been at, but I don't think you've ever met them. Come to think of it, they've been at quite a few functions recently. But for this little hitch, I suspect it would not have been long before new wifey had a press agent and the Drapers made their big move from New Jersey to New York high society."

"Why is it always a new wife that starts the social ball rolling?"

"Because the first wife had chapped hands from taking in washing, I suppose," Reuben answered. "Besides, think of all the worthy organizations in this city—many of your favorites, by the way—that depend on parvenu money."

"You mean like Su—"

"No names, Cynthia. Heaven knows when you may be imploring her to support one of your worthy causes."

"Support for the arts is a very democratic thing, dear," she answered. "But anyway, how certain do you think it is that Draper is the murderer?"

"I think my policeman friend, Luis, is pretty convinced, and so am I," Reuben said. "Thank God he's Hispanic, by the way. His conversation in Spanish with Carlos Faghater was pretty hot and heavy, but it got results."

"So you should know tomorrow?"

"That depends on what Luis finds out at the plant. But I think the case is as good as closed." Being able to make that statement, and the wine he had consumed (from a good bottle, selected to celebrate the occasion), made him feel very content.

"What does George Bannard think?"

"I haven't told him."

"Oh, Reuben, you really are naughty."

"Well, he was gone for the day by the time Bautista and I had sorted it out," Frost said defensively. "Besides, his behavior in this whole thing has been a little exasperating. He wants to know about everything but is always running off to Chicago or to a board meeting or whatever despite everything that's going on."

"Well, you'd better tell him tomorrow morning."

"Maybe. But I think I'll wait till Luis gets back from New Jersey."

"He's your former partner, dear. Surely he's entitled to full disclosure, as you lawyers say."

Cynthia had started to clear the table when the buzzer at the front door sounded. Frost went to the intercom and found out that Arthur Tyson was outside.

"What on earth do you suppose he wants, arriving unannounced at this hour?" Frost asked his wife.

"Maybe he wants to confess," Cynthia said.

"Very funny," Frost shot back as he went downstairs to admit his visitor. "Unless this is some sort of batty social visit, which I doubt, I'll talk to him in the library."

"Good evening, Arthur," Frost said, after unlocking the front door. "Come on in."

"Frost, what I've got to say won't take long and I can say it right here."

As he spat out that one sentence, Tyson showed all of his less pleasant qualities—bullying aggressiveness, a splenetic temper and general rudeness. Frost had seen him in fits of temper before, but never had encountered the livid anger now on display before him. It was as if Tyson were again facing down a Big Ten lineman on a crucial play.

"Oh come, Arthur, let's not stand here. Come on up to the library."

Frost led the way up the stairs to the second floor.

"How about a drink?"

"I don't want a drink, you snaky son of a bitch, I want an apology!" Tyson shouted.

Frost was not used to being called a son of a bitch, most especially by a Chase & Ward partner more than fifteen years his junior.

"Arthur, please calm down. You're not making sense," Frost said. "And sit down, as well."

Tyson did so but continued his tirade. "Maybe I'm not making sense, but nobody else is either. First that sniveling drunk Coxe, giggling about how I was suspected of murdering Graham Donovan. And then you, you doddering old fool, playing Dr. Watson to that spic cop.

"All I want to know," Tyson went on, bounding out of his chair, "is why in the name of heaven you gave him my name! Who do you think you are, playing private dick, whispering ideas into that thick cop's head? You're a damned senile Iago!"

Not Siegfried and Benno after all, Frost thought, but Othello and Iago. He was amused but dared not show it. In fact, Tyson was also making him extremely nervous. Frost put his hands out flat and moved them in a calming gesture, but this only infuriated Tyson more.

"All I can say, Reuben, is that I'm not going to put up with it! I'll sue you for slander! I'll have a guardian appointed, since you're clearly senile. How could you do it? How could you possibly tell that dumb cop to interrogate me?"

"Arthur, Arthur, Arthur. This past week has been hell for all of us. Especially for those of us who were Graham's friends," Frost said, regretting at once the implication that Tyson was not. But Tyson was too angry to notice the slight. "I've been cooperating, everybody's been cooperating with the police, trying to get this awful thing solved. Nobody's been running around accusing you, except you yourself. First your behavior at the morgue, which the police knew about quite independent of me, despite the unfortunate joke I made to you about being a suspect. And then your attack on poor defenseless Fred Coxe. Yes, I did tell Detective Bautista about that, but I did it in a context in which I explained that you had a terrible temper which, judging by this little séance, is undeniable. All I can say is that you were better off having me tell him than having him hear the story, at about fourth-hand and luridly embellished, later on."

"Attack, you said," Tyson screamed. "What I said to Fred Coxe was an attack? No, it wasn't! *This* is an attack!" Before Frost could stop him, Tyson had grabbed a vase of flowers from the table beside him and flung it as hard as he could with both hands at Frost's feet. "*That* was an attack! Not like your assault on my character, but still an attack!"

Frost was horrified and frightened. The vase had broken and splashed water on the cuffs of his pants. How was he to get rid of this raving madman before he did further damage to the room—or to Frost?

"Arthur, you've made your point," Frost said, as slowly and as calmly as he could. "And I've made mine. So I suggest we call it a night and that you leave now. Right now."

Tyson was almost gasping for breath, and he seemed to wither under the coldest and most intense gaze Frost could muster under the circumstances.

"All right. That's fine with me. I'll go out. And you can go to hell." His face distorted once again, Tyson abruptly turned and ran down the stairs and out the door.

Frost sat down in a chair, physically and emotionally exhausted and still frightened.

"And what was that all about?" Cynthia asked, as she came into the library.

"Oh, just a courtesy call on a poor old retired Executive Partner—by one of his potential successors," Frost answered. "Help me upstairs, dear, and I'll tell you."

21

REUBEN FROST WAS GRATEFUL ON WEDNESDAY MORNING THAT he had a new drafting project to occupy his time. He wanted to concentrate on the present, forget the unpleasantness with Tyson the night before and avoid speculating on what Bautista was finding in New Jersey. And, if he were lucky, he could plead (however unconvincingly) that he had been too busy that morning to bring George Bannard up to date.

The previous day an old curmudgeon client of the firm, Earle Ambler, had sent him for review a contract for the acquisition of a television station prepared by an in-house lawyer at Ambler's company, named, aptly enough, Ambler Broadcasting Corporation.

Ambler, an old friend of Cynthia's who had gotten his communications industry start practically in the days of the nickelodeon, had years ago become eminently successful as a chain broadcaster, owning television and radio stations in unlikely cities around the country. Ambler had modestly, and with a knowing sense of humor, always referred to his company as "ABC." It wasn't, but over the years Ambler's stations in out-of-the-way places had appreciated in value so that "ABC" was a very profitable enterprise.

Since the earliest days, when Ambler first had come to Chase & Ward at Cynthia's suggestion, Frost had been Ambler Broadcasting's lawyer. Now that it was a settled enterprise, the company had a legal staff of its own, but Earle Ambler still insisted, when more than $3.98 was at stake, that Chase & Ward be involved. And he had further insisted, even after Frost's retirement, that Frost personally handle the business.

In busy times gone by, Ambler's insistence on Frost's personal attention had been a great pain in the neck, and it flew in the face of Chase & Ward's boast that its partners, if not completely fungible, still had a wide enough dispersal of legal skills that no client had to depend—or should be permitted to depend—on one partner. But in his late years as a partner and since his retirement, Frost had no longer been annoyed by Ambler's insistence on personal attention but had instead relished it.

Earle Ambler was a great one for attempting to "up-grade" his provincial empire, so he bought and sold stations as rapidly as was permitted within the confines of the Federal Communications Commission's strictures against "trafficking in licenses."

From the tone of Ambler's letter that morning, Frost gathered that the old man was dissatisfied with the con-tract for the purchase of a television station forwarded with the letter. Reviewing it now, Frost realized that Ambler had been quite right. Sitting at his glass-covered worktable, Frost groaned audibly as he read. The inex-perienced young Ambler lawyer had committed one of the drafting sins Frost loathed: the use of totally extra-neous *whereases, saids* and other "snake-oil" words, as Frost called them, designed to make perfectly straight-forward English sentences appear "legal." But what was worse, the author had based his draft on an earlier agreement that apparently had dealt with acquiring some-thing other than a broadcasting station, since there were none of the clauses Frost knew were necessary when a station was being bought—representations as to the sta-tus of the station's Federal Communications Commis-sion licenses, for example.

Ah, the use—or rather misuse—of precedent, Frost thought. He conceded to himself that every lawyer, good, bad or indifferent, uses a precedent for drafting almost any kind of agreement. But why, why, do mediocre lawyers invariably select a bad model, a precedent that is clumsily written or imprecise or wordy or, more likely, all of the above? And why, if the subject matter of the transaction is a broadcasting station, use a contract for the sale of a shoe store—or whatever—as a model?

Frost had a stack of sharpened number two pencils beside him. He wielded them like scalpels as he cut away at the hapless draftsman's legal prose, attempting to perform surgery that would make the proposed contract viable.

But even though he thoroughly enjoyed drafting, and took great satisfaction in improving the legal writing of others, he still was not able to concentrate fully on the work before him. Graham Donovan's unsolved murder was like very loud music in the background; it could not be ignored, it would not go away and it impinged on everything else that was going on.

By early afternoon—Frost ate a sandwich at his desk (the better to avoid Bannard, who had not called)—Frost had resuscitated the Ambler contract and sent it for recovery to the office word processing center. Bautista barged into the office just as Frost was tossing the heavily edited—or more properly, redrafted—contract into his outbox.

"Sit down, Reuben," Bautista said, in his excitement dropping the formal "Mr. Frost" for the first time. "You won't believe our luck. It turns out my buddy knows the Draper plant well; it's on his regular beat. So we went to see a guy there he deals with a lot—the production supervisor, name of Barlow. Well, it turns out—and this is hard to believe—that Barlow recently had a fight with Draper personally. Over this stock deal, in fact. It seems that old Barlow got wind of the stock offering and that Draper and some of the officers who owned stock in the company were about to make a bundle. Barlow never had been given stock, and didn't know that others had until that registration statement you showed me, which lists the major stockholders, got circulated around the plant.

"Barlow was one mad guy," Bautista went on. "And apparently Draper was not too sympathetic when Barlow confronted him. So anyway, Barlow was ticked off as hell and was ready to tell us anything we wanted to know about Mr. Chairman of the Board. Apparently Draper had been filching painkillers from the plant for years, which not even the Chairman of the Board is supposed to do when controlled substances are involved. Then my pal asked if it was only painkillers, and old Barlow said well, as a matter of fact, no. Only a week ago, Draper had asked for a small supply of the digitalis derivative used to make pernon!

"So there you are, Reuben. I think we've got our man," Bautista concluded triumphantly.

"I'll be damned. The conniving bastard. When will you arrest him?"

"That's up to you. Since he lives in Jersey and the plant's in Jersey, we could go through the rigmarole required for an interstate arrest. Or—"

"Or?"

"We could invite him to New York and arrest him here. Maybe not the most kosher way to do it, but I thought you might like to be in on it. Am I right, Reuben?"

"Yes, I suppose you are," Frost said slowly. "In fact I know you are. But there's one little hitch, I'm afraid. There's no way I can lure Draper to this office; I've never had any dealings with him, and I'm just an old retired crock as far as he's concerned."

"So what do we do?" Bautista asked.

"The only person who can lure him here is George Bannard. To discuss the future of his representation by Chase & Ward."

"You sure, Reuben?"

"Absolutely. But that's all right. It's high time George Bannard did some of the heavy work in this case."

Within minutes Luis Bautista and Reuben Frost—Pat O'Brien and an unnamed actor, Siegfried and Benno, Sherlock Holmes and Dr. Watson, Othello and Iago—

were explaining the new developments to a startled George Bannard.

"What do we do now?" Bannard asked, after he had been fully briefed.

"George, Mr. Bautista has told you it would be neater and cleaner to have Draper arrested here in New York. And you're the only one who can get him here."

"How do you mean?" Bannard said.

"Well, you're the Executive Partner, so you can perfectly well call him in to discuss who's going to replace Graham as his contact here at the firm."

Bannard looked distressed, but he saw the logic of what Frost was saying.

"So what should I do? Call him?" Bannard said, looking at his watch. "It's a little late to try and get him in here today."

"That's all right, Mr. Bannard," Bautista said. "I think tomorrow morning would be fine. That way I can have some support troops here if things get sticky."

Bannard winced. "Tomorrow is awfully inconvenient . . . but I suppose I can shuffle some appointments if necessary. What time did you have in mind?"

"Ten o'clock okay?" Bautista asked.

"Sure," Bannard said, "though he may think he's important enough to discuss his business over lunch."

"Let's try for ten."

Bannard, still showing some reluctance, asked Mrs. Davis to put a call through to Draper. The call was made and Dwight Draper said he would be happy to see Bannard at ten the following morning. "As I said at Graham's funeral, we should get things squared away now that Graham is dead," Draper told Bannard. Indeed, Bannard thought. He told Bautista the meeting was set.

"So when should I be here?" Bannard asked.

"A little before ten is fine," Bautista said. "I'll be here with a couple of helpers around nine-thirty. Do you suppose we could use the office next door? I'd like to have them nearby in case there are any fireworks."

Bannard winced again but immediately called Fred Coxe, asking him if his office might be free early the next day. Coxe said that he would be uptown at a meeting and Bannard was welcome to it, so no explanation of the impending maneuvers was required.

"Officer, you'll be here with me, of course, tomorrow morning?" Bannard said in a hoarse, nervous voice.

"Yes, sir. I'll be right at your side or, if necessary, in front of you," Bautista replied, reassuring Bannard not at all.

Bautista and Frost could scarcely contain their exuberant relief as they left Bannard's office.

"I'm sorry you're going to miss the climax," Bautista said, as they went down the hall.

"Well, if there are going to be fireworks, I think it's just as well for an old man," Frost replied.

"You know, Reuben, unless your Executive Partner screws up, I think we've done it," Bautista said.

"Luis, I think you're right."

Smiling, the aging lawyer and the young detective locked in an affectionate Latin *abrazo*.

22

LUIS BAUTISTA WAS BACK AT CHASE & WARD THURSDAY morning at nine-thirty, this time accompanied by two other plainclothes officers, one a black woman. They first went to Frost's office and then, at his direction, to Bannard's office. Bannard, in accordance with instructions, was waiting for them, and perfunctorily acknowledged Bautista's introduction of Sergeant Imperatore and Officer Rush. ("Where are the sons of Erin?" Bannard thought to himself, as his stereotype of the police force was again deflated.) It was agreed that all three would wait next door until Bannard signalled for Bautista to come in and begin the questioning of Draper. Bannard was decidedly nervous, but Bautista tried to reassure him.

"Don't worry, Mr. Bannard," he said. "Officer Rush is the women's judo champion of the Department. And Sergeant Imperatore used to be a sharpshooter with the Tactical Patrol. Whatever happens, we'll be here to help you."

"I appreciate that, Officer," Bannard said glumly. 'I'm sure there will be no problem."

(And if there is, Bautista thought to himself, and assuming you're still alive, you can always call the Mayor.)

Bannard barely had time to finish a cup of coffee before Draper arrived, promptly at ten.

"Good morning, George, how are you?" Draper said

as he advanced across Bannard's office, hand out-stretched. "Thanks for calling me so promptly, but we need to get a new lawyer assigned to the Draper account. It may not be the biggest at Chase & Ward, but we do pay our bills on time." Draper laughed at his own joke and took out a cigar and lit it. Bannard, as a reformed smoker, suffered in silence.

"What about this young Phelan?" Draper went on. "I liked him and would be happy to have him doing my work. He's a good kid. You ought to make him a partner."

"He's a little young for that, Dwight," Bannard replied. From Draper's comments, it was clear he didn't know much about selecting a lawyer. The late Graham Donovan and Mike Phelan, two years out of Columbia Law School, simply were not comparable. Was Draper really too unsophisticated to know the difference? Or did he want someone naive and inexperienced, but with the protection of being able to say he had relied on Chase & Ward, his general counsel? In view of recent developments, the latter view was probably correct. But didn't Draper realize that "young Phelan" was the one who had uncovered Draper's deception of his lenders?

"He worked with you on your proposed public offering, did he not?" Bannard said.

"That's right. And he did a very fine job. Very good boy, Phelan."

"What's the status of your offering, Dwight?"

"Oh, we've decided to put it off. The underwriters say the market isn't right. I wanted to go ahead, but the underwriters said wait to get a better price, so I have. We'll probably go next month," Draper said.

Confronted with this bald lie, Bannard decided to proceed with the business at hand and surreptitiously pushed the call buzzer on his telephone.

"Dwight, I'm afraid I didn't get you over here to discuss your future relationship with Chase & Ward," Bannard said gravely. Draper looked puzzled and took a long drag on his cigar, but remained silent. "This is Detective Luis Bautista of the New York City Police

Department, who has a few questions for you," Bannard explained, nodding toward Bautista, who had entered the room and stood beside Draper.

"Good morning, Mr. Draper," Bautista said, without shaking hands.

"What is this, George? Some kind of joke?" Draper said, looking from one to the other. "I come over here to discuss my legal business and all of a sudden I'm talking to a policeman. What's going on?" Draper started to rise in his chair, as if to leave because the joke was not to his liking. Bautista did not physically restrain him, but moved his six-foot frame in front of Draper's chair.

"Mr. Draper, as Mr. Bannard says, I have some questions to ask you. You are perfectly free not to respond and I want to warn you that you have certain rights."

Bautista flipped a celluloid-covered card from his pocket. One of the "Directions to Police Officer" contained on its reverse side was an instruction that the card was to be read to any person subject to "custodial interrogation," meaning questioning after a person "has been taken into custody, or otherwise deprived of his freedom of action in any significant way." Bautista conservatively judged that moving his impressively developed, muscular body in front of Draper, who was now sitting back and looking nervous, might fit the "significant way" category, and began reading to Draper the prescribed ritual—not the centuries-old responses to the priest's Latin Bautista remembered mumbling from an embossed card in his days as an altar boy, but a secular ritual derived from a generation of Supreme Court decisions.

"Mr. Draper, you have the right to remain silent and to refuse to answer my questions," Bautista read. "Do you understand?"

"Understand? No, I'm afraid I don't understand," Draper said, attempting to remain calm. "As I said, I came here to discuss private legal business, and instead I have a policeman reading me my constitutional rights. I don't understand at all!"

"Let me continue, Mr. Draper. Anything you do say may be used against you in a court of law. Do you understand?"

Draper was silent.

"Do you understand, Mr. Draper?"

"Really, Officer, this is very silly. Won't you please stop reading from that card and tell me what it is you want?"

Unperturbed, Bautista continued the ritual. "You have the right to consult an attorney before speaking to me and to have an attorney present during any questioning now or in the future. Do you understand?"

"Officer, if I may say so, my attorney is sitting right next to you. Won't you—or can't you—understand that?" Draper attempted to put ice in his voice, but there was a slight tremor that damaged the effect.

Bannard, cowed by the whole proceeding, thought of speaking up and pointing out that Chase & Ward's loyalties were to Draper Chemicals, not to the very nervous individual before him. But this was perhaps not the time to deal in niceties.

"If you cannot afford an attorney," Bautista plodded on, following the letter of his *Miranda* warning card, "one will be provided for you without cost."

"That would be cheaper than Chase & Ward," Draper said. "But let's cut the comedy. If you won't let me out of here, at least let's get to the point."

"If you do not have an attorney available," Bautista continued—this guy was not going to get off because he had not been advised of his constitutional right not to incriminate himself—"you have the right to remain silent until you have had an opportunity to consult with one. Do you understand?"

"Officer, I really am going to stop answering these ridiculous questions," Draper said.

"Now that I have advised you of your rights, are you willing to answer questions?" Bautista persisted.

"I have said so about five times, I believe," Draper replied.

"Good. Now that we've had the preliminaries, it's

time to dance. Dwight Draper, I'm putting you under arrest—''

"Arrest! What the hell are you talking about? You are loco, boy, straight, raving loco!" Draper said, his icy politeness now giving way to hostile anger.

"Let me explain, Mr. Draper. Then you can say whatever you want to say," Bautista said evenly and calmly. "I am going to arrest you for the murder of your lawyer, Graham Donovan—''

"Loco! Loco!" Draper shouted.

"May I go on? On Friday afternoon, September eighth, Mr. Draper, you and Graham Donovan had a quarrel in his office over whether or not you had committed fraud in your dealings with the lenders to your company. You returned to the Draper Chemicals plant in New Jersey, where you obtained from John Barlow, the production supervisor, a quantity of a highly poisonous digitalis derivative used by your company in making the drug Pernon."

Draper and Bannard were utterly silent as Bautista spun out his narrative.

"Three days later, on Monday, September eleventh, you made an appointment to see Graham Donovan again, at two P.M. You arrived at one-thirty, confident that Donovan would be at lunch but that you were well enough known that you would be allowed to wait in his office. That's what happened, and while you were waiting, you poisoned the water in Donovan's water carafe.

"Do you want to hear more, Mr. Draper?" Bautista said. Draper, who had slumped in his chair and let his cigar go out, was silent.

"You thought you were safe. You had been present in Donovan's office several times in the last month working with him on your company's registration statement. You knew his daily habits—when he went to lunch, for example, and the peculiar morning routine with his iced tea. You knew that he would use the poisoned water from his carafe the next day, when you were safe back in New Jersey. You knew that he wouldn't detect the slightly bitter taste of the poison in his iced tea. And you further knew that the poison would have a delayed reaction, reducing the likelihood that Donovan would die in the vicinity of the poisoned carafe.

"So that's why I'm arresting you, Mr. Draper," Bautista said quietly. He and Bannard both looked at the sagging figure sitting before them. Draper sat without speaking, as if struck dumb by the ruinous detail of Bautista's narrative. He gripped the arms of the chair he was in and looked straight ahead with a glassy-eyed stare into nothingness. Neither Bautista nor Bannard interrupted the long silence before he spoke.

"I had to do it," Draper finally said, in a strained, unnatural voice. "I had spent my whole life building my company. I never took anything out of it, just enough to live on. I had just one dream ever since engineering school—to have a public company, with its stock listed on the New York Stock Exchange and its management, me, respected in the business community. I wanted more than anything to be perceived as a clever and successful entrepreneur, not just a run-of-the-mill engineer from a second-rate school in Pennsylvania. That was my dream, and that was what I was working to make real."

Draper wiped away a tear and tried to control himself. "Then this thing happened over my loans. I ran into a bad cash squeeze two years ago—just temporary, but I was running out of cash. I knew Freedom Mutual would take forever to approve a new loan, so I went to Multibank and hocked my receivables. It was a new account for them and they didn't ask any questions. It was all a technicality anyway; Freedom would have let me borrow the money if I'd asked them. And I'll be out of the Multibank loan in another couple of months. But Graham, my old friend Graham, was on my back. He said I'd violated some federal law about debtor disclosure, that the public offering had to be postponed, all kinds of things that would have ruined my company and ruined my dream. So I did what I had to do. Yes, I poisoned him. I had to. I couldn't let my dream—my dream of thirty years—fade away over a legal technicality."

Draper covered his eyes as he finished speaking. Soon

his entire body was shaking as he began sobbing—huge, rending sobs like those of a young child. It took several minutes before he was able to go on.

"And there was more, gentlemen. Here I was, after a generation of friendship with a man I thought was my brother, being accused by that man of being a crook. I simply couldn't go on with my life—my nice, respectable life—as long as there was someone out there who thought, who knew, that I had cheated. I'm sorry, George. Sorry about Graham. But sorry also that my whole life's work has gone for nothing."

Draper broke into sobs again. Bautista signalled Bannard, who in turn pressed the telephone buzzer. The two other police officers came in at once.

"Shall we go now, Mr. Draper?" Bautista asked gently.

Draper, still crying, nodded. The two officers with Bautista flanked him and led him toward the door. No handcuffs, just a firm but gentle hand on each arm. Bautista lingered behind.

"I guess that's it, Mr. Bannard," he said.

"I guess so. How can I thank you for what you've done?" Bannard said.

"Not necessary. I was just doing my job. Except you might mention it to the Mayor the next time you see him."

As the posse went down the hall toward the elevators, Bautista lagged behind and went into Reuben Frost's office.

Frost pretended to be fully occupied with the document in front of him. Neither man was fooled by this pretense of concentration.

"Well, Reuben, it's over," Bautista said.

"He confessed?"

"Yes. With lots of tears, but he admitted the whole thing."

"What can I say, Luis?"

"Nothing. You don't need to say nothing," Bautista answered, the emotion of the encounter eroding his usually correct, school-learned grammar. "I'm the one—or

I should say, the Police Department is the one—that should be thanking you."

"Well, Luis, all I can say is that it was an interesting collaboration."

"Yes. Yes, it was."

"Will we meet again?" Frost asked, realizing after he had spoken that he sounded like a mindless ingenue in a dreadful play.

"Who knows? Maybe. The air up here on the fifty-first floor is pretty rarified for me, though. But maybe. We'll see."

"My wife wants to meet you," Frost said. "Perhaps you could come and have dinner?"

"Sure. I'd like that. You've got my private number."

"I'll call you."

"Okay. Take care."

The detective left and Frost's small office seemed doubly empty without his bulk.

Dinner? Why not? Cynthia would be fascinated. But was there a Mrs. Bautista? Or a girlfriend? Children? Frost realized that he really knew next to nothing about his newfound collaborator and friend. But that could be fixed, he said to himself as he sat down at his desk. That could be fixed.

CLEANUP

ONCE DETECTIVE BAUTISTA HAD LEFT, BANNARD CALLED IN Mrs. Davis to tell her what had happened.

"Don't tell anyone else for the moment, Margaret," he said. "I want to make an announcement to the partners at the weekly lunch today. Tell MacMillan's to serve champagne—Dom Perignon, too—at the end of lunch. But no glasses on the table beforehand. It's all to be a surprise. And ask Reuben Frost to come in."

"Reuben!" Bannard called out minutes later when Frost came into his office.

The man actually seems glad to see me, Frost thought to himself.

"Have you heard the news?" Bannard asked.

"Yes. Bautista stopped to tell me on his way out."

"Thank God it's over. I should have suspected Draper all along. I've never liked him."

"I know."

"Well, it was some experience, let me tell you. Who knows what he might have done? He was clearly desperate," Bannard said.

"I'm sure there was enough firepower in and around your office to take care of any emergency," Frost said.

"I don't want anyone to know until firm lunch." Bannard paused for a moment. "By the way, Reuben, could you come to the lunch today? You should certainly tell the firm your part of the story."

"Of course, George, if that's what you want."

"Yes, it is. We've all been through a lot, and I think we all ought to celebrate a bit."

"Fine. But just this once," Frost said, heading off Bannard before he could make a gauche remark to the same effect.

"I suppose we have some loose ends to tie up. One is Grace Appleby. I guess I must call her in and fire her. I want to have that done and over with before our lunch."

"I have a couple of loose ends to tie up, too, George. So I'll see you at lunch."

"Good. And thank you, Reuben. You really have been a great help to me."

"Glad to oblige, George. Any time."

Frost went back to his office, amused at the prospect of returning once more to the partners' lunch. But what would he include in his side of the story? Merritt's dreadful tax dilemma, now solved? Tyson's irrational outburst at Frost's house? He would tell about the latter and not the former, he thought, unless something could be worked out in the meantime.

With that in mind, he took the elevator up two flights and went to Tyson's office. He entered unannounced.

"Reuben. What a surprise!" Tyson said from behind his desk. All traces of the irrational anger displayed less than two days earlier had disappeared.

Uninvited, Frost took a seat. "I thought you ought to know, Arthur, that Dwight Draper has been arrested for Graham's murder."

"My God. Tell me!"

"No, Bannard wants to keep it a surprise and unveil the details at lunch. But I thought you should know that you are no longer a suspect."

"I guess I never really was," Tyson said, laughing nervously.

"That's not how you were acting at my house Tuesday night."

"I guess I was a little hot under the collar."

"Yes. And that's really why I'm here."

"I apologize, if that's what you're after," Tyson said sulkily.

"No, Arthur, I want more than that. I'm now retired and so Chase & Ward doesn't mean much to me financially anymore. But it is the firm where I spent my active life and I don't want to sit by in my old age and watch it fall apart. I love the people here too much."

"I don't follow you."

"Then let me be very explicit. George Bannard retires as the leader of this firm in two years. Graham Donovan, as the senior corporate partner, would by tradition have been his successor. But he is gone. It's also no secret, Arthur, that you would have liked the job, and I assume you still do."

"Oh, I don't know, Reuben. I've thought about it. I won't deny it. But who knows what may happen?" Tyson said.

"That's always true, Arthur. But I'm here to get your assurance that at least one thing won't happen."

"What's that?"

"I want your ironclad assurance that under no circumstances will you become the next Executive Partner of Chase & Ward," Frost said, slowly and deliberately.

"Why should I agree to any such thing?"

"Because, Arthur, you are temperamentally unsuited to run this firm. You've demonstrated that once to my satisfaction in recent days, and, I understand, once again when I was not present. You're a fine lawyer, Arthur, everyone concedes that. But with your temper this place would be torn apart."

"And if I don't give you the assurance you want?"

"I will include in my narrative of recent events, which Bannard has asked me to give at lunch, a meticulous account of your beavior at my house Tuesday night. After which I suspect you might not even be head of the trust and estates department, let alone a candidate for Executive Partner."

Tyson angrily swiveled his desk chair away from Frost. After staring out the window for a moment, he turned back.

"You're a clever old bastard, Reuben. And you certainly give me a lot of choice," Tyson said.

"Does that mean I have your word that you will never accept the Executive Partnership?"

"*Never* is a big word, Reuben."

"I know. And I use it advisedly."

"Then never it is. You meddling bastard."

"Thank you, Arthur. I'll see you at lunch."

Frost was pleased and relieved as he returned to his office. Pleased because he had neutralized Tyson, relieved because he had not had to withstand another torrent of rage. As he came to his office, he asked his secretary to call in Perry Griffith. For the fourth time in a week, Griffith answered the summons.

"Well, Perry, these little sessions are getting to be a habit," Frost said.

"Yes, they are. What is it this time?"

"I just wanted you to know that Dwight Draper was arrested for the murder of Graham Donovan about an hour ago."

"Really? So Phelan was on to something," Griffith said.

Frost laughed. "He was, but I don't think he quite knew what was going on."

Frost recounted the whole story for his associate.

"Needless to say, Perry, I am immensely grateful for your help. You kept your ears open as I asked you to. I thank you."

"Well, Reuben, I'm glad you feel obligated."

Frost frowned slightly. Did Griffith think he could parlay his recent help into a partnership?

"Don't worry, Reuben, I'm not going to cash in in any big way," Griffith said when he saw the look on Frost's face. "Alice has been after me for some time to relocate. She's from California, you know, and she's got a chance to do some very interesting research at Stanford Medical School next year. I'd been fighting the idea until recent events here, thinking I still had a chance at being a partner. But in thinking about it the last few days and talking it over with Alice, I don't think I'd have a chance even if I were personally responsible for Graham's resurrection. The cold fact is Graham didn't like me, and nobody in the firm is going to go against the judgment of their murdered partner."

"I'd have to say I think you're right," Frost said.

"So I'm going to try and get a job at a good firm in San Francisco."

"That should be easy enough," Frost said. "You'll be the smartest lawyer in the whole city."

"I don't know about that. But I'll probably be asking for recommendations to firms out there fairly soon."

"That's easy, Perry. I'm sure things will work out, and we'll do anything we can to help. Keep me posted and let me know what I can do."

While Frost was tying up his loose ends, Bannard talked to Grace Appleby.

"Miss Appleby, I have three things I want to talk to you about," he said after the woman had seated herself in his office.

"First, I'm sure you'll be happy to know that Graham Donovan's killer has been found. Dwight Draper was arrested for the murder earlier this morning."

"Mr. Draper! I can't believe it! He was devoted to Mr. Donovan. They had been friends for years!" Miss Appleby said, clearly surprised at Bannard's announcement.

"That may be, Miss Appleby. But Graham's devotion to the law was greater than his loyalty to Dwight Draper. And Draper, when pushed to the wall, couldn't accept that."

"What do you mean, Mr. Bannard? I don't understand."

Bannard told the Draper tale, in somewhat abbreviated form. Then he turned to another subject.

"Now let me get to my second point. I was wondering if you've come to any decision about your future here?"

"No, no, I can't say that I have, Mr. Bannard," Miss Appleby replied.

"Have you thought about early retirement?" Bannard asked, in a seemingly casual way.

"I would like that, but I'm only fifty-eight and the firm's retirement plan doesn't provide for early retirement until sixty."

"Well, suppose we were to bend the rules in your case, Miss Appleby, and let you take early retirement right away. Would that interest you?"

The woman was silent for a moment. "Yes, I believe it would," she said finally. "It would be very hard for me to start afresh with a new boss at my age. And a cousin of mine has been after me for at least two years now to come and live with her in Arizona. But are you sure this can be done?"

"Miss Appleby, the Pension Plan Committee is an independent group of partners, but I think in view of your service"—he almost said "loyal" service—"they will be willing to waive the age requirement in your case."

"There are only two conditions, Miss Appleby. One I'll get to in a few minutes. The other is that you must promise us that you will never work for another law firm, or any business or financial organization, ever again. Retirement must be full retirement."

"Well, it would be, of course. But what a strange request! What do you mean by it?" Appleby assumed an air of almost girlish perplexity.

"You bring me to my third point, Miss Appleby, which is a very difficult one for me to discuss. You remember the difficulty we had over the Stephens Industries press release a while back?"

"Yes, I remember it very well."

"I think you probably do, Miss Appleby. Since there is every reason to suspect that you were the one who leaked it to Bennett Holbrook & Company."

"Me? Why that's absurd, Mr. Bannard! Why would I do such a thing?"

"For the simple reason that you had sold ten thousand shares of Stephens Industries short, Miss Appleby. To make sure the word got out as soon as possible about Stephens' problems. You thought the leak of the press release would send down the price, so you could cover and take a quick profit."

For the second time that morning, Bannard saw the look of a person defeated. But this time the reaction was that of a cornered animal.

"So you nosy bastards found out, did you?" The girlish visage had disappeared and the woman's face was contorted with hate. "Well, so what? It's very easy to be sanctimonious and pious when you make as much money as you make! If I took home half a million dollars a year, I'd play the market fair and square too. But I took care of a sick father for seven years—kept him at home, paid for his care on my salary. No dumping him in a nursing home for me. *I* paid his bills! Not the State of New York! Not Uncle Sam! *Me!* Fifteen-thousand-dollars-a-year Grace Appleby, loyal legal secretary!

"Well, when he died and I realized I was fifty years old and had no money, no real estate, nothing, I decided it was time for little Grace to come into her own. I took a course in the stock market and began investing what few dollars I had—five thousand dollars from my father's insurance, a couple thousand of my own. I took risks, but I used common sense. I did very well until the downturn a year ago, when everything I had went down, down, down. So I needed a sure thing or two and I found them—the Stephens transaction and two before that that your snoopers presumably haven't figured out yet." The woman stopped speaking, hoarse and out of breath.

"Miss Appleby, I was afraid we'd have a scene like this. Needless to say, your conduct is inexcusable and I would have fired you without any question this morning if you had not elected to retire. But I'm going to stick by my offer of early retirement and strongly suggest you take it."

"You said there were two conditions to my retirement. You told me one. What's the second?" she asked, her calm returning.

"That you donate your profits from the Stephens transaction and the other two you mentioned—which I don't even want to hear about—to that hospital you do work for, St. Blaise's. And I guess there's a third condition too."

"Yes?"

"Be out of here by the close of business today."

LUNCH WITHOUT MURDER

24

RUMORS AT CHASE & WARD OFTEN SPREAD LIKE WILDFIRE.
But Detective Bautista and his fellow officers had apparently been so discreet in removing Dwight Draper that his arrest was not generally known. Thus there was great surprise at the weekly Thursday firm luncheon at MacMillan's when champagne glasses were produced at the end of the fish-in-peanut-oil main course. (A couple of the more astute partners had already figured out that something was up when they saw that Reuben Frost was present. When one of the bolder ones asked him why he was there, he answered simply that "George Bannard invited me.")

The idea of a drink of any sort at a Chase & Ward luncheon was unprecedented. Bannard kept his counsel until the champagne was served.

"Ladies and gentlemen, I hope you don't think we're setting a precedent today. The champagne is for this day and this day only. But there is reason to celebrate. Graham Donovan's murderer was arrested in my office earlier this morning."

Bannard paused for effect—and got the response he desired. Audible murmuring arose from the group seated around the U-shaped table. "Who was it?" someone called out.

"Graham Donovan's client, Dwight Draper, confessed the murder to me and a police officer."

Frost, having not been in on the denouement, wondered how much Bannard had had to do with the confession. His guess was very little.

"We have been through a very trying few days here at Chase & Ward. The death of our partner and friend, Graham Donovan, tragic enough in its own right, was made even more so by the fact that it was murder. I am sure that Graham's murder raised doubts and suspicions with many of us—doubts about some of our employees, some of our associates and, frankly, about each other.

"But the murderer was, thank heaven, not one of us," Bannard went on. "Graham, as Draper's lawyer, had insisted on a standard of conduct for Draper and his company that Draper was not prepared to live up to. Instead he put poison in Graham's water carafe the afternoon before Graham died, and murder was the result. It's a complicated story, which I will ask Reuben Frost to tell. Reuben has once again performed a great service for this firm. His assistance to me—and to the police—was vital in solving the case. Reuben, will you tell us about it?"

All eyes turned to Frost, who was sitting not at the head table but amid the groundlings along the side. Slowly and methodically—and savoring the attention he was receiving—Frost recounted the story from the beginning. It was a complete, if judiciously edited, account, omitting Bannard's clumsy handling of Bautista, the suspicion that had fallen on Grace Appleby and Perry Griffith, the Merritt episode—and Arthur Tyson's displays of temper.

As he neared the end of the narrative, Frost was about to cede the floor back to Bannard and then thought better of it. It was obvious that Bannard had in mind making a toast; Frost now mischievously decided to preempt him.

"Graham died for the high principles that we like to think govern the conduct of all of us here at Chase & Ward," Frost went on. "As I often said when I was one of you, as your Executive Partner, this firm and the principles that guide it are bigger and more important than any of us as individuals.

"My dear friends, you will not be as strong as a firm because Graham Donovan is gone. But Chase & Ward will surely be a more resilient firm for having survived the awful events of the last ten days.

"George Bannard seems to have supplied us with some nice champagne here. I hope it hasn't gone flat during my long talk," Frost said. Then the old man rose and raised his glass. "So, ladies and gentlemen, let me end by proposing a toast—to the memory of Graham Donovan and to the firm, to our beloved Chase & Ward!"

About the Author

HAUGHTON MURPHY is the pseudonym of a partner in a Wall Street law firm. He lives in Manhattan with his wife.